D0952215

SNOW ANGEL

SNOW ANGEL

A Novel

JAMIE CARIE

B&H
PUBLISHING GROUP
Nashville, Tennessee

IBSN: 978-0-7394-9420-2

Published by B&H Publishing Group,
Nashville, Tennessee

To my dad, Jim—
who smiled, nodded, and then laughed his
victor's laugh as I dreamed out loud.

To my mom, Donna—
who showed me Christ and the cost.
If I've done anything beautiful . . . it was born
in the both of you.

And to Tony, my husband, my Noah—
What would I be without you? I cannot imagine.
This is for you.

Acknowledgments

To my editor—Thomas Walters: Thank you for believing in me and loving Noah and Elizabeth's story. It finally happened because of you!

To my wonderful agent—Wes Yoder: Thanks for taking me on when there was no reason for you to. You are depths of wonderful advice and endless graciousness.

To the fiction team—David Webb and Karen Ball, wonder editors: I'm so blessed to have you both working on these next books.

Kim Overcash Stanford, Robin Patterson, Julie Gwinn, Diana Lawrence, David Schrader, and Mary Beth Shaw: You made it all come together and I'm so grateful for each of you!

Prologue

New York City, 1879

Jane jerked upright at the pounding on the nursery door. Her gaze darted nervously to the dark, curly hair of her daughter who sat happily, so innocently beside her stacking wooden blocks into towers of tottering glee. She repressed the urge to snatch the child up into the protection of her slight bosom and cling to her, to hide them both from this horrible thing that was to happen, wishing for some miracle, some magic that would make them invisible or transport them to an exotic land where all was well for an unwed mother. Instead, with trembling fingers she smoothed Elizabeth's baby-fine hair, closing her eyes briefly, feeling the strands slide between her fingers, willing her mind to make the imprint.

Remember the silken texture. Remember that too.

The pounding came again, short and hard and angry—always angry. She forced herself up on shaky legs, weakened from the strain of living on little but nervous energy and stomach-wrenching dread waiting for just such a knock. There had been comments from the few people she'd been allowed to see, servants mostly. "Miss Jane, you're so pale" or "You must eat something, Jane," and the reproving glare of "You'll only make yourself sick, Jane—what good will that do the child?" All of these comments left her drowning with guilt. As if she couldn't see for herself the ashen paleness of her face in the mirror every morning, the purple-hued smudges under her eyes, and the way her clothes hung loose and forlorn from her shoulders. She hardly recognized herself these days.

She turned the knob. The door swept wide by its own weight, such a well-made door with its fancy engraving work and beveled-edged molding, one of the thousands of carefully thought-out details in their much envied townhouse. She forced herself to look at his face, into the eyes of her father. He never came to this room, had never even seen his grandchild, nor much of her since she'd had little Elizabeth nearly two years ago. How fitting, she thought bitterly, that despite the whimsical wallpaper and cheerful curtains, this room had more a sense of a tomb than of bright beginnings. The brightness was cold, the light harsh, the empty echo from the hardwood floor an accompaniment to the resonant thudding of her heart. Today this nursery meant death to the deep places of Jane's soul. After this day, she believed, she would live in body alone.

"The people from the orphanage are here, Jane. Bring the child and her belongings. I will give you ten minutes." Her father's voice was flat, his eyes hard.

She simply stared at him, as though a fog had settled over her brain. His face, though, was reality—unmovable, insurmountable reality. The look in his eyes penetrated the daze until all she could hear was the pounding of her blood in her head. How could she do it? Her only joy—taken. It was impossible. Her body refused to obey him, rooted to the floor like a sentinel.

"Did you hear me, Jane?" He spoke to her like she was five, his chin jutting forward, his eyes squinting in anger with that stern, sneering tone that had always terrified her and compelled immediate obedience. She felt the familiar fear of him and took a step back in defeat, hating herself as she moved but knowing that when Howard Greyson made up his mind about something, nothing and no one ever stopped him.

Jane sank to her knees in defeat. It was no use. The time for pride, for hiding behind the facade of independent bravado, was over.

Her eyes filled. Her tears spilled over. "Please, I beg you, don't take her from me." Her voice shook so that she could scarcely continue. "Please, I'll do anything."

Judge Howard Greyson's lip curled in disgust. "Not another one of your scenes, Jane. You can and you will. We've discussed this. Now quit groveling and get that child ready. If you don't do it yourself, I'll have a maid do it, and you won't even get to say good-bye."

He started to turn away, to turn his back on her like all the other times. But this time Jane stopped him by pulling hard on the hem of his gray trousers.

She felt impotent rage swell and fill her chest. Her weapons were so few, so futile; still, she tried to penetrate his impassive will. "I'll never forgive you! Do you hear me?" She stood in stiff outrage and backed away from him as if he were a foul presence in the room. "As soon as I get away from here, I will find her. I will get her back."

Unmoved, her father gave the scene a loathing glare. "You are a spineless fool, Jane. I am only doing what is best for you. Since you are in no condition to bring her down, I'll send Mary up to get her." He turned on his heel and strode down the hall.

She was glad to see his back this time. She would never look him in the eyes again.

Little Elizabeth had listened to the scene in innocent confusion. As the door banged shut, she began to cry. Jane rushed over, picked up Elizabeth, and clasped her child hard to her chest, swaying lightly back and forth. The tears streamed one after the other down her cheeks and into the child's ebony hair.

If only there were a way of escape, she would take it. But her father had taken care of that too. She had been locked in the house, kept under guard by a sharp-eyed, starched housekeeper since he had told her of his plans to marry Jane into an affluent family in his world of politics and law. The unwanted bastard granddaughter was to be secretly banished, as if she were the thief of Jane's innocence. That they had successfully kept her pregnancy and, later, the child hidden from society for nearly two years was a fact she still could hardly believe.

Jane glanced at the nursery window in desperation. With Elizabeth pressed close, she walked to the window, parted the yellow checked curtains, and looked down. They were three stories up—an impossible height. She looked down into the little round face and the deep brown eyes of her darling girl and knew she couldn't risk it.

Elizabeth reached up and traced a tear on her mother's face with a chubby finger, saying, "Mama?"

"Yes, mama," Jane whispered back, knowing it would be the last time she heard it. "Always your mama."

The midafternoon sun fell across the child's face, illuminating her fair skin and shining black hair. Jane caressed the soft hair with shaking hands. She outlined the little dark brows, the softly rounded cheeks, the tiny chin that could pucker with stubborn determination, and then, her favorite, the deep brown eyes that could express outrage, glee, and hundreds of still undiscovered emotions that Jane would not see. Determined, Jane blinked out the pools of tears in her eyes and gazed at her child, memorizing every line and curve for the years to come.

"Mama loves you, Elizabeth. I want you to always remember that," she choked out softly before pulling the child to her chest again. "I will always love you, and I will find you. Someday, I'll come for you." Then fiercer and low she declared, "I *will* come for you."

The door opened softly, allowing Mary into the room. With a sympathetic look, she pried the child from Jane's arms. Elizabeth cried out immediately and held her arms out for her mother, kicking her legs in the beginnings of a fit. The maid tightened her grip, causing Elizabeth to struggle in earnest, then carried her out of the room and shut the door behind them.

The last image Jane saw of her daughter was the confused distress in those dark brown eyes. Distress that turned into angry wails.

The last sound Jane heard from her daughter was her cries fading down the hall. With a wail of her own, Jane collapsed to the floor in a puddle of despair. Hands over her ears, eyes tightly clenched shut . . . Jane began the years of mourning.

One

Alaska, 1897

Cold. Hard and relentless, the icy shards of snow and ice swirled, encompassing the slight, young woman in their fury. The wind screamed about her, haunting music that rose and fell in an eerie melody, as if the conductor had fled and the orchestra gone mad. Time turned its head toward her and paused, deigning to notice her struggle—an impassive but patient enemy observing the meager strength of this lump of barely breathing clay to battle the tempest, waiting for her to give up so that it could number her among the vanquished. And at the center of the scene, as if she were the star in a stage play, the young woman stumbled through snow so deep it reached her knees, making simple steps impossible while profound tremors spread from her core in great waves of teeth-chattering misery.

Can't stop, she repeated over and over to herself in a mind that felt stupid and sluggish. *Can't stop . . . can't . . . stop.* Her breath was snatched away so fast she couldn't say it aloud, but she wanted to, needed to. A tremor turned sobbish, ending in a half-sane laugh. *Won't stop . . . no . . . by God, won't stop.* She stopped, as another wracking tremor-sob overtook her, the frigid air reaching way down deep into her lungs, making them ache and spasm. *So cold . . . so frozen solid through . . . can't go on . . . can't stop.* Wandering thoughts flitted and fled, self-pity fighting resolve. She bent her head against the gale and took another small step forward, unable to tell if she was really moving ahead or only standing against the wind. The desire to lie down and give up surged through her—like a man in shaking, sweating need of a strong drink, it beckoned, softly warm and smiling, promising and seducing.

Wouldn't take long to die. Sleep . . . rest and warm. Always and forever warm.

Emboldened, the fix grew insidious, smile turning to sneer, causing the still, frozen part of her brain to wake up and recognize its traitorous nature.

Can't stop . . . can't stop . . . she began the chant again, not really knowing if she had stopped moving or not. It must be a bad thing, this inability to tell what her body was doing, but somehow she couldn't seem to care much. Rubbing cold-stiffened hands across her eyes, the thin leather of her gloves doing her little good, she lifted her head with fresh determination and struggled forward.

Was that a light? A flicker . . . a light maybe . . . yes . . . yes. The swirling mass of white shifted long enough to glimpse . . . something.

Light . . . life, yes, choose light-life.

She blinked rapidly, trying to see, trying to blink past the thick, wet veil, her heart pounding with hope and then fear that it was only a blind man's dream. She saw it again, wavering yet strong, and something else—something solid and sure and huge surrounding it. A house. With sudden energy she plunged forward toward the yellow glow. She couldn't feel her feet any longer, nor her legs or hands either, but salvation was just steps away. Just a few more steps away.

She stumbled in her hurry, falling into a heap, quickly becoming buried half-alive. She tried to stand, drowning in snow, thinking her arms and legs were floundering but seeing that they were just lying there, realizing in a daze that her knees wouldn't bend, that her legs had turned to wooden posts no longer acknowledging the authority of her brain.

Get up! Everything inside her wailed it. Her throat worked with the effort to scream it aloud, making incoherent sounds of distress, a desperate, discordant harmony in what now appeared a tragedy. Panic set in. She had to concentrate. She had to make her sluggish brain command her legs to push her up. She struggled, clawed, and climbed, digging herself in deeper, trying to stand, but her legs were unable to support her weight. *Get up!*

She stopped suddenly, her breathing rasping and shallow from the effort, and fell back into the snow in defeat. She couldn't do it. Couldn't get up. She gazed up at the sky, where the dark black of night peeked through the shifting white. She felt strangely warm and comfortable. She would be buried now. Detached, she realized that the icy sensation on her cheeks were tears freezing in their trickling tracks. Her face was quickly becoming covered with flakes—soon she wouldn't be able to breathe—but she couldn't find a reason to brush them away. A voice long recognized as her strong self chided her, *You shouldn't cry; you never cry.* Everyone died sometime, and this was her time. Another part of her, so long suffocated by sheer will that the voice was faint, spoke softly, sadly. She was going to suffocate now, with her light just ahead, with salvation right around the corner. Like so much of her life, it all was too little too late. She would never be strong enough or brave enough or good enough. It was hopeless to try.

Crawl.

The thought came startlingly clear, as if heaven had decided to reach down and take her hand. But she was warmer now, and she was sleepy.

You have life in you yet. You could crawl.

Yes . . . maybe. She still had some feeling in her arms. She lifted them, feeling funny like they were waving around instead of brushing snow off her face the way she wanted them to. Taking a few deep breaths, she managed to sit up and then turn onto her stomach. She laughed. She did have some strength left. Rising up onto her hands, she rocked back and could see that even though she couldn't feel her legs she was on her knees. Looking ahead she felt another spark of hope. The wind changed sides and became her ally, shifting again, giving her another glimpse of the light. Bending her head, she inched forward, looking up every now and then, catching occasional flashes of the light. Half-crawling, half-dragging herself through snow that reached her chin, she fought on, swimming in snow, swimming for her shore. She couldn't quit. She wouldn't quit this time.

Straining forward, every muscle stretched, reaching toward the light. Her heart pounded louder and louder, faster and faster, a crescendo in the music, straining toward climax. *Where is the light?*

Suddenly, her head smacked hard against a sturdy object. Reaching up, she felt solid wood. A wall. She breathed thick and heavy, her hands pawing at the surface, icy tears of relief blinding her completely. *The door. Must find the door.* Groping with unfeeling hands and unseeing eyes, she edged around a corner. Finally the wood changed, indented long and rectangular. This must be at a door. She tried to stand, but her knees buckled. Taking a steely breath of the frigid air that made her lungs crackle inside, she pounded and pounded and pounded with the last of the life still in her.

"Please . . . God . . . ," she whispered before collapsing.

NOAH WESLEY SAT BY A crackling fire, reading and drinking hot coffee to help shut out the bitter cold. He glanced up at the muffled sound at his door. *Just the wind,* he thought, not wanting to leave his warm fire and let in an icy blast to check. Anyone he knew would just come barreling through in this weather. No one in their right mind would knock. His broad finger absently traced the words down to his place and he began to read. Once absorbed, he was startled to hear an inner voice say loudly and distinctly, *Noah, go and open the door.*

Noah glanced at the door, a vertical line creasing between his dark, bushy eyebrows. A sudden inexplicable urgency came over him—someone was in trouble. He hurried to the door. Dragging the board from underneath, he turned the new porcelain knob he'd recently installed and pulled the door wide. Snow, getting deep fast, was all he could see. He stuck his head out, trying to see through the swirling winds as they shifted and blew ice into his face. He called out. Nothing answered but the howling of the wind, so sharp it snatched his breath away. He called again and yet again, trying hard to make out any forms in the cascade of white, anything at all. Finally, shaking his head, he stepped back to shut out the cold that was fast seeping through his thick, woolen shirt when he heard the voice again.

Noah, open the door!

"Nothing is there but the wind," he answered aloud in a confused voice, but he opened it anyway. He took a deep breath and shouted.

"Hello-o-o! Anybody out there?"

Hearing nothing, seeing nothing, he took a step forward. Something soft yet solid moved under his foot. He jerked back, knelt down, and quickly unburied the still form at his doorstep. "My God . . ."

He lifted her, noting how light she was, how air-thin her bone structure felt, as if she had been made for flight instead of this earthly gravity, and brought her inside, slamming the door with one hand. Carefully, he carried the seemingly lifeless bundle to the sofa, the only store-bought piece of furniture he owned, and laid her on it. He brushed snow from her chest, revealing an ice-encrusted cloak. The frogged clasp was frozen stiff and unmovable. Noah pushed the folds of the cloak aside and placed his ear over her heart. It took a moment to find it—yes, he heard a faint but steady beat. Taking out a pocket-knife, he cut the frogging of the cloak, slid it from under her, and tossed it aside.

Like some angel born of the storm, she was as pale as the snow he had taken her from. Dark, curling, shoulder-length hair tossed wildly about her head. Her face was delicately made, small and sweet. Upswept brows and long, closed lashes made dark slashes of color against the bleached skin in deathly beautiful contrast. Her bloodless lips reminded him how very cold she was. He touched an icy cheek with the backs of his fingers, noticed her wet clothes, and realized the gaping needs of a lone woman in a blizzard with nothing but thin clothes on her back. She was a living, breathing miracle . . . for the moment, anyway.

Hastening to his hand-hewn bed, Noah jerked off a quilt. Next, he went to his dresser and rummaged for a warm shirt and some woolen socks. She would be lost in the shirt, but it was the best he could provide for the moment.

Kneeling beside her, he carefully covered her with the blanket and began removing ice-encrusted clothes from underneath it. He barely glanced at her garments but noted in the back of his mind how well used they were, as if they had been scrubbed too many times with too much vehemence. A thin white blouse with tiny gray stripes and too many buttons—*confound the thing*—a gray skirt, one plain white petticoat, gray stockings, and badly worn black ankle-boots completed the ensemble and marked her a greenhorn. Noah shook his head in wonderment at her foolishness. How she had made it to his cabin, which was partway up the slope of a mountain and miles from Juneau, in a snowstorm, wearing no more than this getup, was nothing short of miraculous. Who she was and where she had come from were questions begging answers—answers Noah didn't know if he ever would learn. She seemed as frail as a spring flower caught in a sudden, mean frost.

Noah dried her and dressed her in his warm garments, his hands clumsy at the task, the back of his neck turning warm at the unfamiliar intimacy. Then he covered her with the quilt. She looked so lost and little in his red flannel shirt, too bright against the white of her throat. He didn't like it against her small-boned beauty, but it was the warmest thing he owned and he wasn't about to take it off her now. He reached out to her, first touching her cheek with the backs of his fingers, then brushing gently at the ice in her hair.

She was out cold and Noah knew enough about thawing to be glad for this. It was a painful process. He only hoped it was happening in time. For reasons he really didn't want to probe, he hated to see her marred in any way by this experience. Blackened feet to hobble on for the rest of one's life would not set well on this one. Those things belonged to grizzly miners with gap-toothed grins and greedy eyes, not to recently rescued snow princesses.

The teakettle began to whistle, bringing him back to his kitchen and the immediate need of warming her extremities. At the stove, he poured steaming water into a deep porcelain bowl and refilled the kettle from a bucket, putting it back on the stove for the next round. He would need lots of hot water if he were to have a chance of saving her feet. Taking up a soft cloth, he hurried back and knelt down beside the end of the sofa, lifting the bottom of the blanket. He slipped his arm beneath her knees, lifting her legs so that her feet dangled, half-crossing each other. Gently, he lowered her feet, immersing them in the warm water, his eyes taking in the daintiness of her toes and arches of her feet, his gaze traveling up her ankles to slim, shapely legs. Once again, he marveled that someone so thin and elegant could possess enough strength to find his cabin, on foot, in such weather.

As soon as the water cooled, he lifted her feet, dried them carefully, and wrapped them in another blanket. They had reddened in the process, but he wasn't sure if that was a good sign or a bad one; it was a bad case of frostbite, anyway.

After laying a couple of logs on the fire to keep the room warm, he concentrated on the next greatest concern, her hands. Kneeling beside her, he began soaking the reddened, chapped hands. Hard-working hands, certainly, but something more. One wrist had a long scar around it. He stared at an especially ugly welt on the inside of the other wrist, thinking of a burn he'd once had, but this was much worse. It looked like a recent injury. He wondered what might have caused it, and indignation and protectiveness rose within him. This wasn't caused by physical labor; she had been mistreated, he was sure of it. A deep disquiet settled over him as he immersed one hand at a time, warming them in the water. He then rubbed a sweet-smelling ointment into her wrists, his thumbs making tiny, gentle circles where pieces to her past lay vulnerable to his gaze. Her skin turned rosy under his care, making him feel slightly better.

Tired, Noah pulled the rocker over to the sofa, fell into it, and stared at her. If only she weren't so still. If only she would shiver or move, anything aside from the tiny rise and fall of her chest. Then he could breathe easier. Then he could find his own rest.

The minutes that held the answer to whether she would live or die ticked loudly from the mantle clock. *Time would tell.* It sounded so deceptively easy, that phrase. The waiting was anything but easy, but he had done all he knew to do. He needed more than the raw, elemental laws of wilderness survival. He needed help. His head fell back against the chair as he prayed for her—prayed that her life would be spared, prayed that her feet would recover, prayed pleading mantras, not knowing better words except to remind God of the many miracles He had done and ask Him to do another.

It was a struggle to stay awake. He let his eyelids fall shut. Just to close his eyes for a little while. Just to rest them.

He must have fallen asleep because the next thing he knew he was jerking upright in his chair with dreams of snow angels fading from his mind. He looked toward the girl.

She was so still—too still. Coming fully awake in a panic, he realized her chest wasn't moving in the faint but steady rise and fall of the past hours. Falling to his knees, he moved to her side and laid his ear upon her chest. He could feel how cold she was, even through the thick shirt, sending a spike of fear through him. Something was wrong. She seemed *worse* than an hour ago. The clock's ticking was louder than her heartbeat, making him wish for something to throw at it to still its insistence. He gripped the edge of the sofa with one hand and leaned over her, pressing his ear harder. Just as he was about to back away and give up, there it was. So faint, so erratic—her heart sounded like it was . . . freezing. Behind his closed eyes he saw it in his mind, he could see her heart seizing up and freezing solid.

"No," he cried, leaning over her and roughly gathering her into his arms, willing his own warmth to seep into her flesh. "God, no. Don't let her die!"

Suddenly, he was tearing open her shirt and then his, turning her toward him as he climbed up to lie next to her on the sofa, side by side, pressing his warm chest to her shockingly cold one. He pulled the quilt over their heads and then grasped the back of her head with his hands—hands that had hacked a life out of frozen wilderness, hands that had unsuccessfully worked the plow and then fallen back on the knowledge of the smooth barrel of his hunting gun, hands that had been lifted in worship and made fists to the sky in desperation, hands that had known the struggle between life and death in the hard place that was Alaska—he grasped her silky hair, bringing her head to his, her lips to his, so that he could breathe his own warm, living breath into her. He didn't know what he was doing. It was crazy, it was wrong . . . but it seemed right.

Call to her.

"Call to her? I don't know her name!" he screamed.

Then something took over, a calm panic of sorts, and he began a rhythm. A breath into her mouth and then, in a deep, commanding voice, "Wake up." Another breath. "Wake up, Come on, wake up!" Another breath. "Come back, sweet one. Come back." Another breath. "Wake up. Come back to me." On and on and on until he began seeing odd red dots in his peripheral vision. It was dark under the blanket and hot. He felt the sweat trickle down his back, felt the doubts assailing his mind, telling him how foolish he was, but he kept breathing and talking, breathing and talking until he needed a breath of fresh air so badly, he had to lift the blanket to allow a crack of light and air into their cocoon.

As the light crept in, her face came out of the dark and into shadows. There was enough light to see that she was flushed and a sheen of sweat shone on her forehead. There was moisture on her upper lip, evidence of his efforts. Lifting the blanket a degree more, he saw the small rise and fall of her chest. She was breathing again, breathing on her own.

The hope that had been flickering inside him flared to full life. "Thank you," he cried out, his voice hoarse from breathing his life into her. *Thank you.* He lay back down beside her, pulling her close into his arms and sighing heavily into her hair. *Thank you.* His chin rested on the top of her head. She would live. He didn't know how, but he was sure now. She would live.

It was the last thought he remembered thinking before a deep sleep overcame him.

✳ ✳ ✳

July 7, 1880
Dear Miss Greyson,

I have received your request for my services in locating your daughter, Elizabeth, and am most glad to tell you of my devotion to your cause. Please be assured that I understand the discreet nature of the investigation, and while we may never meet in person, I will keep you abreast of my inquiries and future proceedings by letter.

I have begun my investigation with the names of the local orphanages and schools you supplied in your letter. Please know that your plea has touched this humble investigator's heart and I will make returning your daughter to you my utmost concern.

Sincerely yours,
Jeremiah Hoglesby
Private Detective for Hire

Two

hiteness, brightness, hurting her eyes. Conscious thought tried to assert itself, but she quickly rejected it, thinking she must be dreaming still, that the strange sound resonating from the area of her chest couldn't possibly be a man's snoring. All she knew for certain was warmth, inviting and cozy. She snuggled her face and then her body deeper into the big pillow at her side, and with a deep sigh she flung an arm around it and drifted back into the cushions of sleep.

Her next sensation was a burning in her feet. She squeezed her eyes tightly closed, vaguely wondering what she had done to them. What kind of scrape had she gotten herself into this time? Elizabeth opened her lids a slit, saw white light, groaned, changed her mind, and squeezed her eyes closed again. Her feet felt on fire. That was the cause of this rude awakening, she realized as she surfaced from one of the deepest and most profound sleeps of her life. Whatever had she done? With an inward sigh of resignation, she turned her head toward the ceiling and tried opening her eyes once more.

13

Disjointed memories assailed her. Mountain . . . blizzard . . . so much snow . . . so much cold. Had she actually survived it? Her heart pounded in fear that she wasn't even really alive, that this warmth, this burning, was some form of the afterlife. Then she heard it. A groan and a sudden movement by . . . by her pillow!

Her head jerked toward the sound and she came face to face with a snoring mouth.

She tried to scream. She really did. Wanted to so badly, but all that came out was a croaky pig-like squeal. She pushed against the huge chest, knocking him from the bed . . . or sofa, she amended, half-sitting in stultified shock, taking in the surroundings of a cabin. *Good heavens, where am I?*

The man sat up, suddenly, and looked at her, both frantic and disoriented—as if she were some kind of crisis. Sleepy eyed, tousled golden hair, with deep dimples in lean cheeks . . . then he frowned at her. Panic hit her hard in the stomach. Who was he? Where was she?

Her gaze dropped to his chest where his shirt hung open, revealing golden skin. Then she noticed the width of his shoulders, the strength of his arms . . . the size of his hands. She tried desperately to remember . . . anything. He could break her with little effort at all. Not that she wouldn't fight. She knew how to kick where it did the most damage and run or hide, still as night, for hours if need be. She could manage him if she had to. Abrupt dizziness hit, making her head pound as if this stranger wielded a hammer. She leaned back against the cushions, a sound of distress escaping her throat.

The man was rubbing his hands over his face, through his hair, and then looking at her with such intensity that she suddenly thought she might be sick.

He made a sudden move toward her, causing her to shrink back into the cushions of the sofa. His hand was outstretched as if to touch her . . . she swatted it away before it could reach her, making her hand ache almost as bad as her feet.

"What do think you're doing?" she croaked.

He seemed confused, as if she couldn't possibly be talking to him.

She sat back up abruptly, determined to take charge of this astounding set of circumstances, but sitting up all the way was challenge enough. Dizziness overwhelmed her and a hazy blackness loomed in her vision. She quickly dropped her head to her knees, as she knew from experience to do, waiting for it to dissipate. When she felt ready, she cautiously tried again, sitting quietly for a few moments to regain her senses. The man remained quiet, watchful.

The blanket slipped. Elizabeth felt a draft of cold and glanced down, then gasped in shock. She was wearing nothing but a shirt, and it was not even buttoned up . . . at all. Outrage rose to the surface, making her hot with embarrassment as the thoughts connected themselves. She looked up at him, grasping the sides of the shirt together so tight they threatened to strangle her.

"You! You beast!" She wanted to brand him with every foul-mouthed word she knew or had ever heard, but she was breathless with anger and nausea. And her feet—they felt as if she'd stuck them into the fire and left them there. She tried to reason it out and glare with mortified hatred at him at the same time. The storm had caught her off guard. So stupid! Hours of walking, searching for anything to save her. And then she had seen a light. And then a house. She didn't remember anything after hitting her head against the wall. But the evidence was obvious. This man had . . . well, she didn't know exactly what he had done, but to take advantage of her unconsciousness was contemptible. She looked around the cabin in desperation, noting the door, windows with casings that would open, and places to avoid where she could easily be cornered and trapped. It was all so neat and clean. Her gaze scanned the kitchen area. What she really needed was a weapon. She had to get a weapon.

The man looked at her intently. His gaze dropped to the shirt she was wearing, *his* shirt, and then back up to her face. A telling red flush filled his face as he looked into her eyes.

"Where are my clothes?" she demanded. "What have you done? Tell me what you did while I was asleep."

He shifted his weight from one foot to the other, looking at her and then behind her at some spot on the wall above her head, as if he couldn't quite look her in the eye. "Um . . . I had to get the wet clothes off you . . . that is . . . you nearly froze to death. I had to . . . put on some dry . . . my shirt was the best I could do."

She glared at him. "Then why didn't you button it? It couldn't keep me warm like this, could it?" She buttoned the shirt with shaking fingers as she talked. There had to be more and she would know it or see that he died a slow, painful death, she promised herself. "What about your shirt? What were you doing sleeping with me like that?" His chest and stomach were in full view. She dragged her gaze back to his face as he tried to explain.

"It was buttoned. But I . . . that is, you were so cold and you . . . during the night you stopped breathing, I couldn't find your heartbeat. I'm sorry. I just acted. I thought . . . well,

I just thought the only way to warm you was . . . my body heat against you." He looked down at his own bare chest and quickly pulled his shirt closed, reaching for the top button. "I'm sorry." He looked at her, really looked into her eyes, and said, "I did the only thing I knew to do."

She didn't know what to believe. Had he saved her life? Had it really been so innocent? "Why didn't you button it up after, after you saw that I was breathing? Why did you stay with me like that?" she pressed, feeling close to tears and hating herself for it.

"I fell asleep. I'd been up since dawn chopping wood, and it was well past midnight."

"Where are my clothes?"

He took a long breath, pointing toward a washstand beside the four-poster bed. The cabin was small, one large room serving as a living room, a kitchen, and a bedroom. Elizabeth looked to the bed covered with a patchwork quilt and saw her clothes hanging there, dripping, giving credence to his words. "They're hanging over there, drying. In this cold it may take a while, but I expect they'll be dry by tomorrow. You really shouldn't be getting up yet, you know."

"And why shouldn't I?" she said, latching on to the anger that rode so high, so easy. "You can't tell me what I can do. I'll get up if I please." She attempted it even, so determined and unwilling that he see any weakness, before falling back with a cry of pain.

The man cleared his throat, ran his fingers through his sun-streaked hair and tried again. "I'm real sorry, miss. I only meant that you had a close call out there in that storm. You will probably need some time to regain your strength."

Looking pointedly at her feet he added, "And you should stay off your feet."

Her feet *were* hurting, they felt numb and fiery at the same time, and the rest of her body ached all over, like she'd wrestled with a bear in the storm instead of ice and snow. But she felt too trapped to admit it.

He leaned a little toward her and asked, "How do you feel?"

She shifted on the sofa, clutching the blanket to her neck. "Fine," she said concededly, "except my feet hurt."

"Good . . . I mean, that's a good sign. If they hurt, they'll get better, which means they weren't frozen. They'll likely hurt for a day or two."

He turned and stretched, flexing broad shoulders and a wide upper back and then walked over to the low-burning fire to add some more wood. Elizabeth could still hear the storm raging outside, whistling through unseen cracks in the walls of this man's cabin and howling, making the glass rattle in its panes.

She wanted to ask where she was and who he was, but she didn't want to be the one initiating questions. He seemed to know her thoughts as he said, coming back over to her and thrusting out a hand, "I'm Noah Wesley. I sure would like to hear how you made it halfway up the mountain to my cabin in a blizzard." He paused and smiled, like he admired her. "And your name . . . I sure would like to know your name."

Noah. She had never met anyone with such a name. It sounded so . . . ancient. But he didn't look ancient; he looked very much in his prime. She considered lying about her first name but thought better of it—too complicated.

"Elizabeth," she stated simply, refusing to offer more.

He stood there, towering, so that she had to tilt her head back to see his face, and said, "I was going to make some breakfast. Could you eat a little?"

Her mind raced back to her last meal. She had been searching for information in the saloons of Juneau, wandering really, having left the main group after they all heard that the freeze had settled into the tributaries of the Yukon River and they would have to wait until spring to finish the trek to Dawson City. She hadn't known where to go or what to do next but had decided that she must find a party of prospectors to join. Her fellow passengers might have the resources to winter in Sitka or Juneau, but she didn't. She needed to get to the gold.

It couldn't be too late. It just couldn't. Not after everything she had been through to get here. There had to be someone in this town going to the Klondike where gold nuggets as big as her hand lay ready for the taking. One barkeep had seen the hollow of her cheeks, taken pity on her, and ordered a beefsteak fried up. Then hearing of her mission he'd smiled, not unkindly but with a definite hint of doubt. Taking her over to a window, he'd pointed toward a mountain, this mountain she'd somehow conquered. Halfway up was a supposed full-fledged mountain man, a guide. If anyone could make it to the interior this time of year, he could, she was told. That had been yesterday, noon. It seemed like a lifetime ago. Was she even the same person?

"Yes, breakfast sounds good." Her brain felt sluggish, still frozen.

When she tried to get up, Noah shook his head. "Just sit tight. I'll bring it to you. And I'll need to take a look at those

feet later, so you might want to start getting used to the idea."
He grinned at her.

It was so unlike any grin she'd had directed at her. It was
kind, like he understood her vulnerability and wanted to put
her mind at rest. Like he could see her fears and her courage
and her will to pull them together into a whole person . . .
and he still liked her, admired her even. Yes, that was it—it
was a kind, restful sort of grin and it made her want to cry.
Cry that she was alive. Cry that she'd found this place and,
yes, this man with his kind, blue eyes. But she wouldn't cry.
She would not cry.

Feeling drained from the monumental effort of sitting up,
flustered by the way he teased her, and a little breathless by that
smile, she sat back but watched carefully as he moved about
the kitchen. She couldn't get the image of him lying beside her,
pressed against her, out of her mind. She had never slept the
night through with a man before. Had he really been so noble?
She didn't like it. And he looked entirely too comfortable standing in front of the stove, wielding his pots and pans, humming
a song that sounded vaguely familiar.

The pan soon made a sizzling steam, and the smell of
fried meat drifted to her nose. She closed her eyes in exhaustion, the peace of this place beckoning to some hidden part of
her. Unbidden, a feeling of yearning washed over her and a hazy
memory of being rocked and sung to gnawed at the corners of
her mind. No one had ever sung such a song to her, she chided
herself . . . and yet it was achingly familiar. She thought back
to the "mothers" in her life. Margaret had certainly never rocked
her. Besides being much too old for such things by the time she
was adopted, Margaret hadn't a maternal bone in her body. And

the orphanage . . . it was possible she had heard the song there, but somehow she didn't think so. Her memories were so gray, shrouded like a death march toward an accidental birth, that she had neither the strength nor the will to resurrect them. But the need to know what the song was grew until, before she knew what she was doing, she blurted out, "What is that song?"

The man swung his head toward her. "Song?"

"Never mind," she said quietly, embarrassed.

"The song I was humming? Just an old hymn, I think. Do you know it?"

Elizabeth slowly shook her head. "I don't know. I thought maybe I had heard it before, but I'm not sure where . . ." She let her voice trail off, mortified that she'd let her thoughts out into the open air where they could be questioned . . . examined.

Noah gave her a half-smile and a look of understanding, then he turned back to his cooking, as if it was nothing special, that look, and stirred something around in the black iron pan. "If my singing bothers you, I'll stop."

Elizabeth could only shake her head and sink back down into the cushions. She wanted to hide, bury herself in the covers and block out this man who could give her his heat and then revive such a memory. Was he real?

He was soon finished and brought her a heaping plate of meat and two huge sourdough biscuits, with thick brown gravy poured over the whole contents of the plate.

Elizabeth could only blink at the giant pile of food, feeling a little queasy. There was enough food on the plate to feed her for a couple of days. Looking up at his immense size, she couldn't help but smile and ask, "I'm certainly hungry, Mr. Wesley, but do you think I could lift that plate?"

He stood there speechless, looking at the plate and then back down at her. As he looked at the plate again, he burst out laughing. He was the kind of man who laughed at himself, she realized, surprised again. "You're right, of course. What was I thinking? Guess I'm used to cooking for men. We don't get many young ladies visiting in this part of the country."

A fine, upstanding young lady. Of course, that is what he would expect. She scrambled mentally for the role.

Carrying the plate back to the table, Noah moved half the contents onto another plate. Returning it to her, he held it out and said with a grin, "This better?"

She nodded. "Thank you."

Noah settled into the chair with his own food and said between bites, "If you're up to it, I'd like to ask you a few questions and maybe I could answer a few for you, too."

Elizabeth paused, her fork midway to her mouth. Stiffening inside, but rising to the challenge, she took a deep breath and nodded. He wouldn't find out. There was no way he could know that she was running from a detective, Ross Brandon, who had turned out to have tormenting plans for her. No way he could possibly discover that her adoptive parents were searching for her, possibly to pin a claim-jumping murder on her. What other reason could they have for actually paying Ross to find her? She was an adult now; they had no parental rule left over her. The thought of going back to them or seeing that evil detective again made her stomach twist in fear. No, this Noah would learn nothing to give him reason to throw her back into the blizzard.

The man had begun speaking again, so she concentrated on paying attention.

"I've lived up here for seven years now, and you are the first visitor I've had show up in the middle of a blizzard. I sure would like to hear how you found me in this storm."

Elizabeth shifted with the shadows of truth and deceit, all the while shivering with the memory of the cold. "I can't really remember very much. I think it was your light." She pointed to the window. "From that window, I saw a light through the snow, and I followed it here."

The man named Noah shook his head. "It's a miracle you could see anything in such conditions. Experienced men with the strength of ten of you have been found frozen solid, cowering under moldy hay bales in the aftermath of such blizzards. Do you have any idea how lucky you are?"

Elizabeth did know, and as she looked at the handsomely disheveled man in front of her she felt a flush of gratitude. "I believe so. Thank you for having your lights burning in the window." She smiled at him. "And for building your cabin here."

He looked shocked for a second, and then his laughter rang out in the room and wrapped around her like a warm, comforting blanket. She looked for malice behind the laugh, some sign of sarcasm, the bite of accusation, but it wasn't there. She couldn't find anything amiss in those deep blue eyes.

He was still smiling but with concern as he asked, "You were alone? Where is your family?"

Elizabeth poked at the food on her plate, sighing inwardly. It was a question as old as she was. He would want to know that she came from a wonderfully fine family, so of course he must not be disappointed. She slipped into the role of solemn orphan, as easily as a woman slips her hand into a well-worn glove. "I was alone. I don't have any family living."

He searched her face. "How did you come to be in this part of the country?"

"My last home was in Seattle. I heard that gold had been found here and decided to join everybody else going to Dawson City."

Noah leaned forward in his chair, "Alone? Don't you know what could happen to a lone girl in a mining town?" He paused . . . then his brows rose. "You're not a prostitute, are you?"

Elizabeth raised her chin. "Certainly not! I grew up in the gold fields, sir. From Utah to California, I've followed rush after rush. I can take care of myself and not by earning my living on my back." That much was true. She had been gold mining with Margaret and Henry since they adopted her years ago.

Noah settled himself back in his chair. "I'm sorry. Please, go on."

She took a determined breath. "When I arrived in Sitka, I found out, as all of us aboard the ship did, that we were too late to go on to Dawson City. The Yukon River apparently freezes in October. We had no choice but to wait until spring." This news had been frustrating to most, but it was terrifying to Elizabeth. Most couldn't feel the hot breath of vengeance breathing down their neck.

Noah nodded. "More often it freezes in September, in some places anyway. I saw a group heading out in August. Those steamers are probably locked in the ice right now. It's a cold way to spend the winter. Good thing you waited. So you left Sitka?"

Elizabeth clasped her hand into a fist. "Yes, but I was still determined to find an expedition to join. Still am determined.

When I arrived in Juneau I asked around and was told that a man lives up here who might be able to help me. Unless there is another cabin on this side of the mountain, I believe they were talking about you."

"Me? I have no intention of going to the Klondike. Most people who know me know what I think of panning for gold."

Elizabeth felt the final threads of her hope snap. Why did nothing ever work out the easy way? "But a barkeep in Juneau said the man who lives on this mountain might take me, or know of a Tlingit guide who would."

"I have several friends among the Indians, and yes, a guide might be bought. But I would not be a part of sending a woman into the treachery of the Alaskan interior during the winter. I don't think you understand this land, miss. In my opinion, those trails are no place for a woman, and that's during the good months."

"Mr. Wesley, you have no idea how determined I am."

Noah gave her that disarming half-smile. "If your trek up to my cabin in the middle of a blizzard is any indication, I'd say I have an idea, Elizabeth."

Despite her anger, she felt a sudden and unexpected melting inside at the way his deep voice spoke her name. Her next words came out softer than she intended. "When I started out, there wasn't a cloud in sight. I may be a woman, sir, but I'm no fool."

"Glad to hear that." Noah frowned. "But refusing to wait for spring thaw would be a dangerous mistake, fatal even. Everyone else is stuck down here, what's your hurry?"

A hundred answers rose to her lips, but she swallowed them all . . . except, "I want my share of that gold."

Noah looked into her eyes, and she knew he was searching for something deeper than her words. This man wanted the truth—all of it—and that was something she just couldn't give him. Inwardly she felt the fire of a fight spark, and she knew it blazed from her deep brown eyes. Looking defiantly at him she made her challenge, but something strange happened. Instead of feeding her anger she noticed his eyes, noticed how blue they were . . . and clear of anything except concern and calm. A sudden feeling of connection with him startled her, causing her to rear back on the sofa and cross her arms over her chest. His voice was low and reassuring, and she felt it all the way to her toes as he spoke.

"Gold will still be there in the spring. And then you'll have no trouble finding a party to join up with. For now, though, you need to rest."

He rose, so tall she thought it a wonder his head didn't brush the golden wood of the ceiling. Gently, he took her plate from her.

"Go back to sleep, Elizabeth. You're safe now. We'll have plenty of time to talk later."

Stunned, she did as he asked.

September 17, 1881
Dear Mrs. Rhodes,

I have received your letter and may I congratulate you on your recent marriage. After many months of inquiries I had nearly given up hope, but I am thrilled to report that

I have tracked down a housemaid named Mary who was recently let go from your father's employ. Upon questioning the woman, who was quite afraid to speak to me, she admitted to hearing that Elizabeth was taken to an orphanage in the state of New York.

I immediately began correspondence with the orphanages in our state and have recently received a reply from a teacher at the New York Orphan Asylum asking for more information. I promptly wrote her of our situation and am awaiting her reply. My instincts say we are very close, ma'am. I shall write immediately upon discovering any further leads and will travel to the orphanage if I receive word that your daughter may be there.

You mentioned dark brown hair and eyes? Would you happen to have a photograph of her?

Sincerely yours,
Jeremiah Hoglesby
Private Detective for Hire

Three

Alaskan blizzards were anything but predictable. Sudden starts appeared out of a clear, blue sky, catching off-guard folks going about their lives fishing or hunting or just walking across the street in town to catch the local gossip at the trading post. Other storms stole in, pretty like and soft with glittering flakes of a million shapes and sizes, only to turn nasty with deep cold and swirling winds that tore the roofs off houses and blew ice down chimneys. And then there were the times a storm started, sputtered and stopped, only to start again and blow for days, making the townspeople wonder if the wind knew its own mind. But always it seemed a living thing, alive and brutal and capable of most anything.

Elizabeth had experienced a few blizzards in her lifetime; she was not totally unprepared for Alaska. And yet, something was different here. Nature reigned in Alaska, winter its king, not satisfied to borrow a climate for a few weeks or months of the year. No, here it ruled with a wildness that existed only in the lands of the Arctic Circle, and this recent wildness seemed somehow directed at her. The storm outside haunted her, invading her dreams, dogging her with its desolate moans,

making her curl in a tight ball at night and cling to the edge
of the narrow sofa with her arms pressed hard up over her ears.
Like a mother who knows the subtle variations of her infant's
cries, Elizabeth grew to know the wind. Sad and then angry,
mournful and then vengeful—extremes of intensity, much like
her emotions these past days, tripping between peaceful seren-
ity and restless unease, being trapped in this cabin with this
strange-wonderful man. It lingered, this storm, not caring that
it confined her in this loving place that made her want to run,
run with the power and speed and flight of such wind. Would
it ever end?

At dawn of the fifth morning the storm stopped just as
suddenly as it had started, leaving behind more snow than
Elizabeth had ever seen and a kind of quiet that left an odd roar
in her ears, making her wonder if something was wrong with
her hearing. The cabin had been nearly buried in drifts, keeping Noah, a man who seemed afraid of nothing, busy for days
shoveling a path between them and the animals in the barn,
taking care of all their needs.

Elizabeth lay on the sofa, slowly surfacing from sleep, looking around the bright room, hearing faint sounds of water splash-
ing. She felt anxious but didn't know why, her mind scrambling
for a foothold. Sitting up, she looked about the room. There he
was, at the dressing table beside the bed, shaving, his movements
sure and steady, his stance strong. As soon as she saw his lathered
reflection in the small, round mirror hanging beside his bed, the
fear dissipated, as if her equilibrium had been righted.

After a moment, the realization that *he* was the reason
for her sudden calm sank in through the layers of comfortable
denial. A deep unease settled in her stomach. She had allowed

herself to become dependent on this man. She'd relaxed her guard and let him mean something to her. Sinking quietly back down into the warm covers, she sternly lectured herself, replaying in her mind the faces and ways humankind had failed her—thinking of Ross Brandon, then Margaret and Henry Dunning, then back further, face after face, until she saw the wraithlike image of her own mother, an image she never let herself see. She forced herself to recognize that here in this cabin, with this man, was a new kind of threat, one that could destroy her far more thoroughly than the others. She had to get away from him before she never wanted to leave.

With new determination, she sat up on the sofa and tested her feet. They were much better, though not well enough for the long walk back to Juneau. She didn't ever again want to plunge back into snow that reached her waist, but she would think of something. She must think of something. She glanced behind her and saw that Noah was wiping the soap off his face, looking at her.

"Good morning," he said. The outer corners of his eyes crinkled in a smile, genuinely happy to see her.

It was such a domestic thing to say. Had anyone ever said that to her before? She felt anger overtake her. Quickly turning away she said in a stiff voice, "Before you go and ask how I'm feeling, let me tell you. I'm stiff and sore from lying down so much, and I don't smell very good either. I'm hungry and I need a bath. Is there any possibility I can get a bath?"

Noah's brow creased and with a wavering smile he said, "Sure, I have a tub. I'll fill it up for you and set it in front of the fire. It will take awhile to warm though, so if you want to go over to the table, I'll cook you some breakfast while you wait."

She gritted her teeth in frustration. He was so good! So unable to understand her response that she wanted to scream. Why couldn't he be like everyone else and shout back at her? She would know how to respond to that. Instead he made her feel churlish and whiny by being so patient.

"Thank you," she said in a low voice instead.

Noah only nodded and set about getting her breakfast of sourdough biscuits and gravy on the table, all the while talking to her like . . . she was his friend, like she was his equal.

"I'll need to go back out to the smokehouse for some more meat today. It's a good thing the storm finally blew itself out. We're running low on wood, too."

His list of his chores made Elizabeth feel guilty. Her bath would no doubt put him behind schedule, but he wasn't complaining. He never seemed to protest the ebb and flow of life's changing moments.

"I should get back to Juneau." It sounded harsh in the face of his kindness, but she couldn't help it she was disrupting his life.

He paused in the act of making biscuits—something she couldn't help but feel she should be doing for him.

"I've been thinking about that." He sounded hesitant, like he knew she wouldn't like it. "I'm not sure you're ready to travel yet."

"No, maybe not yet. But soon."

He nodded. "Let's get you a bath set up. We can figure out your plans later."

He clearly didn't want her to leave. She pondered it, wondering what he might want with her. What could a man who had everything want from a woman like her? But she remained quiet, watching him hurriedly eat his breakfast and then rush out to fetch a big metal tub stored in the rafters of his barn. She watched quietly as he hauled it through the door, placed it in front of the fire and then set to work hauling buckets of snow. The snow piled high in the tub made her shiver. It would probably take some time to melt, all that snow.

Spearing another forkful of fluffy biscuit and swirling it in the brown gravy, she took a bite, a spectator from her comfortable seat at the kitchen table. His cooking was really good, just enough salt and not a lump in sight. She had watched him prepare the dough for the biscuits using his clay pot of sourdough starter to make the bread rise. Every morning he mixed the dough, let it rise, and then rolled it out and cut it into biscuits. Coming fresh from the oven for breakfast they were wonderful, light and flaky and oozing with butter. She knew the importance of a good batch of starter for sourdough; it could last forever and keep a person alive on the trail. His biscuits were just about the best she'd ever had, which again brought to mind this puzzle—he was just too perfect. There had to be a chink in that shining armor somewhere, and she was going to find it. She would find it and then push and push on that spot until he pushed her out of his cabin back to the safety of the strangers in Juneau.

After filling the tub to the top with snow, Noah went to the stove and carried a large pot of boiling water over to the rim. Every so often he glanced over at her at the table. He would smile or comment on some small matter, but what his eyes spoke to her sent new tremors through her body. For some reason she couldn't fathom, this man liked her.

The tub emitted a great hissing sound as the steaming water melted the snow into slushy piles that soon turned into lukewarm water. After another fifteen minutes, Noah had another pot ready and poured it in. Then another and another until the cold, harsh, deadly snow had turned into something inviting, something desirable. Elizabeth could hardly wait to get in.

Clearing his throat Noah said, "I have chores to do in the barn, then I plan to chop some wood, so I'll be gone awhile. The soap and a towel are in the top drawer of the bureau. Is there anything else you'll be needing?"

Elizabeth looked down at the shirt she was still wearing—his shirt—and asked in a rush, "Are my clothes still here?" She hadn't seen them hanging to dry for days.

"Of course. They're in the bottom drawer." He pointed to the bureau, pulling on his winter gear as he talked. "Well, I'll be back around noontime."

With that he was out the door.

Elizabeth drew a deep breath. Forcing herself up, she walked unsteadily over to the bureau and looked for her clothes. There they were, practically her only possessions in the world, folded into neat squares and lying on top of some other shirts like the one she was wearing. After closing the drawer, she opened a narrow top drawer and started digging around for the soap. She found it, a big, flaky cake smelling of lye that she could hardly grip with one hand. The washcloth was easy to find, right beside the soap, but a towel . . . hadn't he said the towel was here also?

Still rummaging through his things, she found a pocketknife with a sharp blade. Staring at it for a moment, she made her decision and dropped it onto the top of her pile. She could hide it on her person after her bath. She might not need it here, but there was always tomorrow. She would need it someday.

Glancing around, she saw the towel draped over the wash-bowl. He'd probably forgotten he had already used it this morning after he shaved. It must be his only one. She reached for it, noting it was still damp and lifted it to her nose. It smelled like him. She closed her eyes and inhaled the scent . . . manly, woodsy, like the land and a man melded. It reached something inside her, making a warmth come over her that startled her. Quickly she lowered the towel, wishing he had another, something sterile and free of . . . anything. Without that choice she hefted it with her other supplies and hobbled over to the steaming tub of melted snow.

Piling her goods on a nearby chair, she dipped a finger into the water. Perfect. She could hardly wait. How long had it been since she'd had a real bath, one of life's few pleasures? Wresting the large buttons from their holes, she worked the plaid shirt from its place. *Ugh.* It was practically stuck to her back, she'd worn it so long and slept in it so soundly. She peeled off the itchy socks he'd given her, staring at her feet and feeling another rush of thankfulness that they weren't ruined. Then gingerly, with a breath of anticipation, she stepped into the water. A loud sigh of pleasure escaped her as she sank down into the depths. She was surprised and pleased to find that she could almost stretch out completely, with her head leaning against one curved end. Closing her eyes, she let her thoughts wander— wander from the small room to Noah, outside chopping wood.

How strong he was. How strong and good. Had she stumbled upon a saint's doorstep?

＊＊＊

BY NOON NOAH'S arms were aching and his stomach was growling. She must be done bathing by now. After stacking the logs against one of the cabin walls and making a trip to his small smokehouse for the last of the deer meat, he headed back.

Cautiously, feeling like a visitor in his own house, he opened the door, his face shielded by a load of wood with the bundle of wrapped meat stacked on top.

"I'm back," he announced hesitantly.

He was walking into the kitchen to deposit the meat on the table when Elizabeth surprised him by saying pleasantly, and in a suddenly silkier voice than he remembered her having, "If you will lower the wood, I'll take that bundle off the top for you."

He automatically did as requested, disgruntled with himself that his mind had seemed to stop working. After feeling the weight lifted, he turned, carried the wood to the fireplace, and busied himself by stacking it and building up the fire. After a time, curiosity got the better of him and he turned around. Instead of a sulky girl lying on the sofa in his excessively large shirt, he saw a radiant young woman, dressed in her own dry and very becoming clothes, busy cooking in his kitchen.

Well, he amended after smelling the air, *trying to cook.* As he stood staring at her, she burned a finger on the handle of the iron skillet and let out a yelp. The noise shocked him into movement. Full of only good intent, he walked over to help. He reached for her hand. "Let me see it," he commanded softly.

She didn't extend her hand toward him as he expected. Instead, she held it to her tight, shaking her head. "It's fine. My own foolishness."

He reached for it. Taking her hand in a firm, steady grip he uncoiled her fingers so that he could examine the wounded finger. There was a red welt but no blister. He'd had enough of both in his early bachelor days to know the protocol. Noah wordlessly backed her to a wooden chair by the table, picked up a cloth, and went to the front door to pack it with snow.

She didn't resist this time, only looked at him with big brown eyes. She wasn't at all sure she wanted him handling her, but she bravely held the offended finger out to him anyway.

He smiled deep inside, seeing this small measure of trust, hoping to be worthy of it. "Hold it in the ice a few moments." He gently wrapped the cloth around her finger, his eyes on the welt. Then he raised his gaze to hers, felt himself drowning in the deepness of her, seeing his reflection and then deeper, into her soul for a brief moment before she quickly looked down.

"Just sit a minute. I'll finish dinner."

He could sense Elizabeth's eyes on him while he tried to save her meal.

"I'm not much of a cook," she said unnecessarily.

Noah nodded in silent agreement as he took the char-broiled meat from the pan. The potatoes, lying next to the meat, were black in places, but still raw inside, and the biscuits . . . well, he guessed that's what they were. He was afraid to ask.

✳ ✳ ✳

ELIZABETH THOUGHT HIS silence meant he was angry. Aha, a chink in the armor. He wasn't fond of anyone messing with his kitchen. A strange chink, but maybe it would qualify. With a sigh she asked, "I suppose you were born knowing how to cook?"

Noah was looking at her as if he couldn't really make out this new side of her. He cleared his throat and responded hesitantly, "No, I've lived alone for a long time. A person learns to cook after doing it for years." His ears were red.

"Well, I haven't been in a kitchen much, but I'm sure, someday, after years of practice, I'll be as competent as you."

"Sure you will, but in the meantime if you would like me to show you some basics, I could."

"OK." She shrugged and smiled at him. "How long have you lived up here?"

"Seven years now. Came up from Montana in '90 to start a trading post with my friend, Will." His eyes took on a faraway gleam. "My pa was a trader before he started ranching. He taught me everything he knew."

"What made you decide to come to Alaska?" Suddenly she wanted to know everything about him.

He threw some fresh steaks into the pan as he talked, warming to the subject. "A friend of mine, Will Collins, came up first. We grew up together. When he got back to Montana we would sit around and talk about Alaska. Will couldn't wait to get back here. He said I would feel the same once I came here, and he was right. I scouted around Juneau for six months before I found this place. It was summertime. You wouldn't recognize this valley in the summer, it's so different. Anyway, I was following Gold Creek. Usually I would go south and follow the road all the way to the Silver Bow Basin and Jumbo, the mine down that way. But that day I pushed east and found Granite Creek. I passed an amazing waterfall and then came into this lower basin. That's where this cabin is now. The valley and lower slope are covered with wildflowers and berries in the summer. It was perfect. I knew it was the place I'd been searching for. I can't imagine I'll ever leave. It's wild, unspoiled. It's home." He paused and gazed out the open window to the mountains, and Elizabeth suddenly understood why the windows had no curtains.

"I guess the land has become a part of me, in my blood." Looking suddenly sheepish, Noah snapped his attention back to the skillet on the stove.

Elizabeth felt herself drawn to him even more. She'd never met anyone so sincere, so passionate about something.

"I like it here, too," she said softly.

Noah turned toward her with his piercing blue eyes and said, "But you like it for its gold."

Elizabeth felt mesmerized by those eyes. Smiling deep into them, she said softly, "It's called 'gold fever,' and I've had it for years. That's what is in my blood."

※ ✳ ※

November 29, 1881
Dear Mrs. Rhodes,

I have just received word from my correspondent at the New York Orphan Asylum. She writes of a child, about four years old who matches your daughter's description. I leave tomorrow with the great hope that we have found her. I will, of course, write immediately should I locate her. You didn't mention the photograph in your letter. Does this mean that you don't have one?

Thank you for the extra funds sent by personal messenger. It is my great pleasure to assist you.

Sincerely yours,
Jeremiah Hoglesby
Private Detective for Hire

Four

"Y ou really pan for gold?"

"Sure. I've been mining since I was fourteen." She paused, steel threading her next phrase. "I know I can do it if I can just get a claim."

"And you plan on going to the Klondike?" Noah asked with his brows raised.

"Yes. I admit I haven't mined alone before, but I did my share of the work. I can pan and work a sluice or a rocker. I know how backbreaking it is. If I can get my hands on a decent claim, I'll hit pay dirt, I know I will."

Noah sighed and gave her a patronizing grin. "OK, you're a miner. But do you have any idea the hardships on a trail like this one? There are mountains to traverse, lakes and rapids to cross. The Canadian Mounties won't let you into the Yukon Territory without a ton of supplies that you have to pack there on your own back. Horses and dogs can only help some of the way, and only if the weather is just right for them. I've heard one of the trails has become a horse graveyard, so many of them have slipped and fallen into the ravines along the way. The trail is a muddy ice bog in the spring, and with all that melting snow, the rapids are so fast you can barely get a vessel down them with your life and supplies in tact. It's no place for a woman."

Elizabeth pressed her lips together. "I'll have you know I've traveled from one end of the West to the other. I've crossed mountains, streams, and rivers, and I'm as capable as any man. You just watch me tackle that trail. Just . . . you . . . watch."

Noah held up his hands in surrender, "Now don't go getting your feathers all ruffled. If you want to risk your fool neck, well then I guess there's nothing I can do about it. But it seems to me you still have one big problem: What are you going to do until the spring thaw?"

Elizabeth hadn't quite figured that out yet, but she wasn't about to let him know. "I'll get a job in Juneau. Wait if I have to." She shrugged. "It will just take a little longer than I originally planned."

Noah made a discouraging sound. "You'll be lucky to find a job with so many others in the same situation. Do you have enough money to hold you over and buy all the supplies needed for the journey?"

Elizabeth didn't. She only had what little she had been able to take from Ross, the investigator who even now might be in Alaska looking for her. After the ship's fare to Sitka, there wasn't much left for precious supplies. She did need a job, and she would have to save every cent she made. But she really didn't appreciate this line of questioning and attempted to change the subject, nodding toward the stove. "I may not be much of a cook, but doesn't that smoke coming off the pan mean it's done?" She raised her brows questioningly, as he had done earlier.

Noah quickly saved the second batch of deer steak. Cutting off a small piece for her, he put it on her plate alongside some beans and leftover sourdough biscuits from breakfast. He seemed deep in concentration, so Elizabeth kept quiet. She watched him give her a plate with carefully small portions and sit down across from her.

NOAH SAID A prayer of thanks, lifted his head, and took a bite. He chewed thoughtfully and watched Elizabeth, her big brown eyes still downcast, looking at her plate. She was the prettiest thing he'd ever seen, and she seemed to get prettier every day. But what was he going to do with her?

Elizabeth interrupted his musings by asking, "How much land do you own around here, Noah?"

Noah shrugged and answered, "About 160 acres."

"So you own some land close to this Juneau gold mine, then?"

Noah nodded, "Yes, very close to it. My land starts at the head of Granite Creek and goes east and north up the slopes of Mount Juneau. I also own part of a big chunk of rock on Mount Olds. Why?"

She toyed with her food a moment and looked at him thoughtfully. "Have you ever prospected on your land? I heard Juneau had its own gold rush a few years ago."

Noah nodded, chewing his food. "Yes, it did. Two fellows, Richard Harris and Joe Juneau, found gold on Gold Creek in 1880. But from what I heard, they really owed their success to a Tlingit chief named Kowee. I missed the rush that followed.

But I don't think it lasted long before all the placer mining was panned out and the lode mining began. Most of the gold around here was in hard rock. The big companies moved in with heavy equipment and set up mining camps like the Jumbo. It was destroyed by a snowslide in 1895. There's talk of rebuilding it, but I don't know that they will." Noah shrugged. "Will wanted to start a trading post for the miners, and it didn't take much for him to convince me to join him in that venture. But to answer your question, no, I didn't prospect my land. Between lack of time and, I guess, lack of faith that any gold was there, I didn't give it much thought." He frowned and took another bite. "Though I'll admit that with all the excitement of this new rush, I've begun to wonder . . ."

"Noah, you could be sitting on a fortune! Are there many creeks or streams on your land?"

Noah nodded. "Several. Granite Creek is the big one."

Elizabeth shook her head in disbelief. "And you've never even checked them?"

He shrugged with one shoulder. "They were probably mined out during the rush. Besides, I don't know the first thing about gold mining."

Elizabeth huffed. "Neither do most of the greenhorns who stampede. It doesn't take long to learn, though." She cocked her head and smiled. "I could help you."

The idea of hiring her as a prospector had already occurred to him, but the notion had its problems. For one thing, he didn't know if she was telling the truth about being a gold miner. He really needed an expert since he knew next to nothing about it. He wasn't sure he trusted her, either. It would be foolish to hire someone he didn't trust, and yet . . . something about the idea appealed to him.

Trying not to show his excitement, he said, "We'd have to start in spring when the streams thaw out."

Elizabeth shook her head. "I can't wait that long. All the good claims will be gone if I stay here. I need to leave for Dawson by first thaw."

"Elizabeth, I hate to be the one to tell you, but all the good claims are already gone. They were gone a year ago."

She bristled as he knew she would. "Then why are all those millionaires still getting off the ships in Seattle?"

"Those men panned that gold a year ago. In August, last year, three men discovered gold on Rabbit Creek. They renamed it Bonanza Creek and staked their claim. Word spread up here about the findings, but winter was just around the corner. When the Yukon River froze, it trapped the prospectors up there near Dawson. That's why it took so long for word to reach the outside. By the time Alaska began to be flooded with gold seekers, most of the good claims were gone."

Elizabeth stood abruptly and walked away from the table. With her back to him she said, "I'll find a way. I always do."

Noah sighed. He knew he was hurting her, but the thought of this fragile-looking woman taking on the man-eating northern trails and the Yukon River made his stomach lurch. Softly he said, "Elizabeth, you may know a lot about panning gold, but this is Alaska. The ground up there is frozen—not in inches but in *feet*. Maybe even miles. I heard the men in Dawson are building fires every night to thaw out a few feet of earth at a time. They have to dig it, haul it up with buckets, and then build another fire in the hole and do it all over again. In the spring they'll have a ton of earth to wash. A ton. They have nothing better to do with their winter, stranded as they are, but I do. If we wait until spring thaw, we can check out all the streams on my land. It may take awhile, but who knows? We might find gold."

She turned, eyes blazing. "Yes, *your* land. What kind of future am I supposed to make for myself prospecting for someone else? I need to strike it rich on my own."

Noah motioned for the chair. "Elizabeth, please sit down and listen to me. You would be a partner, not just working for me."

She ignored the chair, "What *exactly* would being your partner mean?"

Words and plans that he hadn't even let himself think through started pouring out of his mouth. "Come spring, we decide on a spot and you help me mine the land. I'll split any gold we find, say 40/60."

"40/60? Why not 50/50?"

"I'll be providing the food and shelter. That should count for ten percent. It's a gamble, you see. You could end up paying a lot for food and board or next to nothing, depending on how much we find. What do you think?" Noah smiled broadly, knowing it was sound reasoning.

"What do I do until spring? You seem to have my future sewed up tight."

She sounded so resentful, Noah had to suppress his smile. It was killing her to accept his offer. "Actually, I did have a thought on that, but only if you're agreeable to it."

"Well?"

"In another week or so, when you're ready to travel, I'll take you down to Juneau to the trading post. With all the added business of the miners, I know Will and his wife would welcome the help this winter. Then, when spring thaw breaks, we'll pick our ground, set up camp, and if all goes well, maybe hire a man or two to help."

Elizabeth closed her eyes briefly. When she opened them Noah could read the resignation, but she didn't like it. "Since I'm not in a position to bargain with you, Mr. Wesley, I will accept your offer, but I'd like to make one thing perfectly clear. This is a business partnership, nothing else." She turned away from him and spoke toward the stove, "I'll have my own shelter."

Noah's fist came down on the table, making the plates jump. "Confound it, woman! I—I wouldn't offer anything like that. You'd have your own, well, you know, shelter. You didn't really think I was . . . I mean, I might, but not unless we were married . . . that is . . . well, you know what I mean." He broke off in frustration. "And don't call me 'Mr. Wesley.' It's just plain Noah."

Elizabeth had turned in shock when he began his tirade. Clamping her open jaw shut, she said, "OK. I just wanted to be clear on that." Looking down at his empty plate she ventured, "I'll be glad to wash these dishes and do any other chores to help out while I am here."

Noah was still flustered and it took him a moment to grasp the turn of topics. Too gruffly he asked, "Are you sure you're ready to be on your feet? I nearly froze my feet a couple of times and I know it takes some time to heal."

"Oh, and I'm sure you just laid around the cabin for days while you were waiting for your feet to thaw, right?" she asked, her head cocked to one side and a curtain of dark hair falling over one shoulder.

Noah answered with a shrug, "I guess not, but you're a woman."

Elizabeth's lips pursed together. "And hardier than you think, which I will prove soon enough. But for now, I'll start with the dishes. At least let me help you while I'm here."

Suddenly Noah understood. Her pride was at stake, and he couldn't say that in the same position he would feel any differently. Looking around the orderly cabin, he spied a basket under the bed and smiled. There was one household chore he could never get his hands adept at. "I'm not much at mending. Can you sew?"

Elizabeth nodded. "Yes, I can sew. What do you want made?"

Noah stood and walked to the bed. Bending down, he reached under the frame and pulled out a willow basket overflowing with all kinds of garments. He talked as he sorted through the pile. "Just some mending. I can't seem to fix holes, and they've kind of piled up over the last few years." Glancing over his shoulder at her he added, his voice quieting a degree or two, not wanting to hurt her feelings, "You'll be needing some warmer clothes yourself, to see you through till spring." He looked back down at the bed. "I have some nice furs you could use. You'll need them for the journey back to Juneau."

He held his breath in the ensuing silence and then was relieved to hear, "That's very kind of you, thank you." When he turned around, she had busied herself by pouring water from a porcelain pitcher into a pot to heat for dishwater.

Noah put one of his piles, the one with long underwear and other more personal items, back into the basket and stuffed it under the bed, leaving the other pile on top. "Well, just take your time on these things. I need to scout out some dinner, so I'll be gone for about an hour, going around the perimeter of the cabin checking for prints. I'll probably spend most of tomorrow further out, if the weather holds." He smiled at her, trying to put her back at ease. He found he would rather see her spitting mad any day than see her humbled like this. It would be good to leave for a while and give her some breathing room. Shrugging into his coat, Noah had to check the sudden urge to kiss her on the forehead before he left. He shook his head slightly as he bent down to tie on his snowshoes. "I'll be back soon." With a wave, he was out the door and shutting it tight behind him.

Walking to the barn to feed the animals, Noah smiled as he thought of Elizabeth. For such a little woman she sure had a lot of courage. She was really something. It hit him suddenly how much he would miss her when she left. He didn't want her to leave. He didn't want his life to go back to what would now seem lonely, almost desolate. Glancing up at the beamed roof of the barn Noah whispered, "I never thought I'd ask it, but . . . could You send another blizzard?"

January 14, 1882
Dear Mrs. Rhodes,

I regret to inform you that the woman with whom I have been corresponding was no longer employed at the orphanage when I arrived. The other teachers claimed not to have ever known her. I believe they are being dishonest and that Elizabeth was here, but someone has learned of our inquiries and they have moved her to another location. No one will speak to me except to claim they've never seen or heard of an Elizabeth Greyson with your child's age and description. I have carefully searched the area for both the teacher and Elizabeth but have not been able to locate any knowledge of them. I must tell you, ma'am, this is too coincidental to be accidental. Do you have any enemies I should know of?

> *Sincerely yours,*
> *Jeremiah Hoglesby*
> *Private Detective for Hire*

Five

When Noah returned he was surprised to find Elizabeth in the kitchen again.

She turned toward him as he walked in, wiped tendrils of curls from her forehead with the back of her hand, which held a long-handled wooden spoon, and said, "I'm glad you're back. I was beginning to worry."

With that announcement, she turned back toward the stove, as though she said such things to him every day. Stirring vigorously, she shot him a smile over her shoulder—the kind of smile that held him fastened to the floor.

"I'm boiling rice. I didn't think I could mess it up too badly, do you?"

Noah was entranced, despite himself. To think that just a few short days ago she was a pale and lifeless girl to him. Now she was a vivacious, warm woman. He liked the way she moved about his kitchen, with feminine gestures and graceful tilts and lifts to her arms. She was so different. He decided he had been away from women too long. He could only shake his head and slowly pull off his gear as he watched her move, light-footed, around the kitchen. Finally, he walked over and stood behind

I could hardly see to get home at night. When I heard about this gold rush, I jumped at the chance to make a real future for myself."

"And risk your life in the process!" He was nearly shouting, shouting at the unfairness of it all. That she had to be so strong all the time. That she didn't want him. That he might never be able to scale the walls she'd constructed around her heart. But she didn't know that.

"*Because* I'd have to risk my life in the process," she said low and fierce and whisper-thin. "I had nothing else left to lose."

He shoved away from the table, not knowing how to answer that except to say, "Dead people don't have futures, Elizabeth."

What did it matter to him what she did with her life, anyway? It wasn't as if he could do anything about it. Stalking over to the hook on the wall, he pulled his coat down and shrugged into it.

"I'm going to feed the dogs."

❅ ❅ ❅

ELIZABETH WATCHED HIM go with an angry glare. How dare he try to tell her about her life. If he knew about the things she'd done, he would be finished with her. She imagined the shock and even disgust on his face had she told him of the agreement she'd struck with Ross. She shook her head slowly. She couldn't think of that.

There were many other, lesser transgressions to shock him with that she knew by heart, like a creed, the mantra of her existence: the subtle lies, the petty thefts, the calculating maneuvers to get what she wanted, what she needed to survive to the next

her to peer over her shoulder into the pot. She sure did smell better than the rice.

"It looks good," he said. "How long has it been boiling?"

Elizabeth shrugged, her shoulders brushing up against his chest. "Only a few minutes," she said softly.

She had stiffened a little, at his nearness he supposed, but he wasn't willing to step back just yet. Above and in front of her sat a shaker with salt in it. He reached for it, saying, "You'll need a little of this." His voice was huskier than he meant it to be, and he cleared his throat. It had been a long time since he had felt this awkward around a woman. He had been sixteen when he'd had his first crush on a neighbor's daughter. She had been the fickle sort, only interested in him as long as he ignored her. The moment he'd noticed her that summer she suddenly filled out her dress and looked at him with subtle challenge in her eyes, when she knew she'd snared his attention, she'd suddenly turned uppity and unreachable. He was left with hot dreams and thin air. It had been a good lesson, though, and he'd been more careful of appearing too eager after that. There had been a few others since that time. A woman in Montana had caught his eye. Now older and wiser, he'd courted her with some finesse. But in the end, she just hadn't seemed the right fit. She would have been a practical choice, but he could only see himself living the daytime hours with her. He'd broken it off, feeling wretched in the face of her tears. In Alaska he'd been "set up" a few times by well-meaning friends. He'd gone along with it, but none had captured his heart or, truthfully, any other part of him.

He looked down at the woman in his cabin and inhaled as quietly as he could. Now, *this* woman. This woman captured his imagination. He could not get enough of looking at her or listening to the outlandish things she said. At night, hearing her soft breathing just steps away, he lay awake wanting to go to her. Sleep only made him dream of her, even dreaming of how she smelled with her clothes drying beside his bed. He lay there wanting, dreaming of touching her again, touching her in ways that would bring her to life . . . again . . . but in another way. She was all he could think about.

Elizabeth stood there, stiffly enduring, slowly stirring the swirling bits of rice. Finally, with quiet force she stated, "You may think you want me, Noah, but believe me, you don't."

Her tone shocked him more than her words, so much so that he took a step back and then another. "What do you mean?"

She turned and looked at him with eyes as old as the earth. "You don't know me."

It took courage, in the face of those eyes, but he stepped back toward her and took her hands into his. "I want to know you."

She laughed. It was brittle and made his heart sink. What had made this young woman so fierce? So unreachable?

She laughed again, this time making light of it. With a shrug of one shoulder she turned back to her rice and asked, "What do you want to know?"

Noah felt his throat constrict. How could she change like that, from one moment to the next, into someone else? He grappled with a hundred questions, half wanting to run out into the familiar territory of his frozen land. But he couldn't give up. There must be some key, some way to unlock her barriers. "What kind of family did you have?"

She stiffened, almost imperceptibly. Had he not been focusing on every nuance of her stance he would have missed it.

"Oh, you know. Just the normal kind."

Noah pressed on. "How old were you when you lost your parents?"

Her head was bent over the pot in apparent concentration. She had knotted up her dark hair and some curls had fallen, making the back of her neck look vulnerable in its graceful beauty. He wanted to kiss her there more than anything he could ever remember wanting. His body ached to take her into his arms and kiss her.

"I don't remember. My grandparents raised me. We lived on a farm in Illinois."

"I thought you were from Seattle?" he managed from a tight throat.

Elizabeth turned from the pan, brushing past him and busying herself setting dishes on the table. "I am from Seattle. I moved out west after my grandparents died."

"All alone?"

"Yes, well, I had friends. And I made a decent living for myself."

"Panning gold?" he asked with more heat than he meant to express aloud.

"Yes, and doing other odd jobs. I was a seamstress at a dress shop in Seattle."

"At least that was a respectable job."

Elizabeth snapped, "I am sorry to offend your high moral standards, but I did what was necessary. I couldn't pay the boarding house and feed myself on what they paid me to work fourteen-hour days, sewing until my eyes were so blurred

day, the men on the goldfields . . . lonely men, who were so easy to take advantage of. She'd grown overly confident, thinking she could play the game without paying a price. And she'd been very successful, until Ross.

No, Noah could not possibly understand her—he was from a different world. He certainly wouldn't want her as his business partner, and she needed him to believe she had agreed to his plan. She needed the help of his friends to get through the winter. Never mind that for the first time she felt the emotional upheaval of a dull pain in her chest and enormous guilt when she looked into his clear blue eyes as he, hopeful and excited, spoke of their partnership come spring. She squashed the emotions. A conscience was something only the rich could afford.

Throwing elk steaks onto the hot skillet, she attempted to cook the meat. The steam and sizzle coming from the blackened pan sounded like she felt. Why must he probe and poke at her? He knew nothing about the black, empty hole that gaped inside her where his questions lurked. What had happened to her parents? As if she hadn't wondered that a thousand times and then determined to wonder about it no more. Why did he have to make her think of it again? But she couldn't seem to help it. The one memory locked deep in the recesses of her mind, a place she hadn't visited in years, mercilessly surfaced. A woman . . . soft, warm, comforting, motherly embrace. A smile that had beamed at her. Eyes that had glowed with love. Had she imagined it? She was afraid to dwell on it, that it might disappear into nothing but a wishful daydream. No, it must have been her mother. Her real mother.

Then the memory of aloneness—feeling so utterly alone and frightened, with no one to come when she called. Dark rooms and loud voices and children crying, all blurred together for the first years. She'd learned the value of disappearing into silence those years.

The memories were clearer around age five when, she had since concluded, she must have been moved to a different orphanage. She'd received a good education and plenty of food, simple and repetitive though it was. The girls were like girls anywhere, she supposed, some kind and loyal, some spiteful and mean. It hadn't been bad, really, but it would take more humility than she possessed to tell Noah about it. She didn't want or need his piteous stare.

The real trouble had started later when she was adopted. She ground her teeth, turning the meat over in the pan, stabbing at it with a sharp fork, as she thought back on pinch-faced, evil-eyed Margaret Dunning and her shiftless husband, Henry. She repressed a shudder, remembering how they had inspected her, making her stand and turn around, examining her teeth and then her body before taking her home with them. It didn't take long to figure out what the Dunnings had really wanted. With them, she'd learned all the colors of dirt, how hard clay was and full of rock, how little by little even a skinny girl could move mountains. She learned to hide food in her pockets and then, when they'd found that, in underclothes and broken-down boots. She learned the sting of a switch, the sound it made as it slashed through the air depending on its thickness, and the haphazard aim of blind anger.

It had taken six long years before the Dunnings had finally realized that, even with her, they still couldn't make a living off the dirt. Henry came home one day, drunker than usual with more than whiskey. He'd been struck by gold fever. He'd heard of a strike in San Juan, Utah. The next instant, it seemed, they were moving west. It had been her first ray of hope. Out west she could run away. There would be opportunities and, like the prairie schooners she watched sail by, she intended to float away on the first one that came along. But the unexpected happened: Elizabeth caught the fever. Gold was all she thought about. The next big strike was always just around the corner, hope a heavy aphrodisiac. And it was contagious. All three worked doggedly to find the mother lode. Elizabeth had been sure that gold was the answer to all her problems.

One day Henry had shown up in camp after a long absence with a toothless, ear-splitting grin, as excited as she'd ever seen him.

"Where you been? What you been up to?" Margaret had asked suspiciously, eyes narrowed. "You're hidin' somethin', I know you."

Henry shook his head, grinning, something he rarely allowed himself to do because of his blackened, rotten teeth. He dug into the pocket of a pair of faded tan pants. What he pulled out left them both speechless. It was the biggest chunk of gold they had ever seen, laying right in the center of his dirty palm.

The air whooshed out of Margaret as she snatched it out of his hand. "Where'd you get that?" she demanded, looking at it with amazed glee in her eyes.

Henry's chin rose up and his chest puffed out with pride. "I found me a new claim, woman. Gold showing on the surface, thick as my wrist."

Elizabeth was aghast. Henry never spoke to Margaret like that, as if he demanded her to respect him. Margaret quickly burst his bubble.

"You? A new claim?" she shrieked. "Why you no-good, lying thief. You stole that or did somethin' evil to get it."

Henry shook his head but didn't look her in the eyes. "N-no," he stammered. "I didn't do nothin' wrong. Now you two pack up. We got to get back to that claim afore' someone else takes it. I covered the gold, so's I could come back for the both of y'uns. Didn't have to do that, ya know. I could'a left you, woman. Gone off and got rich on my own. But I didn't. I came back for you." He turned suddenly toward Elizabeth, eyes mean and hard. "And you, girlie. We got plenty of work for you to do, so be quick about it and get this camp broke up."

Elizabeth turned away before he could see the flare of rebellion in her eyes and began gathering supplies. Had Henry really struck the mother lode? It seemed impossible that he'd had such luck. Like Margaret said, he had probably done something bad, terrible even, to gain possession of that nugget. But maybe, just maybe, something had finally gone their way.

They packed up that morning and started west, Henry muttering about a dirt trail head that he had marked with a large rock. Three long, exhausting days later they came to the new claim. Elizabeth could not believe what her sight told her. Under an overhanging cliff, there was a vein of gold showing on the surface of the rock that trailed in a glittering path from their feet to higher than Henry's head with no end in sight. It promised to be a fortune.

She hadn't been fooled though. A person didn't stake a claim on a spot that had already been mined as this one had, especially if gold was showing on the surface. Only an idiot would part with a claim like that—or a dead man.

Margaret must have thought the same, for she accused Henry of murdering a man to jump the claim. Henry had at first denied it, for days stuck to his story and then, in a sobbing, drunk fit, admitted to the deed. What Elizabeth overheard later that night had sent the first real, chilling fear for her life coursing through her entire body. Husband and wife had talked at length of how they would blame the murder on Elizabeth and concocted an elaborate story to support their claim. She'd known then that she had to escape. They would never share the wealth with her anyway. She forced herself to see the truth— that they would use her, use what little strength she had to help dig out the gold, and then horde it for themselves and blame the murder on her.

In the end, she heard that a man's body was found downstream from the claim. The body had a bullet hole in it, and some men had recognized the miner. They were looking for the killer. All she knew at the time was that Henry had suddenly become nervous. The end had finally come. Elizabeth had to get away from the Dunnings and whatever law would eventually catch up to them. That's when she'd escaped. The man and woman had been so distracted by the gold that it had been easy.

At seventeen years old she had crept away in the middle of the night and joined a family going to Northern California, telling them her parents had been taken by typhoid. It was a common enough occurrence and they hadn't questioned her.

Reaching California, Elizabeth had finally broken out on her own. She'd mined here and there for as long as the gold lasted, alternately panning and sewing for a living. Then she'd gradually worked her way to Seattle and the edge of the continent. After settling into a meager existence as a seamstress, she'd met Ross and learned that the Dunnings were looking for her. The knowledge terrified her, wearing grooves of fear into her mind. What if they were still trying to convince the law that she was responsible for the murder? Miners hung men for stealing, much less killing. It wouldn't matter that she was a woman, either. Both Henry and Margaret were experts at lying and swindling. If they had made it look like she'd done it, then her only chance was to get as far away as possible. And she could never see Ross again. What he had done to her . . . no, she couldn't think of that.

Then, in the middle of July, just before her twentieth birthday, her salvation came. Word of gold in the Yukon Territory of Canada reached Seattle. *Gold* was waiting, hidden in the streambeds of a place so vast, so treacherous, so forbidding that she could lose herself. Something told her, in the pit of her stomach, that she would find what she was looking for here, in this icy wilderness laden with streams of gold.

January 5, 1884
Dear Mrs. Rhodes,

I apologize for the length between letters. I have not given up hope, but thus far I have found no other clues as to the whereabouts of your daughter. Rest assured, I shall not stop trying.

Thank you for the additional payment. I am considering another trip to the New York Orphan Asylum. Sometimes, after the passage of time, people will begin to talk again.

Sincerely yours,
Jeremiah Hoglesby
Private Detective for Hire

Six

The sudden opening of the door interrupted her retrospection. A boisterous shout followed the noise. "Noah, come on man, get the door open!"

Noah pushed through the door with another tall man and a big, beautiful white dog following close behind.

"Wesley, you old dog, how're you doing up here on this slab of ice?"

Before Noah had a chance to answer, the blond man went on in an accent unfamiliar to Elizabeth. "I just returned from Seattle, can you believe little Juneau? That town is booming." His voice trailed off as he spotted Elizabeth by the table. Letting off a long whistle he said, "Didn't know you'd gone and gotten hitched." He gave Noah a leering grin. "Can't say as I blame you, though. She sure is pretty." Raking his floppy brown hat from his head, he nodded and said, "Hello there, ma'am."

Elizabeth only nodded to him and looked at Noah questioningly.

Noah cleared his throat and said, "Uh, she isn't my wife, Jacko. She's . . . a friend." Walking over to Elizabeth, he took her hand in his and led her over to Jacko. "This is Elizabeth, and this is an old trapping buddy of mine, Jacko Cherosky. And this fellow"—he ruffled the thick fur of the dog's neck— "is a Semoya named Kodiak. A Russian through and through, both of 'em."

The blond man smiled with dazzling white teeth. His dog was beautiful, all white with a thick ruff about his neck and a curled tail. Kodiak frisked around the room, sticking his nose into everything, including Elizabeth's skirts. Jacko stretched out his hand. "Glad to meet you, ma'am."

Looking at Noah he boomed, "You better snatch her up while you can. She might just be the prettiest single woman in the whole Alaskan territory. The place is full of men, and she won't last long!"

Elizabeth didn't like the way he was talking about her as if she wasn't even there. "I didn't come out here to catch a husband," she said coolly.

"Well then, what did you come out here for?" There was a twinkle in his eyes that lit up his face.

She could feel Noah watching her as she straightened her shoulders and lifted her chin. "For the gold, of course. A woman has as much right to that gold as a man, doesn't she?"

Jacko laughed and dramatically gripped his heart. "She's wounded me, Wesley!" Then he stopped and looked at her with a slow smile. "But in answer to your question, ma'am, any woman that has the grit to mine for gold deserves to hit the mother lode."

Elizabeth gave him a stiff smile. "I'm glad to hear it because that is exactly what I plan to do." She turned to Noah. "Shall I serve dinner? Your guest is probably hungry after his long trip."

Noah nodded, strode over to his chest of drawers and pulled out the bottle of liquor he kept around for his friend. "Some whiskey to warm you up, Jacko?"

Jacko threw his big parka over the back of the sofa and settled into a chair, "Of course, of course. It's cold enough to freeze the ba-a"—he glanced at Elizabeth and continued—"um, that is, the tail off a shaggy beast such as Kodiak here." Grinning broadly he shrugged. "The usual."

Elizabeth glanced over from the kitchen and frowned at the slushy tracks from the big stranger. Again she marveled how remarkably neat and clean Noah was in comparison to most of the men she knew. It would be interesting to see if his manner changed much around another of his kind. Her gaze wandered to the friend seated in a low wooden chair by the fire. He was a good-looking man, as tall as Noah but not quite as wide in the chest, with his long legs stretched out in front of him and crossed at the ankles. Jacko. *Hmmm, the name fits him.* His voice and mannerisms bordered on boisterous, making wide sweeps with his hands as he talked with Noah. Then Noah told the story of how he had found her barely alive on his doorstep.

NOAH FOUND HIS attention wandering to Elizabeth. He couldn't seem to concentrate on Jacko's litany of the boom going on in Juneau. And, confound it, he was usually so glad to see his old friend. They only saw each other once or twice during the winter months. And when Jacko came to stay, he usually stayed at least a couple of weeks.

Noah returned his gaze to his friend and felt heat steal up his face for only the third time in his life that he could remember, two of them in the last few days. Jacko was looking at him with knowing eyes and a mocking grin. Noah wondered if he looked like the lovesick puppy that he was beginning to believe he was. No doubt he did. Shifting in his chair, he determined to give his friend his full attention when her sweet voice called out, "It's ready!"

Jacko laughed heartily as Noah jumped out of his chair. "Looks to me like your bachelor days are numbered, my friend. That is, if she'll have you. She could certainly do better."

Noah would have taken exception to that remark, except for the sparkle in his friend's light blue eyes. Jacko was going to have a good time teasing him about this, no doubt about that.

"You wouldn't be thinking an old scoundrel like you would make a better catch, now would you?" Noah asked, with just a little more aggression than he meant. They were nearly locking horns by the time they made it to the kitchen area, where Elizabeth was standing with her hands on her hips, glaring at both of them.

"What makes you two giants think I'd take either of you?"

She slapped the plates of food on the table with a bang for effect and turned back to the stove, trying to hide a smile. She lifted the heavy bowl of rice and moved it to the table, pulled out her chair, and sat down next to Noah. Folding her hands in her lap, she bowed her head and waited expectantly for Noah to bless the food.

Jacko cleared his throat and quickly ducked his head.

Noah said a quicker grace than usual and began to eat.

"So, Mr. Cherosky, what is the news from Juneau concerning the gold rush?" She darted Noah a look. "Noah may not be interested, but I'd like to hear anything you can tell me about it."

"Well, ma'am, I was shocked when I got back to this area. It's a regular boomtown, as you probably know. I've been in Seattle, doing a little trading and stocking up on goods. I was barely able to get passage back up here when I did. The ships are loaded, and the price of fares is just plain thievery. But I had to get supplies for the trading post if this crowd is going to weather out the winter in Juneau. Has Noah told you we're partners?"

Elizabeth looked at Noah and raised her eyebrows. "No, he seems to have left that out."

"Well, we and a third man, Will Collins, own the only trading post in Juneau. We arrived before anybody was here but the natives and a few miners from the Juneau strike, which was about ten years ago, and it's already paid off, hasn't it, Noah?" He looked briefly at his friend with a wolfish smile.

Noah only nodded and continued to chew. He thought it best for his own self-preservation if he just kept his mouth shut for a while.

"Anyway, I was elected to go south for a heavy run of supplies, miners' supplies and food mostly, to hold all of us through the winter." Turning toward Noah, he exclaimed, "You wouldn't believe some of the schemes and gadgets they're trying to pawn off on those green, would-be miners. There's a cure for the scurvy, steam-powered sleds, and I even brought back a pair of 'Klondike boots' for a good laugh on Will." He laughed uproariously. "They have spikes on the bottom and armor plating on the outside. A man wouldn't get a mile in them! You have to see them."

Turning back to Elizabeth he said, "There's more than one way to strike it rich in this gold rush." He winked at Elizabeth and cut into a big chunk of meat.

"Well, I must say, you have a hand in all the pies, Noah. You really should have let me know this before we agreed to become partners. I may have had a different answer."

Jacko looked back and forth between the two of them, asking with raised brows, "You two are partners?"

Noah was hesitant. A man didn't really like to admit that he had a woman as a business partner. He knew what Jacko would think—was already thinking. "Oh it's nothing really. She wants to mine for gold, so I thought we would take a look at the streams on my land come spring." He hoped that sounded neutral enough to suit both of them, but looking at Elizabeth, the way she sat straight up and stiff in her chair and didn't meet his eyes, he knew he had made a mistake.

Noah felt a rush of anger. The thought of not having an excuse to see her again after he left her in Juneau didn't sit at all well with him, and yet, with Jacko questioning their plans, making him speak them aloud, they sounded exactly how they really were. He just wanted her to come back; he just wanted *her*. Confound it, what was she doing to him? She wasn't right for him. She didn't have any of the qualities he needed in a wife. She was feisty, unpredictable, too young, too fragile, and worst of all, she tied his stomach up in knots half the time. It'd be a living hell. What was he even thinking? Shaking his head, he looked down at his now-empty plate, wishing there was more food to keep his hands busy.

Elizabeth must have seen his confusion. She looked at him with a small smile, understanding, and something else in her eyes, like she was considering something, weighing it. It made him anxious, thinking he had really angered her.

She stood, taking his plate, walked to the stove and placed another steak on it. Setting it in front of him, she stated, "We're even. You may have filled my plate too full, but now I haven't filled yours full enough."

Noah nodded at her and cut off a thick piece.

She turned to Jacko. "Would you care for seconds, Mr. Cherosky?"

The blond nodded and winked. "Call me Jacko and I'll call you Liz. How about that?"

Elizabeth smiled at him. "I suppose that would be all right."

Noah grasped the handle of his knife tightly and sawed at his meat, noticing how warm and inviting that smile was. She never smiled at *him* like that.

Taking his plate to the stove, Elizabeth dished up the last of the meat. Then she refilled all their coffee mugs and sat back down.

Between bites Jacko asked, "So, Liz, Noah said he found you on his doorstep in the middle of a blizzard. I must say, the good Lord must have had a guardian angel looking out for you that night. It's a miracle you found this place."

Elizabeth nodded, cup suspended under her lips. "Yes, I was very lucky. I do believe Noah saved my life."

"I didn't do that much," he heard himself remark, remembering all that he had done. God help him, he was turning into an idiot right here in front of her. Fighting for control, he made himself lean back in his chair, keep his mouth closed, and drink his coffee.

"I'm sure that isn't true," Elizabeth said sincerely, looking him square in the eyes. "I will be forever in your debt, Noah Wesley." Her voice had softened and taken on an almost seductive tone.

The room was silent. The undercurrent of emotion between them was impossible to repress.

"Noah mentioned you'll be going back to Juneau? Can I help with anything?" Jacko asked with grinning enthusiasm, breaking the tension.

"Actually, yes," Noah replied. "It would help tremendously if you could stay here and take care of the animals while I take Elizabeth down to Juneau. I'd like to stay in town two or three days to get supplies and help her get settled." Looking over at Elizabeth he said, "If that's all right with you."

Elizabeth nodded, giving him that unreadable look of hers.

"Sure, I'd be glad to help out. I was planning to stay at least a week." Patting his flat stomach, Jacko added, "I need to get back to the wilderness anyway. Keeps a man on his toes, and I could use a little toughening up after being in Seattle for a month. The climate's downright balmy by comparison down there."

Looking back and forth between them, Jacko asked, "When do you leave and what's the plan once you reach Juneau?"

"I'll get things ready tomorrow. We can head out early the next morning. The days are so short now, and I would like to make it in the daylight. As far as the plan, I'm taking her to the trading post in Juneau. Will and Cara have their hands full with all the miners waiting out the winter. I'm thinking they could use the extra help."

"You're probably right. I forgot to mention it before, but Cara's expecting. She would be glad to have an extra pair of hands, especially after the baby's born."

"When is her baby due?" Elizabeth asked.

Jacko shrugged as he took a bag of tobacco from his front shirt pocket. "Didn't ask, but I could tell she was carrying so probably not too long."

Directing her gaze to Noah, Elizabeth inquired, "What will I be doing at the trading post?"

Noah shrugged. "You would probably learn to measure gold dust on the scales and trade it for the goods the miners need to buy. With your experience, you could help outfit a miner with supplies for the trail."

Jacko looked thoughtfully at her and added, "Will wouldn't hide you in the back, that's for sure. He's one to take advantage of an opportunity to make extra money, and with a pretty woman dishing out the goods, he'll figure you to be good for business."

Noah saw the nervous look in her eyes and reached out to grasp her hand. "You'll be fine with Will and Cara. Will is like a brother to me, and Cara is a wonderful woman. They will take good care of you, I promise. I wouldn't take you there if I didn't know that for a fact. You understand?"

"Yes, of course. I guess it just took me by surprise, so soon and all." She closed her mouth, hesitated, and said, "I guess I'll miss you."

Noah looked at Jacko and then back at Elizabeth, flushing around the collar. Would the blushing ever stop now that it had started? "I'll come and see you as often as I can," he assured.

Jacko laughed, "And I'll stop by, too. Why, I live right in town. I can stop in every day if you get lonesome."

Elizabeth squealed as Jacko dodged a bone that suddenly sprung up from Noah's plate and propelled itself toward his head.

Jacko roared with laughter. "OK, OK, I'll only come every other day."

❄ ❄ ❄

May 24, 1885
Dear Mrs. Rhodes,

Please know my desire to be of service to you is unflagging, but I have unfortunately been unable to find further clues. The New York Orphan Asylum has threatened to have me arrested should I show up again. This, of course, makes me all the more determined. I am sure they are covering up the unsavory details of Elizabeth's flight, and I suspect they are being paid for their silence as they have just finished an additional wing from an anonymous benefactor. The more I have prodded into the details of the addition, the more threatening to my person the orphanage and builder have become. I have begun to carry a gun. At the risk of sounding cracked, I sometimes feel as if something dark is looming over my shoulder. It's very disquieting, really, but again, makes me more determined than ever. Rest assured, we will not stop until we have found her.

Sincerely yours,
Jeremiah Hoglesby
Private Detective for Hire

Seven

She couldn't sleep. The room was cozy warm with the perpetual fire crackling and popping, the quilt tucked up tight under her chin. Tomorrow they would prepare for the trip to Juneau and the next day they would leave. Just two more days with him.

Noah had given Jacko the bed, while Noah slept on a thick fur between the fire and where she lay on the sofa. He had fallen asleep right away tonight, with the kind of deep and even rising and falling of his broad chest that spoke of easy contentment, of a peaceful, steadfast nature. His blanket was another long, dark fur. Elizabeth couldn't help but think about what it would feel like to lie between those two silky surfaces. She turned away and closed her eyes. She didn't want to watch him. She told herself it was impossible to consider anything with Noah other than a surface friendship, a sham business partnership. But still, she couldn't sleep. She could hear Jacko's loud snoring from the bed. A movement from Noah regained her attention. He had rolled over onto his back and the fur had slipped down a few more inches. Firelight danced over his dark form, illuminating then shadowing, revealing and hiding, mesmerizing her. Turning her face to the ceiling, she squeezed her eyes shut. What was wrong with her? Not even Ross, the only man she had *believed* herself in love with, had made her feel like this man did. Turning back she stared at him, trying to reason it out in her mind.

His feet must be cold, sticking out from the bottom like that. Glancing around she saw the heavy cotton shirt she had mended after dinner while the men talked. He would probably kick it off, but she thought it was worth the effort. After all the care he had given her, he could use some in return, couldn't he? She slipped out of her makeshift bed and sidled over to the shirt. Whisking it from the back of the rocker, she crept over to the sleeping form and spread out the shirt, letting it float gently onto his feet.

She jumped when a hand suddenly clamped around her wrist. "Elizabeth?" the groggy, deep voice asked. "What are you doing? Is something wrong?"

She'd been caught. Biting her lower lip and standing in her thin undergarments, she started shivering, her teeth chattering. "I-I-I w-wasn't doing any-anything," she said, trying to pull away from the grip on her arm.

Noah easily drew her closer until she was kneeling in front of him and whispered, "You were doing something. Why are you up? Are you all right?"

Elizabeth looked down at his chest and sighed. She couldn't possibly tell him the truth. It was ridiculous.

NOAH WAS FULLY awake now and growing more uncomfortable by the moment. She was sitting there in front of him with the firelight casting dancing shadows on her curves, her gown tangled up around her bare legs. Forcing his eyes to her face, he concentrated on keeping them there. But all he could see was the top of her silky hair. Putting a thumb under her chin he tilted her face up. That was a mistake. When he saw the smoldering depths of her eyes, he knew. God help him . . . she wanted him.

He fought a quick internal battle and lost, unable to resist her quiet call—had even been waiting and hoping for it in some innate part of his soul. Slowly he pulled her toward him, her knees sliding across the silky surface toward him, until she was close enough to touch him. He leaned up, bracing himself with one arm to reach for her, leaning toward her until he could feel her quick breaths across his face. He lifted higher, feeling the fur slip down to his waist, feeling the cool air in front of him and the warmth of the fire on his back, feeling the rush of blood pound in his ears as he reached for her lips.

They were cold and she was still shivering. Whether from cold or something else, Noah wasn't sure, but he wanted her warm and comfortable. Putting a strong arm around her waist, he pulled her closer, down into the fur nest with him, feeling her stomach come flush against his, feeling the small mounds of her breasts against his chest, and all the while pulling the fur over them where it could warm her.

"Elizabeth," he whispered into her hair, next to her ear, sending a shiver through her body.

His lips grazed the line of her delicately made jaw, then into the crook of her neck, then back to where her breath mingled with his. His hand slid up to the back of her neck and then around, his thumb caressing her cheek. Their breaths intermingled, becoming one. Her eyes looked like dark pools, their depths unreadable, unfathomable. Her lips were still as he touched them, wanting a response, wanting what her eyes just moments ago had promised him.

An eerie feeling assailed him. Something was not right. He lifted his head and gazed into her eyes once again. Noah suddenly knew she was somewhere else, that she wasn't in the room with him anymore. He touched her cheek gently. "Elizabeth?"

As reality returned to her eyes she became alive. Bracing her free hand on his chest, she pushed away and whispered desperately, "No. Don't touch me."

He looked back into her eyes, holding her to him by her wrist, to find fear had replaced the nothingness. Some sense told him fear was the better of the two. "What's wrong, Elizabeth? I won't hurt you."

She shook her head and tried to pull away. "No, I'm sorry . . . I didn't mean . . . you can't."

He abruptly let go of her wrist. "Elizabeth . . . what's wrong?"

When she didn't answer, just looked confused and terrified, he reached out for her, but she scrambled farther away. "You know you can trust me, Elizabeth. I would never harm you."

She shook her head, tears gathering in her eyes and whispered, "Good night, Noah." She went back to the sofa and rolled away from him, pulling the quilt up to her neck.

He looked at her slight form under the blanket and felt like cursing. What was wrong with her? What was wrong with him? Just when he thought they were going to get closer, she once again closed herself off. Would he ever really know her?

Why Lord? Why did I have to fall in love with this woman?

❄ ❄ ❄

AS AUTUMN ASSERTED itself, darkness crept increasingly into the daylight. It was mid-November and Noah hoped they would have enough daylight to make it to Juneau, although he and his lead dog, Shelby, had made it in the dark before. Looking across the room, he saw that Elizabeth was still asleep. Rising, he folded the furs and walked quietly over to where she lay. He gazed down at the translucent creamy skin, the dark hair spread around her pillow. He didn't want her to leave, wished he had time to court her and make her want to be in his arms. He wished he had time to help her conquer the demons that seemed to hound her. She needed him.

Common sense told him it was a good thing Jacko had come when he had, though. He knew that after last night he shouldn't be spending the night alone with her. He'd prayed for a blizzard, which would have gotten him into a lot of trouble, being holed up alone together for days, but instead Jacko had shown up ready to watch the place, leaving Noah without an excuse to put off the trip. Her feet were much better, and it was time to take her back to Juneau. But he promised himself he'd make as many trips into town as the winter would allow. He wasn't about to let her get away.

The day went by as if weights were dragging the clock hands. He'd been grouchy all morning and had barked orders at both of them while packing for the journey. Elizabeth was quiet and somber, meekly accepting his gruff commands. But Jacko . . . Jacko was enjoying every minute of Noah's distemper.

Noah tried once more at noon to get Jacko away from Elizabeth. "Why don't you come see the dogs, Jacko," he grumbled. "I could use your help."

Jacko winked at Elizabeth and said brightly, "Naw, we've got plans for this afternoon, don't we, Liz?"

She looked from one to the other and compressed her lips.

Noah wanted to drive his fist right into Jacko's smiling mouth. He wouldn't look so pretty with a few front teeth missing. Growling, he shoved away from the table. "Suit yourselves." He swung into his coat and stomped out the door. He strode to the barn, balling his hands into fists and muttering, "Who needs them anyway." Plans! He knew just what kind of plans Jacko would like to have with Elizabeth. Never mind they were very similar to his own. The man had no scruples; he'd seduce his best friend's sister given half a chance.

Swinging the barn door open, Noah walked over to his horse and picked up the brush. With more energy than needed he applied his frustration to the supple, brown coat. The repetitive action heartened him.

He was nearly finished when Elizabeth burst through the door, shouting, "Noah, come quick, the cabin's on fire!"

"Fire?" Noah burst out as he dropped the brush and dashed out of the door, Elizabeth at his heels. Fire was a dreaded thing in Alaska. Shelter could mean the difference between life and death, especially during the winter months. Noah threw off his parka as he ran, having on an old pair of work overalls underneath. He burst through the open door and took in the scene.

The smoke was thick, but Noah quickly determined the flames were concentrated near the stove. Jacko was beating out flames on the floor with his foot. What jerked him into action was seeing a trail creep toward his bookcase and precious books.

"There's no more water in the cabin!" Jacko shouted. Noah swept the quilt off the bed. With his boots and the blanket he stomped out the fire on the floor and turned toward the stove. Elizabeth ran in the door with a bucket of water from the barn sloshing over her sleeves. Noah moved just in time as she threw the water onto the stove, making a long hissing sound and sending steam and smoke into their faces.

It didn't take them much longer to extinguish the fire. After the last flame was out they checked the cabin thoroughly for hidden flames. Finding none, Jacko and Noah followed Elizabeth to the yard, taking deep breaths of the cold air.

"Are you OK?" Noah asked Elizabeth.

She nodded, hugging herself in answer.

"What happened?" Noah asked, looking first at Jacko's blackened face and then Elizabeth's smoke-ringed eyes.

Jacko coughed and held up his hand. "It was my fault. I was trying out a new recipe."

Noah scowled at him. "A new recipe, huh? What kind of concoction were you mixing up in there, Jacko?"

Jacko grinned, unrepentant and Noah growled at him knowingly. "I was just showing Liz here how to make a little miner's punch. The knowledge could prove valuable to her at the post. You know how much Will likes my punch."

Noah shook his head and turned his penetrating gaze on Elizabeth.

She grimaced. "I'm sorry, Noah. He said to add pepper-sauce, and when I did the fumes nearly took my breath away.

I backed up into the table and knocked over the lamp. The kerosene caught fire right away."

Noah nodded. He had seen the broken glass of the lantern and had suspected a kerosene fire.

Jacko said, "I tried to get to her and knocked over a bottle of grain alcohol that was sitting on the stove. It must have met with the kerosene, 'cause the flame caught it. There was a nice little explosion when it met with the puddle on the stove right next to the pot of punch." Jacko shrugged. "It all happened so quickly. We kind of just stood there in shock, staring at the whole thing. Then I started beating out the flames with my boots and Liz went for you. You know the rest."

Noah sighed heavily. "Let's take a look at the damage."

They walked in, the three of them standing just inside the doorway, staring at the mess. Water lay in puddles on the floor and the table. Broken glass was everywhere. The quilts were ruined, lying in smoke-stained heaps. Everything smelled of smoke. The wall behind the stove was permanently blackened, but upon further inspection, Noah was thankful he wouldn't have to replace any boards. With a good cleaning, the place would be almost as nice as before. He was beginning to wonder if his cabin would survive his houseguests. Looking over at Elizabeth, his heart softened. She was close to tears.

He squeezed her around the shoulders and said, "Don't fret about it, Elizabeth. No great harm was done, and at least you and Jacko weren't hurt."

She looked up at him, guilt heavy in her eyes. "After all you've done for me . . . I'm really sorry."

While they were talking, Jacko had gone over to the stove and lifted the lid on the pot. Taking up a wooden spoon he stirred it around. Dipping out some of the mixture he blew on a steaming spoonful. Noah and Elizabeth watched in silence as he closed his eyes and tasted it. He grinned and nodded his head. "It's perfect." He winked at Elizabeth. "Guess we'll have to add a little kerosene to that recipe."

❄ ❄ ❄

December 20, 1886
Dear Mrs. Rhodes,

I am most pleased to tell you that we have had a break in the case. The woman with whom I had been corresponding from the New York Orphan Asylum, Beatrice Timbale, stopped by my office today. Elizabeth had certainly been there. It seems that soon after they discovered our inquiries, Elizabeth was moved and Miss Timbale was let go and given a sum of money to disappear. She says she couldn't sleep, hasn't slept a wink since she left the orphanage, and finally decided to use the last of the money to locate me. Even more fortuitous, she overheard the superintendent and his wife discussing moving Elizabeth to an orphanage in Illinois. She did not discover the name of the institution, but I shall begin writing letters of inquiry immediately.

I remain your devoted servant.

Sincerely yours,
Jeremiah Hoglesby
Private Detective for Hire

Eight

The view from the upstairs window of the trading post revealed a town draped in white, the streets showing through as long lines of brownish gray. Two women hurried by, skirts flapping around their legs, heads bent forward in the wind, hands clutching at bonnet strings. Juneau could have been any northern, snow-nestled town, except for its view. With the bay at one side and mountains surrounding them on the other three, Elizabeth had the feeling of being enclosed, protected, yet more island-living than inland.

The panes of the window rattled and made low whistling sounds as the wind forced its way through the cracks, gusting against the sides of the building, making Elizabeth glad for shelter, glad Noah had brought her here and that she wasn't wandering those cold streets looking for work. She pressed her forehead against the glass and breathed a sigh of relief. Will and Cara Collins had agreed to take her on as a shop girl. The trip back to Juneau had only taken about three hours with Noah's dogs and sled. She'd felt a little as though she was awakening from their own private world and back to reality. With it had fear had come flooding back, though she insisted to herself that everything would be fine.

Will and Cara were everything Noah had said—kind and concerned for her and more than willing to give her a job. Cara had been eager to have another woman around, especially during her pregnancy. Will was slow, methodical, thoughtful . . . he might prove more difficult to handle, but he had not hesitated to trust Noah and take her on, only asking a few questions about her past work experience. There was no reason to fear they would find out about Ross, she reminded herself, pushing away from the window and the darkening view as night fell.

Turning from the twilight, Elizabeth slipped into her nightgown, borrowed at the insistence of Cara. She would have to go back to the saloon where she'd first heard about Noah and retrieve her trunk. The barkeep had allowed her to leave it in a storeroom so that she wouldn't have to lug it up the mountain. Inside was all she owned in the world—a work dress for mining, an everyday dress similar to what she'd been wearing when Noah had found her, and a good dress for Sunday. Aside from dresses and underclothes, she had a brush, some hair pins, stockings, a little wrist bag with some precious coins in it—all that was left from Ross's money—and a tiny chain necklace given to her by one of her friends from the orphanage when she'd left that place.

Elizabeth climbed into the bed, relishing the clean, crisp sheets, and drifted off into an exhausted sleep.

It was pitch dark a few hours later when the howling wind woke her. She sat up, seeing nothing but the cloud of her breath. The room was cold, much too cold for a nursery, which is what Cara Collins had told her the room would eventually be. She turned to her side and curled tighter into a ball with the coverlet over her head, shivering, trying to go back to sleep. Something would have to be done before a baby slept in here. She wouldn't recommend that anyone sleep in this room, including herself.

The minutes ticked by without success of anything save intense shivering. She drifted to sleep, only to be startled awake moments later feeling like she was in the blizzard again. Afraid of the nightmare, she decided she had to get out of the room. She braced herself for the cold and sat up, swinging her legs carefully over the edge to dangle to the frosty floor. Quickly she wrapped the lone blanket around her shoulders and grabbed the pillow, thinking to sleep downstairs by the fire. She winced as her bare feet touched the floor and hurried to the chair where her clothes were neatly stacked, scooped them up, and fled the room.

Quietly she crept down the stairs so as not to awaken anyone. If she could just get downstairs to the chair by the fireplace, she could get warm. She swerved toward it, her eyes on the promise of the glowing blaze, taking one step, then two . . . tiptoeing across the bare, wooden planks, a much warmer floor than her bedroom.

Suddenly she found herself face-first on the floor, a large object moving beneath her. She opened her mouth with a squeal, but the sound was muffled as a big hand clamped down over her mouth.

"Elizabeth?"

She sagged with relief at the sound of Noah's familiar voice and nodded in answer.

Noah quickly dropped his hand. "Elizabeth? What are you doing?"

Struggling to sit up amidst the tangled cloth of the night-gown, she finally faced him, just able to make out the sleepy features of his face.

"It was cold in the bedroom. I couldn't sleep," she whispered. "I thought I would come down here by the fire." Still sitting only inches away she scooted around to gather her strewn clothes and clutched them to her chest, her back to the low flames. "I didn't know you were sleeping here."

Now that her eyes had adjusted to the light, Elizabeth could see that Noah was still trying to wake up. He ran his hands through his hair and yawned, then stood, wearing only his pants. She couldn't seem to look away as he walked to the room's huge fireplace and added some logs, stirring up the embers with the poker. Turning toward her, his eyes narrowed. "You didn't?"

"Of course not."

"Where did you think I had gone?"

Elizabeth shrugged. "I didn't know. I thought maybe you were staying at Jacko's . . . or the hotel. I was sent off to bed rather early, you know."

"I always stay here when I'm in town." He stirred up the fire and then turned suddenly back to her. "If you were coming down to sleep, why did you bring your clothes?" He lifted a heavily muscled arm to the mantle and leaned into it. "You weren't planning to leave, were you?"

"Why would I leave?" Elizabeth asked in confusion and anger. "I just thought it would be warmer to change into my clothes than stay in this thin nightgown."

Noah dropped his arm and looked down at her. "I'm sorry. Guess I'm not thinking clearly."

"I didn't want to wake everyone by making a fuss." She shivered and stood up.

Noah came over to her, started to lift his hand to touch her cheek and then lowered it suddenly. Instead, he pulled a chair closer to the fire. "I'll go into the back room while you change. I'll make some coffee."

Elizabeth could only nod as she turned to face the warm blaze. She sank a little inside thinking how distant he seemed. Will had been suspicious of her. They'd probably talked about her when she and Cara had gone upstairs. Will must have told him what Elizabeth knew all along—that she wasn't good enough for him. It was true. And better that he understood that now.

With a bracing breath she nodded. It was better this way. They should distance themselves. She would forget him. He would come in the spring to begin their partnership, and she would be gone, gone to the gold fields in Dawson City. He would hate her, and then he would want to forget her.

Hurriedly, she slipped out of the nightgown and pulled on her clothes. Once dressed, she moved closer to the fire and spread out her hands in front of the blaze. Feeling wretched about deceiving him, she gritted her teeth in determination. Closing her eyes again, she retraced her original plans in coming to Alaska. She had been scratching out a living when she'd first heard the rumors of an Alaskan gold find. She remembered that day in July when the *Portland* docked in Seattle. The newspapers claimed a ton of gold was aboard the ship, and Seattle had gone wild with excitement. It was the last golden opportunity, and she'd wanted desperately to be a part of it. The only problem was that she couldn't possibly scrape together the cost of the ship's fare, which had skyrocketed overnight. No one would grubstake a woman. Her efforts to find a supporter had brought her only anger and embarrassment.

Then, as autumn crept in and the weather turned cooler, a young man had started showing an interest in her. Elizabeth knew how to discourage a man's unwanted attention; she'd been around men her whole life. But he seemed different. He was handsome and refined, with slick, black hair combed back from his forehead and a black, well-groomed mustache. Tall and lean, he dressed exquisitely. His manners were refined, and he treated her like a lady, something she had not experienced very much in her life. She was intrigued despite her misgivings. When he finally approached her, he was so polished and charming, like a cool, sweet breeze in the stagnate air of her world, and she found herself charmed despite her efforts to remain unaffected. Within a month he had gained her trust, and she confided in him her desire to go to Alaska.

Even now, she could hardly believe what his response had been.

A few days after telling him about Alaska, he made her an offer. They were standing outside of the doorway to her room after a lovely dinner, and then he took her hand and kissed the back of it. Looking deep into her eyes, he purred, "I may have thought of a way that you could earn your passage to Alaska, my dear."

Interested, she asked softly, "How?"

He moved closer, brushing the legs of his trousers against her skirts. Carrying her hand up toward his face, he rubbed the back of it against his cheek. "If you would be willing to become

. . . say . . . my paramour . . . for a time, I could arrange everything for you."

She stood there for a moment, not comprehending in her shock. As the numbness wore off, she jerked her hand away and then reared back and slapped him as hard as she could. "How dare you," she said through gritted teeth. "Never would I do such a thing . . . never."

His eyes took on a stealthy glitter as he held a hand to his face. With a mock bow, he assured her, "We shall see, my dear. Don't answer me now; you are obviously in some shock, not seeing this proposal coming. Mayhap you expected another, more honorable offer?"

He laughed and raised his eyebrows knowingly at Elizabeth's reddening face. "Poor thing, I can see that you did." Turning suddenly viscous, he continued, "I would never marry a penniless girl who could only give me one thing. However, I'll be happy to pay for that one thing, and neither of us will have the worry of the other afterward. Give it time, dearie. I dare say you'll reconsider."

As he turned to go, she cried out, "Never!"

He didn't even flinch, just kept walking down the street.

The next two days had been agonizing. The reality of her situation was that she had to do something. She wasn't making it on her meager seamstress's salary; rent was overdue and something had to be done or she would soon be joining the homeless on the beach, digging for clams. At first, the idea had been so repulsive that she wouldn't even consider it. But the long hours bent over her piecework gave her more than ample time to dwell on the matter. Gradually, her mind had broken it down into acceptable pieces, rationalizing the result. She refused to let herself think as far as the name she could call herself afterward. She decided she wouldn't think of it at all.

She sent him a note and was ready for him when he arrived at her door, so smug and sure of himself. Nothing would have been more pleasant than to slam the door in his face, but she forced down her pride. He smiled knowingly and suddenly became like a hungry cat that had not had a meal in a very long while.

"Once," she stated, staring him in the eyes with impassive eyes, "and you will pay my passage to Alaska."

He raised his eyebrows and observed, "So you've come down from your pedestal but aren't prepared to stay there."

"Take it or leave it."

His smooth demeanor now sickened her, and she vaguely wondered what she ever saw in him. She'd always been so careful, and yet, here she was, caught in the net of her worst fear, believing in another person, believing someone could love her, and then finding it all to be a trap.

Another mock bow, his fingers brushing the tip of his hat, then he held out his arm. "I'll take it, of course."

She stiffly took his arm. Walking the streets of Seattle, arm in arm, as if they were a happy couple, no one but her knowing the tight grip on her forearm, like a manacle, and she, a prisoner—no one but her hearing the pounding terror of her heartbeat, a lamb to the slaughter. And so they went, a picture of what they were not, to his room at one of the town's best hotels. Once inside, once the door was closed, she knew she couldn't go through with it. Starvation would be better than this bodily sacrifice.

She turned to him, panic stark in her face and in her voice. "I can't do it."

His eyes mocked her. "Changed your mind? After all the back-breaking hours of work to find you, you think I'll just let you walk out of here?" He reached for her.

Elizabeth jerked her arm back from his hand and scrambled out of his reach. "You'll not touch me." She made for the door.

"Oh, you don't think so? Allow me to explain the new rules." With deadly calm he sidestepped her, blocking the exit. Grasping her shoulders, he pushed her back and onto the bed. "You can't leave. I have you here for more than the obvious reason. You see, my dear Elizabeth, I did not come upon you by chance as you surmised. I was hired. Hired to find you."

"Who? Who would want to find me?" The question tumbled out before she could stop it.

He gave a crack of laughter and smirked at her. "Who indeed? For reasons unknown to me, your adoptive parents are searching for you. A seedier pair I haven't run into for some time, I'll admit." He shrugged as though to himself. "But their gold was the real thing. They were most urgent to have you back in the"—he grinned humorlessly—"family fold."

"No, it couldn't be." She was talking more to herself than to him. Why would the Dunnings spend actual money to find her? She thought back to the dead miner and a cold chill crept its way up her spine. A thought—a hope-killing, despairing thought—clawed its way into her mind: *They had pinned the blame on me for the miner's death. Did Ross know about that?* Scrambling from the bed, she backed away from where Ross was standing. With her back ramrod stiff and her chin up, she looked at the man she had thought she cared for and felt newly sick. How could she have been so wrong? She had to hold it together long enough to get out of this hotel room. "I'm leaving now," she stated with quiet determination.

The sickening smile returned to his red lips. With a carefully manicured hand, he smoothed his mustache and regarded her with glittering eyes. "Leaving?" Harsh laughter rang out. Then suddenly his demeanor changed as rage surfaced. Gripping her shoulder in a painful vise, he shoved her back onto the bed. Before she could move, he was on top of her. She flailed and kicked, managing to hurt him but only temporarily slowing him down. He was strong, stronger than she would have thought from his wiry frame. He made it look easy, holding her down with one hand.

White ceiling with a crack running across . . . muffled sounds that she couldn't identify coming from her own throat . . . heavy breathing in her face . . . *Can't breathe . . . can't breathe . . . help me . . . can't breathe.* The rape took only minutes, every second so real she could only numb it by burying it so deep and never thinking of it again.

Breathing hard in her face, his voice a low staccato, Ross explained what he'd planned all along. "Listen carefully. I'm going to wire the Dunnings now and tell them how I've found their long-lost daughter. You will stay right here with me until they arrive to fetch you. Until then, you're mine to do with as I please."

Grabbing her wrist with a pain-shooting grip, he dug in his pocket for a length of rough plaited rope, jerked her hands behind her back, and tied her wrists together with a tightness that crushed her fine bones. He pushed her down on the mattress and began tying her feet together. A handkerchief served as a gag. Then, with casual movements, as if he suddenly had all the time in the world, he adjusted his clothing, turned toward the door, and picked up an elegant, gray flannel hat. He looked over his shoulder at her with a leering grin.

She could only stare back with all the horror she felt.

He laughed and walked out the door saying, "You'll learn to like it, I promise. You'll be begging for it by the end of the week."

She heard the key turn the lock on the outside of the door and looked desperately around the darkening room. Struggling, she rolled on to her stomach and pushed up onto her knees. She had to get out, had to get out, had to get out—a desperate litany that was now her existence. She twisted and turned her hands, frantically fighting the rope. Pulling against it as hard as she could, she tried to stretch some space between her wrists. It was impossible. She felt like an animal caught in a trap and thought of how some chose to chew off an arm or leg to save themselves. She realized now it would be worth it.

With renewed effort, she pulled on one side and then the other. She couldn't bear the thought of what might await her if she didn't escape. She had to get out no matter how much it cost her. Gritting her teeth and with a low growl, she pulled on one arm as hard as she could, the threads of the rope like a dull knife on the outsides of her wrists. Sweat dripped from her hairline as the rope cut into her flesh. Taking quick breaths, she pulled relentlessly. A steady drip of red spotted the white sheet behind her, adding to the other smears of blood, a virgin's blood that should have been her husband's.

She pulled harder, starting to cry and whimper from the pain, but still the rope didn't give. Collapsing onto the bed, she wept in earnest. All was lost. He would come back and how would she endure it? She knew, from the depths of her being, that she couldn't let him do it again. She would rather die.

Rubbing her face into the blanket, she gritted her teeth, then curled toward her knees and rocked up to a sitting position. She wanted to live.

"God, help me. Help me." It came out as a cry and a whisper. She never dared ask anything of God—she didn't deserve His help, but she was too terrified to care now. If He struck her dead for asking, it would be better than what was to come with Ross.

Desperately, she looked up and saw the flickering shadows dancing across the ceiling from the only light in the room. Her gaze swung to the burning candle on the bedside table. Long strands of loose hair hung in her face, but her eyes held an intense determination. For a breath in time everything seemed to slow to a stop inside of her as she wondered how brave she really was, then she thought of it no more.

Slowly, she scooted to the edge of the bed, swung her legs to the floor, stood, and gained her balance. With little hops, her feet inched toward the candle, her eyes never leaving it. Upon reaching the table, she turned her back toward it and stretched out her arms. Looking over her shoulder, she strained to position the rope over the flame. Her immediate reaction was to jerk her hands away from the blue blaze.

Silent tears fell in the silent room as she took a deep breath, felt an odd calm overtake her, and then replaced her hands. Her breathing quickened, became a pant, as the flame danced across the delicate skin of her wrist. She bit her bottom lip until she tasted her own blood. Beads of sweat broke out on her temples, but she was able to keep the rope steady over the flame. She could see the thin band of smoke curling up from the candle, like a snake dancing for its charmer. She could smell the rope and her own flesh burning. She pulled to either side with all of her strength, waiting . . . waiting . . . for the rope to break and free her from this hellish nightmare.

With a loud sob, her head to the side, her eyes tightly clenched, she felt the cord finally give. Her arms hung limply at her sides, her wrists strangely numb. Her whole body shook, her arms quivering as she raised her hands out in front of her. Ugly, bloody welts from the rope were on the outsides, but worse by far was the raw flesh of her inner wrist where the flame had worked. A queasy dizziness overwhelmed her and she was forced to sit on the bed and put her head between her knees. She had always had a strange propensity to faint, but she knew she couldn't allow that to happen now. She had to get out of the hotel before Ross returned.

After slowly untying her feet, she groped about until she found a linen handkerchief and tore it into two halves with her teeth. New tears stung her eyes as she wrapped her wrists, the cloth sticking to the bloody places, and then she bolted toward the door. Tears of panic and frustration rose, blinding her, as she turned the knob over and over. "No, no . . . please no."

It was locked; she should have remembered that. She wanted to beat on the door and scream, but thought better of it.

Instead, she took a deep, fortifying breath and glared at the room. There weren't any windows, nothing, save the locked door. Pacing for a moment, she thought hard, trying not to think about Ross's promise, trying to ignore the screaming pain from her wrists. Scrambling over to the dresser, she started going through the drawers, pulling clothes out willy-nilly, looking for what, she wasn't sure, but there had to be something. Her head jerked up as she dropped a handful of socks and heard the sound of a heavy thud as one hit the floor. Dropping to her knees, she frantically felt around until her hands wrapped around the full toe of a sock. Her hands trembled as she shook out the contents. Her breath whooshed out of her. Money, a fat roll of it, lay beside a shiny black pistol.

She smiled, mirroring his earlier victorious leer. He'd been a fool to underestimate her. Her thoughts were crystal clear now. She knew exactly what to do.

With teeth set, she shoved the wad of bills in the pocket of her dress and tucked the pistol in her other pocket. Taking the discarded bag, she looped it on her forearm, picked up the porcelain water pitcher, and blew out the candle, letting darkness flood the room. Whoever opened that door, whoever proved her innocent savior, they would not get a good look at her.

Walking steadily over to the door, she pounded firmly on it, pain radiating up her arm and into her shoulder. "Hello, hello!" she called out in as bright a voice as she could manage. It was a hotel and she was sure someone would hear her. Her only worry was that it wouldn't happen soon enough. She had no idea how long Ross would be, which was why she was armed with the pitcher. She would like to shoot him, but that wouldn't be wise. The shot would be heard, and much as she would like to hold it to his head and watch him squirm, she didn't need to add a murder to her list of troubles.

There was a moment of terror when she heard a key scrape in the lock. She had just raised the pitcher over her head, breath held, when she heard a woman's voice. "Mr. Brandon?"

Elizabeth lowered the pitcher and waited as still and watchful as a cat with its prey in sight while the woman turned the knob. When the door opened, Elizabeth shoved the pitcher into the woman's chest and rushed out into the lighted hall. She fled down the stairs, stumbling once, then ran out the door and across the dirt street to the uneven boardwalk, hearing the lady calling after her, "Miss! Wait, miss!"

The cool night air had never felt so good, a freedom breeze encouraging her, blowing her in the right direction. It was as if some source of inner strength had risen up and taken charge. She wasn't frightened; she was in control. Back at her room, she put salve and proper bandages on her wrists, packed one small bag with precious essentials, then moved into a distant hotel under a new name, Elizabeth Smith, a name she'd used before when first escaping the Dunnings, a name she thought to use from now on. The next day she found it easy to procure passage aboard the first ship sailing to Alaska—now that she had money. But it hadn't gone as far as she had expected, only enough to buy her passage ticket with a little to spare. But she had to get out of Seattle as soon as possible. She knew Ross would be looking for her. She didn't know if he would be desperate enough to try to track her all the way to Alaska, but if he did . . . God help her . . .

It had worked beautifully. It had been the middle of October, but she was finally on her way. With a rush of adventure pumping through her veins, she'd kept a confident iron control over her emotions the entire trip. She hadn't let herself think of the incident at all. Coming to Juneau had been an unexpected side trip, but she didn't regret it. It was further off the beaten path and therefore safer. She had been an emotionally strong fortress, until the blizzard . . . and Noah. Until this safety net of love had encompassed her. Now the memories flooded back. They were relentless, and tonight she had remembered it all.

She jerked as a hand touched her shoulder. Turning her head, she gazed blankly into Noah's questioning stare.

NOAH'S HAND DROPPED away with shock. Her skin felt like ice, but it was flushed with the heat of the fire. Her porcelain looks appeared chiseled of stone, her eyes, like those of the dead. She was as unfeeling and cold as granite. *God,* he prayed silently as panic gripped him, *help her. I don't know what to do.* He wanted to hold her, but he was afraid. She looked like she would crumble into a thousand pieces if he touched her. Floundering about, he finally remembered the steaming mug of coffee in his other hand. Holding it out to her, he said in even, quiet tones, "Drink this. It will warm you."

He breathed a sigh of relief when she stiffly took the cup and turned back to the fire. Glancing around, he spotted the discarded quilt that he'd been using and picked it up. He spread it over her shoulders, draping it around her stiff, regal back, the quilt in all its patchwork humility a poor excuse for a queen's cape. Noah struggled to speak, say the right words. "Sit down for a while, Elizabeth. I'll make up a bed for you by the fire and when you're warm enough you can sleep."

She nodded but said nothing, didn't move, her eyes staring into the dancing flames.

Noah cast about for more bedding and busied himself setting out the blankets, feeling desperate to banish the ghosts in her eyes. *God, how can I help her?* he pleaded silently as he worked. It startled him suddenly that he expected an answer. He realized that he hadn't talked to God in weeks. He used to talk to God all the time. Like breathing almost, it was, an ongoing conversation with a friend who was always there, waiting to be asked and be heard, to know and be known. And yet "friend" wasn't quite right either. More like a father who knew everything about him and loved him so unconditionally that He let Noah discover things on his own. Like an all-knowing presence that, on the best days, guided his every move. Since Elizabeth had come to him, things had shifted a bit. He'd begun to spend more time with her, have more thoughts about her, and, he realized with a sudden stab of sadness, have more love for her. She had waltzed into his life on snowflakes and wind and turned his heart and his home upside down. Was that why Adam had sinned and eaten of the fruit? Noah had never understood that, but now . . .

While smoothing away unseen wrinkles from the sheet, Noah confronted man's ancient weakness. He faced his own weakness where Elizabeth was concerned—that it was easier, could seem more fulfilling, thrilling even, to love the seen and the touchable than an invisible God. That if he didn't keep his bearings he could become consumed by her.

But what was he to do now?

Sing her a song.

Immediately his heart lifted within him. His God was still there. *Thank you*, his heart beat out the words. *Thank you, thank you.* Later, he would pray and talk to his God-Father. He would make things right.

Sing her a song. OK, sing to her. He knew better than to argue or question the command. Slowly, as quiet as his deep voice could manage, he began to hum, a little self-consciously, a song as old as time to him and as natural as breathing. He didn't look at Elizabeth. Part of him was afraid to, her intensity so frightened him. Finally, as he laid the pillow at one end of the bed, he glanced up. He felt his heart jerk as he saw the glistening tracks of tears on Elizabeth's still face and abruptly quit.

She turned toward him, her face once again that of a real woman. "Don't stop," she whispered.

Noah went over to her and pulled her into his arms, her face nuzzled below his neck, her body pressed close to his. He held on, but her thin shoulders refused to relax, as though more than flesh and bone held her erect.

He began singing again, this time the song he had sung in the cabin when he'd first cooked for her. It did something to her, that song, just as it had before. Noah didn't understand the power behind a simple song, and yet he could feel himself singing it as he never had before. It was richer, fuller, quiet and yet bursting with feeling. It was more real than anything he was capable of, and he realized with a swelling in his heart that the song wasn't from him. It was from God; He was trying to reach her through music. He wanted to tell her how much He loved her.

Elizabeth's hands were resting on Noah's chest in small fists. At first there was no response, just the closed stiffness of self-protection. Then slowly, against her will, she began to beat a fist against his solid chest.

"Tell me," Noah said softly. "What is it, Elizabeth?"

She only shook her head, crying now.

It was as if he was a tiny boat being wildly tossed by the tempest of her emotions and she needed him to be strong and not allow the storm to overtake them. The depth of her suffering seeped into him, overwhelming in its intensity. He could feel the anger . . . the pain with its razor-edged guilt . . . the hopelessness. She was so alone inside herself.

"You're not alone," he heard himself saying. "You're not alone anymore. You are well loved."

The crying finally subsided into long, slow breaths. Wordlessly, Noah sank down on the makeshift bed, pulling her with him. He cradled her body, softly humming as he would to a child, stroking her hair. Gradually, he felt her relax into his body. The soft rise and fall of her breathing told him that she was asleep. He stayed like that for a long time, past the point that his muscles were screaming at him and his throat was raw from singing, past the point of wondering what had caused her so much pain. He just held her and accepted her suffering as his own. And now he knew for certain: He loved her. He would always love her. It was his place in life to love this woman. Finally, he eased her to the blankets and pulled them up to her shoulders. Abandoning his own bed, he sat down in the rocker, but he couldn't sleep.

The air seemed alive and the hairs on the back of his neck rose as he peered sharply into the darkness. He felt the need to stand guard over her, as if some great evil stalked about the room and only he could keep it from her.

✳ ✳ ✳

September 12, 1887
Dear Mrs. Rhodes,

After months of correspondence with several Illinois orphanages, schools, and even a few mental institutions, I am pleased to report a possible break in the case. But alas, bad luck has struck. In my enthusiasm to bring you good news, I proposed to travel to an orphanage in Illinois and locate Elizabeth before writing to you. After several days on board a train, I arrived at the small town of Normal (which in my experience is anything but). I regret to inform you that as I left my hotel, setting out in direction of the orphanage, I was run down by a farm wagon. It appears I have broken both legs and am writing to you while recuperating at a local boarding house. Please pray for my protection, ma'am. As I said in a previous letter, something dark precludes us, watching our efforts. I plan to overcome it.

Please know that even while convalescing, I am working for your cause, asking questions of the townspeople and in general making myself friendly. I'll not make the same mistake I did in New York. This town will never know my real purpose here.

I shall write as soon as I learn anything more.

I remain your devoted servant.

Sincerely yours,
Jeremiah Hoglesby
Private Detective for Hire

Nine

"Elizabeth, could you climb up and get me two tins of crackers, four cans of beans, and some Mertle's Tea, please?" Cara asked, one hand on her aching lower back.

Elizabeth smiled. "Only if you promise to sit down after this customer." Whispering, she added, "You're looking swollen again."

Cara nodded with obvious relief. The place was packed with men preparing for the mad rush to the Klondike, but Elizabeth could tell that Cara had had enough. With only two weeks to go, she was round as a melon and swelling around the feet and ankles. The doctor had been in to see her yesterday and warned her to take it easy.

Elizabeth brought the required items to the counter. She wrapped the bundle in brown paper, tying it with twine with practiced speed before turning it over to Cara. After taking the man's money, Cara slowly waddled to the back room and plopped down in the rocker. Waving to Elizabeth, she said, "I'll be looking at this new mail-order catalog, but if you need me, just call, OK?"

"We won't need you," Elizabeth and Will said together. They exchanged glances and smiled at each other.

In truth they wouldn't. Elizabeth was a shopkeeper's dream come true, or so Will had said once in his gruff way over the last five months. In no time she had learned how to trade goods for the large variety of furs brought in, mostly by Indians, and the ever-present gold dust. She had even picked up a little of the Tlingit language, which she knew impressed Will more than he would let on. Praise from Will was rare, and Elizabeth couldn't help but relish it when it came. She tried so hard to please him. It had been easy to gain Cara's trust and friendship, but Will was cautious and had remained closed toward her for a long time. He was serious and uncommunicative most times, and even though she had gained ground with him, she knew he was still suspicious of her. She caught him watching her occasionally with a thoughtful frown.

He'd come to her rescue a few times too, though. Such as when some overzealous man made insinuations toward her, or the time an Indian had wanted to buy her. She'd been terrified for a moment that Will was actually going to trade her for some furs, but she found out later he just couldn't pass up the chance to tease her. Elizabeth supposed she should be happy that he cared enough to want to tease her, but still, every time that man had come in since, she ducked into the back room. Will just laughed at her and it had become a shared joke.

Glancing over, she saw Will talking with one of the dark-skinned Tlingit Indians. They were deep in negotiation over some thick furs. Elizabeth turned her attention to the man who just walked up to the counter.

"Can I help . . ."

The words died off as her voice froze in shock, her eyes locking with his.

The man gave her a slow, blinding smile showing his even, white teeth. He wore the same slicked-back, black hair and thin mustache. His dark eyes casually looked her over before he answered. "I'm sure you can," his silky voice oozed.

Ross had found her. She gripped the edge of the counter as she struggled for control. Her heart was pounding as if it would burst from her chest, and the room was tilting sickeningly, but she was determined that he not know it. Lifting her chin she glared at him.

The man's smile seemed to melt into an evil leer. "You are looking better than ever, Miss *Smith*," he drawled lazily. "That is your name now, isn't it?"

The wicked laugh that followed sent tremors through her spine.

"I can see you're surprised to see me. Didn't think I would come all this way for you, did you? Thought you were . . . safe?"

He threw back his head and laughed again, causing Will to look over in curiosity. With precise movements, Ross removed a white, perfectly folded square of paper from his pocket and slid it across the counter. Head down, he raised his eyes and looked secretly at her from under straight black brows. "Fill this order, exactly to the letter, and there won't be any trouble."

The lurking grin was back as Elizabeth numbly took the paper and unfolded it with shaking hands. There were three ordinary items at the top and a neatly written sentence at the bottom that said, "Meet me in the parlor of the Juneau City Hotel at eight o'clock tonight. If you fail to show, your new friends will soon know all about you."

Elizabeth dropped the note onto the counter as if it had sprouted a head and hissed at her. She quickly turned away from him to gather the goods. She could feel his eyes boring into her back as she reached up past a tin of shortbread cookies. What was she going to do? At the brink of hysteria, she knocked the tin off the shelf and spilled the contents on the floor. Will glanced at Elizabeth with a frown.

"I'm sorry," she said to Will, keeping her head down so he couldn't read her eyes.

Will asked his customer to wait and leaned down to help Elizabeth pick up the cookies. Softly, he said, "Is this fellow giving you trouble?"

Elizabeth scooped up the remaining cookies, stood, and turned away to get another item. "No, no, I'm just clumsy today, that's all. Thank you, Will."

Will looked sharply at the man and then back to Elizabeth. "If you say so." He wasn't convinced and Elizabeth knew it, but she had to go on as if nothing was wrong. She had to get Ross out of the post.

Finally, she had the items wrapped. "That will be a dollar and thirty cents." She kept her gaze on the package, her hands clasped behind her back, hiding her scarred wrists.

"What's the matter, honey, don't you want to introduce me to that friend of yours?" She wanted to tell him he wasn't worth a second of Will's time. She wanted to rail back at him, but she held her composure. When she neither answered nor looked up, he continued in a hiss, "You're not afraid of me, now are you?"

She lifted her face to his and allowed, for a second, the contempt she felt for him to blaze from her eyes. "One dollar and thirty cents, sir."

He smirked at her, slid her the payment, picked up his package, and turned to leave.

Elizabeth took a deep breath as she watched his slim form step out the door and toward the street. She glanced over at Will, who was closely watching the scene, as was everyone else in the store by this time. Elizabeth took a shaky breath and turned her attention to the next man who was waiting to be helped. With a reassuring smile toward Will and then her new customer, she managed, "May I help you?"

The big, burly man Elizabeth recognized as a regular slapped a meaty hand on the counter. With a broad smile and a lighthearted wink, he said, "You surely can, Miss Smith." He jerked a thumb in the direction of the door. "Was that dandified version of a man troubling you?"

"Uh, no. Thank you, but I'm fine."

"Well, if he does, you just find ol' Charlie here and me an' the boys will take care of him. You got me?"

Elizabeth gave him a shaky smile. "Thank you, Charlie, I've got you." She glanced at Will and received his nod before going on to fill Charlie's order. Somehow she made it through the rest of the afternoon, but as soon as there was a lull in business, Elizabeth made her excuses and went up to her room.

God help her. What was she going to do now? She had never really thought he would find her. When he hadn't shown up immediately, she had lulled herself into a false sense of security. That he would come now, months later . . . she hadn't even let herself consider it. Elizabeth paced the length of her tiny room, her arms crossed protectively in front of her stomach, unconsciously rubbing the scarred skin of her wrists.

But he had found her and, if possible, he would take her back to Seattle and the Dunnings. Or worse, she feared he may want to exact a more permanent form of revenge. She couldn't possibly meet him, but if she didn't he would go to Will, she had no doubts about that. She couldn't bear the thought of them knowing all she'd done. Will and Cara were her friends, her first real friends, and they meant more to her than she had realized until this moment.

There was one thing she was sure of: She had to delay Ross. She needed time to think and plan. Scrambling, she found a scrap of paper and scribbled a note: *I can't meet you tonight. Will is leaving and Cara can't be left alone, with the baby so close. It would be too suspicious. I can't vary my schedule after the scene this afternoon. Give me two days. I go to Raleigh's Bakery on Friday mornings. I'll be there by 10:00 a.m. We can talk then.*

It was a lie that Will would be gone, but she couldn't think of anything else. It had to work. She had to buy some time to make her escape. Elizabeth took a coin out of her small horde of savings in the top drawer of her bureau. She knew a boy who would deliver the note to Ross. She would slip out and give it to him tonight.

Still clutching the drawstring bag that held her savings, she walked over to the bed, sank down, and clenched her eyes in concentration. There was really only one thing to do, get as far away from the likes of Ross Brandon as soon as possible. If he was determined enough to track her all the way to Alaska, his reasons had to be sinister. He might no longer care about finding her for the Dunnings; he might be driven by revenge alone.

"It's time to run again," she whispered aloud to the room.

Noah's face came to mind. He had visited her several times over the winter and early spring, taking her ice skating and sightseeing, dining at the restaurant, and introducing her to his friends like she was a treasure he had found. In the evenings, after dinner, Will and Cara would mysteriously disappear and leave them alone in front of the fire, making plans together for purchasing mining supplies and the best way to set up their camp in the spring. After a while, Elizabeth forgot that she was supposed to be pretending and found herself caught up in the excitement. But it wasn't gold she hungered for this time; it was time with him.

When he would reach for her hand and silently hold it, a new sensation threatened to engulf her, a feeling she couldn't remember ever having and didn't know how to identify until one day, right after Noah had left, Cara had remarked, "You seem to glow with peace after Noah has been here, Elizabeth." Peace. She had never known peace before.

Noah made her feel other strange things too. One time a strong wind had swept through town during one of their walks and he had pulled her into his encompassing embrace, wrapping his arms tightly around her, bending his head so that even her head was covered and then turning so that the wind gusted against his broad back while she felt only his warmth. They had stayed like that until the wind grew slack and then walked on, laughing at such a wind, hand in hand, back to the trading posts. Warmer were the moments when he stared into her eyes and made her secretly wish he would kiss her again.

Strangely, he didn't make her frustrated with herself and the restless dreams he caused. He had made her feel like a part of his life—a part of him. And somewhere along the way she had fallen in love with him. She had started to believe that she might stay and mine his streams with him, that her past would stay safely buried thousands of miles away and that she would start over, be a better person with him and for him. She'd even begun to pray a little—not how she had always thought of prayer, formal and sterile, but talk to God the way Noah did, crying out to Him with her feelings and thoughts, believing He was real and cared about her.

She had let herself dream of a normal life. She should have known better. She would never deserve those things.

Taking a deep breath and wiping away the tears that were coursing down her cheeks, she straightened her spine. It would have grown tired and boring, such a simple life as they would have had. She was forgetting who she was, and it was time to wake up. She balled her hand into a fist thinking of the lost time. Prospecting parties had been stocking up at the trading post for weeks and, like a fool, she had always found an excuse why she couldn't join them. It was nearly May. She could have left by now, *should* have left by now, but she hadn't and that had been a terrible mistake. Now Ross had found her—and he'd brought the truth with him. The truth would never set her free.

Charlie McKay's lengthy list from earlier this afternoon came to her mind. Hadn't he mentioned he was readying a group to leave in the morning? Hadn't he said that if she needed anything to just call on him? What had she come to Alaska for, anyway? To work as a storekeeper? No, she had come to take on the trail to riches—Dawson City in the great Yukon Territory of Canada.

She closed her eyes and imagined the gold, saw the nuggets, black on the outside but with gold showing through—the gold always showed through—calling to her, telling her it was her only salvation.

✳ ❋ ✳

February 12, 1888
Dear Mrs. Rhodes,

I regret to inform you, dear ma'am, that I have been ill, struck down by many hardships in my efforts to locate Elizabeth. If you're a praying woman, please intercede on my behalf. This case has taken on such importance in my life that sometimes, I confess, I would abandon it . . . yet I cannot.

I shall write as soon as I can make further inquiries.
I remain your devoted servant.

Sincerely yours,
Jeremiah Hoglesby
Private Detective for Hire

Ten

Noah rolled back over toward the clock, hoping the hands had moved more than five minutes, which was all they had moved the last two times he'd checked. He finally decided he should end this misery and get up. The time was a quarter till four, and he swore silently to himself. This just wasn't working. He hadn't had a decent night's sleep in weeks. Getting up, he pulled on his pants, lit the lantern, and looked scornfully at the bed. The sheets and quilt were in a rumpled ball hanging precariously off one end. The floor around the bed was strewn with clothes, and when his gaze reached the kitchen, his frown turned to a scowl. Unwashed dishes were piled up in three pails, large portions of uneaten, dried food sticking to them. Tools were lying around pell-mell wherever he had last used them. The wooden floor was no longer a golden honey color, but muddy brown. Books were everywhere, taken down for a momentary distraction and then tossed to the floor or on the growing piles on the sofa when that hadn't worked. His cabin was a disaster! Never in his life had he let things go like this. Where was the discipline that he'd honed to a science? What was wrong with him?

Swinging around, he stalked to the washstand and plunged his fingers into the bowl to splash his face. His fingertips hit the thin layer of solid ice on the bottom and he growled in frustration. He hadn't filled the bowl from his fresh water barrel before going to bed, so the leftover had just frozen up, being so shallow. He gripped the edges of the bowl in frustration. He felt like slugging something. He'd hit the wall if his fingers weren't already throbbing. Looking up into the oval mirror, he caught a glimpse of himself in the lantern light. There was a month's growth of beard on his face. He'd worn a beard before, but it had never looked this shabby. There were bags under his bloodshot eyes and his hair was longer than it had ever been. He didn't think he had ever looked worse. Heck, he was starting to look like an old sourdough. When he thought of what a well-weathered Alaskan (a.k.a. a sourdough) looked like, he almost laughed, but he decided to scowl at himself instead. It better suited his mood.

Walking over to the window, he tugged rather ruthlessly at his beard and sighed. He knew what was causing the problem, and working himself to exhaustion each day was no longer helping. It had barely been a month since his last visit, but he missed her. Just the thought of her face filled him with longing. The icicles were even now dripping from his roof. Spring was just around the corner. If he waited a little longer, just a couple of weeks, the next time he made the trip he could bring her home.

Shrugging into his coat, he spent five minutes looking for his ax and finding it, headed out into the darkness. He gave the enormous woodpile, stacked to the roof around two walls of his cabin, a rebellious glare. So he already had enough wood to last months. He would chop more. The grueling physical labor was his only hope for sleep later. He wouldn't stop until every tree on his property was cut down if need be. Swinging the ax to his shoulder, he trudged into the woods.

Two hours later Noah had worked off enough steam to go back to the cabin. If nothing else, he knew he had to take care of the animals. After gathering up the supplies and food, he made it to the barn, congratulating himself that he hadn't thought of *her* since he'd left the cabin that morning. He shook his head at himself as he watched the dogs wolf down their meat. He was thinking about her again. Nothing worked for very long. Sitting down among his sled dogs, Noah took some comfort in their rambunctious presence.

It hadn't been too bad when he'd first come back. Jacko had still been there, and he had hung around for a few more days, teasing Noah unmercifully about Elizabeth but keeping the loneliness at bay. Once Jacko was gone, a heaviness had settled over him. Noah had never felt so lonely in all his life, and he'd been alone for so long. He just couldn't figure it out. She had only been with him a few weeks, and yet in that time she'd destroyed his life. Yep, that's what she had done all right, destroyed the peace and the disciplined routine that he had prided himself on. With sudden insight, he realized he had thought himself better somehow than other men who weren't complete without a woman. He'd wanted a wife someday, but he hadn't ever really *needed* one before. Sitting on the floor with his knees up, he dropped his head onto his arms and faced the truth. Now, God help him, now he couldn't even eat for thinking about her. He wanted her in every way . . . friend . . . lover . . . soul mate. It was an ache that wouldn't go away and gnawed at him every waking moment. He prayed, he ranted to God, but God had been strangely quiet. So what was he going to do about it? He couldn't go on like this. A man couldn't live on chopping wood for the rest of his life. Confound that woman, she'd ruined him. She had broken him into little pieces of clay, and she wasn't even around to appreciate her handiwork. Shelby licked him on the top of his head, causing Noah to look up and rub his lead dog's face affectionately.

"What should I do, girl?"

Shelby just stared at him with her pretty blue eyes.

"Well, I can't go on like this," he said. "I need to see her." He didn't understand the hold Elizabeth had over him, but he finally recognized that he wanted her home with him—for good.

Once the decision was made, Noah felt like a load had been lifted off his shoulders. He once again had purpose, meaning, and energy poured through him. Later today he would take the goat and dogs to his nearest neighbors, a Tlingit camp, for safekeeping. Then he would pack up his meager stack of furs and light out for Juneau in the morning. Now to clean the cabin. He might just be bringing his woman home, and the place had to be spotless.

IN THE DARK quiet of her room, Elizabeth folded the notes carefully and laid them on her pillow. They were brief, saying only that she had to leave, without any real explanation. If there was one thing she really regretted, it was having to depart before the baby was born. She owed Will and Cara so much more than that. It saddened her to have to leave just when they needed her most. Sighing, she scooped up the bedroll stuffed with her belongings and crept quietly toward the door.

She had pleaded a headache after slipping out to find her errand boy and had remained in her room the rest of the evening. Cara, thoughtful and kind as always, had brought up a tray with her dinner and inquired as to how she was doing. Elizabeth knew Will probably told her about the strange incident with Ross, but she'd successfully convinced her that she just wasn't feeling well, or so she hoped. When Cara left, Elizabeth had written the notes and quietly worked on getting herself ready to leave. If her plan worked as expected, she hoped to be on her way out of Juneau by early morning. *Good 'ol Charlie had better come through,* she thought.

Creeping down the stairs, she silently made her way to the wide wooden counter where she lit a lone candle in a decorative pewter candlestick. Softly, she let her stuffed bedroll slide to the floor and ducked under the bar flap to get behind the counter. She would need all the tools of her trade, and she was in the right place to get them. She pulled out a common list of miners' supplies and scanned it. It was a staggering list— warm clothes, blankets, handkerchiefs, hats, boots, mittens, and gloves. Then there was the food—pounds and pounds of beans, bacon, flour, oats, corn meal, tea, coffee, sugar, salt, and on and on. And that wasn't even taking into consideration all the metal tools she would need. Elizabeth sighed heavily. She wouldn't make it three feet with such a load. To cross over the Canadian border, miners were required to bring enough supplies to last a year. Some said a *ton* of provisions. The edict prevented thousands from dying of starvation when they became locked in for the winter with little to no fresh supplies coming in. But now was not the time to buy supplies like that. She would buy the additional supplies later, when she was closer to the Canadian border. For now, she would just have to take as much of the list as she could. She reached up on a shelf and took down a brown canvas pack. Quickly, and as quietly as possible with the metal pieces clanking together, she filled her bag with a gold pan, pick, hammer, moose-skin pouch (to hold the gold), beans, salt pork, sugar, coffee, tea, flour, rice, baking powder, salt, candles, matches, a canteen, medicines such as morphine and calomel, soap, and toiletries. Walking to the other end of the counter, she picked out the warmest blanket she could find, a highly prized Chilkat blanket of mountain-goat wool and cedar bark made by the Tlingit Indians. It would cost her extra, but she knew it would keep her warm during the cool spring nights ahead. Chewing on the inside of her lip in concentration, she added some tobacco and corn whiskey, which would be valuable for trade and didn't take up much room.

"Elizabeth? What on earth are you doing?"

She jumped, hitting her head on the inside of a shelf.

Turning swiftly, Elizabeth gasped to see Cara at the bottom of the stairs looking at her in innocent confusion. She didn't know what to say. How could she lie outright to Cara? What could she possibly say to explain her actions? They were obvious enough.

Cara seemed to come to the same conclusion in the ensuing silence. "Are you . . . leaving us?"

There was alarm and even hurt in her voice. Oh, why did she have to be so kind and make this so hard? Why couldn't she be evil and mean and heartless like Margaret?

Elizabeth gazed into the kind eyes and nearly blurted out the entire tale, but she stopped herself. Looking down at the mining equipment in her hands, she shrugged and said as carelessly as she could manage, "I've been bored lately. I didn't want to tell you and Will because I knew you would only try and talk me out of it, but I've decided it's time to move on. I have gold fever real bad, Cara, and if I don't go soon, there won't be any left." The words rang falsely in her own ears, but she looked almost desperately at Cara, hoping she would accept them.

"I see." She obviously didn't see. Elizabeth watched her stand there and struggle with a myriad of emotions. "I suppose I should be glad this child gets me up in the middle of the night as it does," she said softly, her hand gliding over her rounded stomach, and then her words trailed off into a little sob as she continued, "or I wouldn't have even gotten to say goodbye." She tried to hold back the cry with the back of her hand.

Elizabeth couldn't bear to see her like this and rushed over to her, straight into Cara's arms, tears forming in her own eyes. "Oh, Cara, I'm so sorry. I just couldn't bear to say goodbye. I can hardly endure leaving at all."

Cara gripped her by the shoulders with surprising strength and leaned back to look directly into her eyes. "Why must you go? Something's happened, I know it has. Something to do with that man who upset you yesterday. Please, Elizabeth, whatever it is, tell me. Let us help you."

Elizabeth pulled away and walked over to the counter, distancing herself from the temptation. She placed her clasped hands on the counter and leaned over them for a moment, wavering. "I can only tell you that I have to go. I can't tell you where or why." Turning toward Cara, she pleaded, "Please, if you really care about me, you'll pretend you didn't see this. You have to let me leave, Cara."

"What about Noah? I know you love him. Are you just going to just walk away and never see him again?"

Elizabeth felt her words, knew them as truth, knew them for the monumental choice they represented. Cara wasn't going to make this easy, proving once again how much she cared. Walking back over to her best friend, Elizabeth clasped her hands and said softly, with as much sincerity as she could force into her voice, "Noah is a good man, Cara, and he has done a lot for me. I'm in his debt, yes, and I feel gratitude and affection for him. But . . ." She swallowed, making her final decision in that moment. "I don't love him and nothing can ever come of it."

She squeezed Cara's hands momentarily, "I left two notes on my pillow, one for you and Will and one for Noah. Please, I'm begging you to go back to bed and forget you saw me here tonight. Find those notes in the morning, as late as possible, and give me time to leave. I don't want anyone following me."

"You ask a great deal. How do I know that you are doing what is best for you?"

Cara was almost in tears again and Elizabeth hugged her briefly.

"You don't. But you have to believe that if there was another way, I would take it. I'll be safe, I promise. Please . . . let me go."

After a tense moment, Elizabeth could feel Cara nod against her shoulder. She almost broke down completely when Cara lifted her head and said, "At least let me help you pack."

They finished the job silently together, Cara giving all that Elizabeth would take and refusing the money Elizabeth had planned to leave for the supplies. She embraced Elizabeth fiercely and then helped her into her coat. Cara's parting words were ones that Elizabeth knew she would always remember and cherish. "You are welcome back here anytime, no matter what. I love you, my dearest girl."

Elizabeth turned and stumbled out into the cold, dark night, forcing her reluctant feet to keep moving. Gathering the tattered shreds of her resolve, she hoisted her pack over her shoulder and trudged through slushy snow toward the Hawk Eye Saloon, where she thought to find Charlie McKay.

Working at the post had been the best place Elizabeth could have chosen to find out the latest happenings of the community. After filling an extensive order for Charlie this afternoon, he had rambled about his most recent job. Charlie, as she had discovered, was a guide for hire and even a packer when needed. A packer's job was more strenuous than any other Elizabeth could imagine. The Chilkoot Pass, one of the only routes over the mountains and into the Yukon Territory, was impossible for dogs or horses to navigate in most weather. Many of the Indians and men like Charlie would hire out their backs to haul, in several trips, the miner's provisions to the top of the pass. Further down the trail, along the banks of the Yukon River, entire Indian families worked for pennies per pound packing supplies down the trails for those who chose to portage their supplies instead of risk the rapids.

Charlie had mentioned that a group of four men had hired him to take them as far as the Chilkoot Pass, where he would stay and help pack their provisions over the mountain. Once safely over the worst of a very dangerous and oftentimes deadly mountain pass, Charlie would collect his pay and set up temporary residence in Sheep Camp, where he would pack other miners' supplies over the pass. Back and forth, up and over that mountain again and again. Elizabeth couldn't understand why someone would want to travel all that way, with all the hardships of the trail, never to mine for gold. But she supposed, as Jacko had said, there was more than one way to get rich. Packing just seemed one of the hardest.

Finally, she came to the rough, plank back door of the saloon. Music and the mixed sounds of feminine squealing and deeper male voices could be heard clearly. Elizabeth was no stranger to saloons. She had lived in too many boomtowns to be shocked by very much and had been pulled along with Margaret many times when searching for Henry. She knew that if she acted like a lady, for the most part, she would be treated as one. And besides, she knew most everyone in town. She just hoped someone would hear her banging at the back door. Going into the actual saloon wasn't part of the plan. The fewer people who saw her and learned she was leaving town, the better. It didn't take long before the door swung wide and John Kingly, the owner and barkeep, opened the door with a scowl on his face.

"Who the . . . Miss Smith? That you?"

Elizabeth stepped quickly into the dimly lit back room. "Yes, Mr. Kingly, it's me."

"Is the baby comin'? If you're looking for one of the docs, they aren't here."

"No, no, it's not the baby. I'm looking for Charlie McKay. We weren't able to finish some business at the post, and I was hoping to find him here."

John looked slightly perplexed, but shrugged and said, "Yeah, Charlie's here. You want me to go and get him?"

"Please, and Mr. Kingly, don't let anyone overhear you telling him who it is, if you please. I wouldn't be here like this if it weren't necessary, but I'm sure you understand that I wouldn't like it to get around." She raised her eyebrows, waiting for comprehension.

He looked around for a moment and then nodded. "Oh, yeah, I see what ya mean. I'll keep it real quiet."

"Thank you, Mr. Kingly. I'll just wait right here." She walked over to a tall stool in the storeroom and perched on the edge.

It wasn't but a half minute before Charlie bungled his way into the room. Elizabeth smoothed back the smile that rose to her lips. Charlie was well into his cups and hopefully that would work to her good. Rising, she met him halfway into the room.

"Why, Miss Smith. What a surprise this is!" He shook his head for a minute as if to clear it and then asked, "What you be wantin' with me at an hour like this, and you coming to a saloon? Something happen at the post?"

Elizabeth led him over to the stool as she said all syrupy and sweet, "Why, Mr. McKay, I can't believe you've forgotten already. Didn't you say that if I had trouble I could count on you?"

"Well, course, ma'am, but I didn't expect you to have trouble so soon. What's the problem?"

Elizabeth took a deep breath. If she could get through this next part, she would be well on her way out of Juneau. "Charlie . . . may I call you that?"

At his distracted nod, she continued, "Do you remember that polished, rather well-groomed looking man at the post yesterday?"

"That peacock? Why, sure I do." He slapped his thigh in an aggrieved way. "He upset you, I know he did, and so did everyone else in the post watchin' him. He's a no-account, slick weasel, if you ask me, Miss Smith. I'd watch out for that one, yes siree . . . why—"

Elizabeth interrupted. "You're absolutely right, Charlie. You must be an excellent judge of character to have picked up on that so soon. You see, he's a distant relative of mine and he's trying to convince me—rather persuasively and by force, I'm afraid—to go back with him to Seattle. Charlie, I must tell you, I have gold fever. I only planned to work at the post until spring, till I could join up with a group and go out to the Klondike like everyone else. Charlie, I can't leave Alaska!"

"You? Go to the gold fields in the Yukon? Why, Miss Smith, men twice your size and age tremble at tackling that trail. Only the best and hardiest make it to the Klondike."

His alarm seemed to be having a sobering effect on the big man. Gazing around, Elizabeth spotted a half-full bottle of whiskey on a shelf and brought it over to him as if he'd just asked her for it. "I understand all that, Charlie. But, you see, I have something that makes up for my lack of size: experience. I've been mining since I was fourteen. I know how to pan and work a sluice or a rocker with the best of them. I'll admit that the journey might be a little hard on me, which is why I came to you. I knew if anyone could get me through that pass and away from that horrid man, it would be you. You know the kind of man he is; he wouldn't have the courage to follow me on a trail like this one. Won't you let me join your group heading out tomorrow? I'm packed and ready."

Charlie took a long swallow from the bottle and wiped his mouth with the back of his hand. He stared off into space for a moment, seeming deep in thought. Finally, Elizabeth tried to regain his attention. "Charlie?"

"Huh?" He jerked around and looked at her strangely for a moment. Then finally he nodded his shaggy head. "If you're bent on going, I guess I'd be better than most to see that you get there in one piece. You'll have to pay the same as the others, though, or there'll be trouble with the men. They ain't gonna like having a woman join the group."

"Of course I'll pay you." Reaching into her pocket, she took out the necessary bills and handed them to him. He reached awkwardly for the money and rose from the stool. "Meet us in front of the saloon at six sharp."

Elizabeth gazed at his departing back, feeling excitement mingle with fear at her success. Now to find a place to sleep. Glancing around, she spotted a hammock hanging in the corner and climbed into it. It would do, unless someone kicked her out of it. The motion relaxed her, causing Elizabeth to fall asleep to the brash tinkling of the piano.

October 6, 1889
Dear Mrs. Rhodes,

My most sincere apologies at the lack of information I've been able to obtain. After my legs healed, I contracted food poisoning and for a time was terribly ill. Fearing for my life, I have moved to a nearby town to continue my work. I am happy to report that I have met a sweet-tempered widow with four children and now share in the institution of wedded bliss. While busy as a new father, business here is surprisingly brisk. But never fear, ma'am, my main concern, the one that has me lying awake at night staring at the ceiling in unblinking thought, is finding Elizabeth. I shall not rest until I've accomplished it.

Next week, I shall pose as a custodian and work a few weeks at the orphanage. This should give me ample opportunity to obtain information about your dear girl.

I shall write as soon as I learn anything more.

I remain your devoted servant.

Sincerely yours,
Jeremiah Hoglesby
Private Detective for Hire

Eleven

It was still dark the next morning as Elizabeth struggled with her pack and bedroll toward the front of the saloon. Three men were standing there, talking in low voices, their heads together. She stood a small distance away, watching them, undecided what to do. With relief she spotted Charlie coming down the street, leading a pair of loaded pack mules by red harnesses. He didn't look to be much affected by his stint with the whiskey bottle the night before. Dragging her outfit a little closer to the group, she pasted a bright smile on her face and prepared for battle.

The men didn't notice her as they grouped around Charlie, their excited voices affirming that this was indeed the party she had joined. Charlie's face was animated with good humor until he saw her. She saw his smile waver and a pucker form on his forehead. *Oh no, he doesn't even remember,* she thought with sudden panic. Bracing herself, she let her pack drop onto the snowy surface and strode with an almost swaggering quality up to the men.

"Good morning, Charlie. Wouldn't you like to introduce me to our traveling companions? I sure am eager to meet them."

She smiled her sweetest smile for all the gaping faces around her.

Charlie sputtered, "Well, heck, Miss Smith, I thought I dreamed that. You don't really want to go gold mining in the Yukon, do ya?"

Elizabeth looked up into his broad, perplexed face. With his dark brown hair sticking out from beneath a floppy hat and his equally long, droopy mustache, she thought he resembled a hound dog.

"Yes, I want to go and I will mine for gold."

She barely resisted the urge to stamp her small, booted foot. "Whether it's with these men or not, I'll let you all decide. But I will go, with or without you."

She gave him a piercing stare that a mother might give a reluctant child. "You did say that if I needed your help, you would help me. As much as I dislike asking, for I'm as independent as any here"—her gaze swept regally over the men standing in a semicircle around her—"I am asking. Are you taking back your offer to let me hire you? You did accept my payment as I remember, and I thought we had a bargain."

Charlie cleared his throat and looked uncomfortably at his boots, "Well now, ma'am, you know I'd had me a few drinks last night, and I wasn't thinking as clearly as I might have been. But now I ain't one to go back on my word, no matter what condition I was in when I gave it." He eyed the group. "As long as these boys here don't mind, I'll let you in with us."

Had the situation not been so serious, Elizabeth might have laughed at the look of relief on Charlie's face as he passed the burden to the other men in the group. She suppressed the urge, instead turning to stare fiercely into each set of eyes.

While they were talking, a fifth man had joined the group. He was a tall, thin man, garbed entirely in brown, but well-dressed in well-fitting clothes, with an ease about him that seemed almost peace-filled. He stared back at her with a set of steady, solemn eyes that searched her emotions, seeing, for an instant, beneath the facade of bravado. He was introduced by Charlie as William Cleary, a preacher from Colorado. She looked quickly away and caught the stare of two of the other men who, she was startled to realize, were identical twins. She had heard of it before but had never seen such a thing. They were both white-blond, had the palest blue eyes imaginable, and wore the same crooked grins. They looked at her with good-humored curiosity, reaching out at the same time to shake her hand. Giving them a sweet smile, she grasped the hand closest and then the brother's, thinking they wouldn't put up too much fuss at her presence. The last man, a dark half-breed she had seen in the post, didn't bother to conceal the scorn in his eyes. Elizabeth met the insolent stare evenly and lifted her chin before sweeping back around to face Charlie.

"Why don't you talk it over with the group, Charlie. Call me when you've come to your decision. I'd like to get a move on before dawn." With a toss of her head, she marched over to her outfit and sat down.

The waiting would have been the worst part, except that she could hear almost every word they said. *The fools don't know how to whisper,* she thought with a tight smile. Charlie and the half-breed wanted her out. She could only thank whatever fate was looking out for her that she'd gotten to Charlie the night before when he'd been drinking, or she would never have gotten this far. The twins were all for having her and argued in her behalf. They mentioned how nice it would be to have a woman around who could cook for them. Elizabeth tried not to groan. They'd find out the truth on that score soon enough. It was a tie, and they all looked to the preacher for the final vote. Elizabeth had to strain and hold her breath to hear the soft intonation of the stately man. He said something about how he believed her when she said she would go with or without them, and that he would rather take her under their collective wing than leave her to the dangers of a lone trail. She was in the group.

Her elation was too great to fear the road ahead. She was strong and smart and desperate. Those attributes had gotten her through before and would get her through again. They had to.

With a few curt words to her, Charlie lashed her pack onto one of the mules along with the others. "You'll have to carry the bedroll on your back like the others," he said in a surly voice.

Elizabeth smiled, confident and cocky as she strapped on her pack for the hike to the steamer that would take them to the jump-over town of Dyea. "I wouldn't have it any other way," she assured him. The temperature was a comfortable 15 degrees, and she could feel the excitement of new adventure in her veins. She wouldn't think of the past or of Cara or Noah or even Ross. She would go forward and carve out a chunk of gold for her future.

THE TRAIL HAD never seemed so slow or tedious as it had on this trip, Noah thought, as he guided his horse into the barn outside the post. Hurriedly, he checked that the water trough was full and added a little hay from a nearby pile to the feed trough.

Later, he would brush the horse down and give him better feed, but for now, he just couldn't wait. He had to see Elizabeth.

With sheer willpower, he made himself walk calmly to the door of the trading post. His look became puzzled and his steps gradually slowed when he got his first good look at the front of the post. Something wasn't right. The place was dark and it looked deserted. An uneasiness swept over him when he found the door locked. Why would Will lock up the post in the middle of the day? He shuffled his feet uncertainly for a moment. Glancing up at the second story windows, Noah's brow creased. The lacy curtains were open and he could see the bedpost of Will and Cara's bed through one of the squares of paned glass.

Suddenly a thought seized Noah, causing him to spin on a heel and stride down the street. Maybe Cara had had the baby. Maybe Will was having himself a celebration drink at his favorite saloon, The Hawk Eye Saloon.

Noah trudged up the narrow street, past the shacks and the lean-tos, the cabins both well built and ill spent, and the plank buildings, the town's businesses with their gaudily painted storefronts in the harsh afternoon sun. The wind was gusty today, and the town had a busy sound to it that was pleasant only in the sense that he heard it so rarely. His boots rang out on the wooden boards as he climbed the stairs to the swinging doors of the saloon. Tinny music rang out at all hours, giving the place a feeling of revelry, but Noah was disappointed to find it nearly empty. Sidling up to the bar, he motioned to the barkeep.

"What can I get ya, fella?" The barkeep seemed bored and in a talkative mood as he polished his eyeglasses on a white apron.

Noah gave him a half grin. "I was hoping to find Will Collins in here. Maybe celebrating the birth of his first child. I went over to the post and it's locked up tight. Can't figure where else he'd be."

The man's face suddenly became animated. "Haven't you heard? That pretty little woman they had working for them up and disappeared night before last. Collins had half the town looking for her."

Noah stood suddenly, numb with disbelief. "What else do you know about this?"

The man shrugged. "I don't know much else." He was about to turn away when Noah reached his arm across the bar and seized him around the collar. Hauling him halfway over the bar to glare into his face, with teeth gritted, he demanded in low, commanding tones, "Tell me what else you know. Anything."

The man's face became red as he wheezed. "OK, OK, just put me down. I . . . I can't breathe."

Noah dropped him abruptly, and the man collapsed to the bar. He quickly backed away out of Noah's reach. Holding his own throat and taking deep swallows of air, he hurriedly explained, "Collins came through here about ten yesterday morning asking if I knew anything about Miss Smith. I didn't know a thing. Then he asked about some other fellow who had talked to her at the post. I'll tell you, I was glad to say I didn't know him. With the look in Will's eye, he was after blood. Anyway, the only thing I really know is that the girl has been gone two days, no one knows where. Speculation has it that it must have something to do with this character who paid her a visit."

Noah scowled and shoved his hands into his pockets to keep them still. Piercing the man with his eyes, he asked. "You're sure you don't know this man's name? Sure you don't know anything else?"

The man backed away even further. "I'm sure. Hey, what's your name, mister? If Will comes back through here, I'll tell him you passed by."

Noah's squinted. "You do that. Tell him Noah Wesley is looking for him."

He saw the man's face whiten as he nodded, but bravery or stupidity must have goaded him on, since he had the nerve to ask. "Aren't you the fellow that lives up on Mt. Juneau? I heard you broke in the Indians around here some years ago. I'm real honored to meet you. Those dirty thieves haven't been near the trouble they could have been for this town if it hadn't been for you."

Noah scowled. "I didn't 'break them in,' as you put it, by thinking of them as dirty thieves. They're men and they've known how to survive in this wilderness a lot longer then we have. They deserve our respect." Noah turned away with barely concealed disgust and strode heavily from the room.

Out in the open air, his heart sank. *God, where is she?*

Elizabeth, his Elizabeth, was gone. Something bad had happened to her, and he hadn't arrived soon enough to help. He could barely contain his feelings of frustration and anger.

Suddenly, a great gust of wind swept through the street. A *williwaw,* Noah thought, grasping the saloon's spindly column with one hand and his hat with the other as the force of the sixty-mile-an-hour wind roared its insistence. He remembered holding Elizabeth in another such wind, breathing in her hair and not wanting to let go even after the wind had died down.

This wind pushed at him, making it nearly impossible to walk toward the trading post and seeming alive with evil intent. It was as if it wanted to stop him from finding her. He didn't know if he was imagining it or not, but he asserted out loud anyway, "You'll not have her." The gale pushed even harder and then, as he stood his ground, it gradually, slowly lessened. His resolve solidified within him, and he felt his spirit rise up for a fight.

❄ ❄ ❄

January 10, 1890
Dear Mrs. Rhodes,

While working at the orphanage I found several answers. It appears that Elizabeth was here and has been here for some years. I regret that I was unable to find her sooner as she was recently adopted. I have not, as yet, been able to find out the name of the adoptive parents but will keep trying. The orphanage is very tight-lipped and rather mean-spirited. I was nearly caught going through their files but managed to hide behind a tall potted plant undetected. While I was in hiding, a woman, the birth mother I believe, came in and demanded information about her child. The superintendent was at first most unpleasant, but suddenly had a change of heart as the woman slid a thick stack of bills across his desk (several leaves were in the way, but I'm almost certain). Your presence here may turn the tide . . .

with some monetary assistance, of course. Could you come to Illinois and assist me?

We are so close, ma'am. I can feel that she is nearby.

I remain your devoted servant.

Sincerely yours,
Jeremiah Hoglesby
Private Detective for Hire

# Twelve

With a mighty push, Noah plowed his weight into the plank door of the post, shattering the wood. Reaching inside, he unhooked the latch and shoved the door open. That's when he heard the muffled sounds coming from upstairs. Taking up the lantern, he flew up the stairs and into the bedroom. Cara lay curled up on the bed, on her side, writhing with pain and clutching her extended abdomen. Noah rushed to her side and knelt down. Touching her shoulder gently, he said, "Cara, it's me, Noah. What is it? Is the baby coming?"

Cara grasped his hand tightly, squeezed with ferocious strength for a few minutes and gasped for breath. When the spasm finally subsided, she gave him a weak smile. "Thank God you're here. Will left yesterday to look for Elizabeth. She's gone. Oh Noah, I didn't know what to do. I let her leave. She was so frightened and nothing I said convinced her to confide in me."

"We'll talk about Elizabeth later. Why didn't you go for help when the pains started? Why did you latch the door?"

"I felt tired and thought I would take a nap. I didn't want any customers, so I latched the door. The pains came on so suddenly. And it's early—I didn't believe it was the real thing at first. I tried once to get downstairs, but when I nearly fell . . . I was frightened. I was going to try again, but then I heard the door . . . oh . . . oh . . . here it comes again."

Noah lent his hand as Cara tensed on the bed. Her head tossed back and forth and her whole body strained, her back arching, then curling inward. Noah only stared, not knowing what to do to help. Awkwardly he reached out and smoothed her sweat-pasted hair back from her brow. "You're doing fine, Cara," he heard himself say and could only credit any sense he had to watching his father help in the birthing of a foal. His father had always tried to keep the animals as calm as possible.

Finally, she relaxed and lay back weakly.

"Elizabeth. Dear God . . ."

"Don't talk," he said gently. "I'll get the details about Elizabeth later. Would you like a drink of water?"

She smiled weakly. "Yes, and a doctor. But I'm afraid there won't be time, and I'm too terrified for you to leave me." She took a deep breath. "Noah, you wouldn't mind delivering a baby, would you?"

Noah felt his throat constrict, but when he looked into her wide, frightened eyes, he gave her his most confident smile. "I'd be honored to be the first to see Will's child. But I'll probably be able to round up a doctor without leaving you. There is bound to be someone milling around outside. And if not, we'll do fine on our own. You just rest in between the pains. I'll go downstairs and gather some supplies and see if I can find a messenger." Seeing the panic in her eyes, he quickly added, "I won't leave, I promise. If you need me, just call."

She nodded, the lines of her face suddenly lax. Her eyelids dropped shut. Noah rose from the bed and headed downstairs for supplies. What supplies he needed, he wasn't sure, but he seemed to remember something about boiling water . . .

He went first to the mangled door, shoved it open, and searched up and down the streets surrounding the post. He saw a boy of about ten, and Noah called out to him. Reaching into his pocket, he took out a coin and handed it to the lad, saying, "Run and get one of the town doctors. Mrs. Collins is having her baby. The boy looked momentarily bewildered, and Noah forced down the urge to shake him awake. "Check their lodgings and the saloons and be quick about it. Spread the word—someone will know where they are."

The boy nodded and seemed to understand because he latched firmly onto the coin and took off, his feet flying out behind him. Noah returned to the store, thinking he had done the best he could. As he heard the gasps coming from upstairs, he searched his dim memory of birthing babies and hurried to gather a few items. Blast it, he wished Will were here. There were very few reasons that would take Will away from the post and his very pregnant wife. He knew it was his friendship and not only concern for Elizabeth that had done it, and he was humbled by his friend's loyalty. He only hoped he could be so noble in this task before him.

After some searching he found clean clothes, a porcelain bowl, and string and scissors to tie the cord with. He filled the bowl with fresh water, stirred up the fire, and put a pot of water on to boil to sterilize the tools.

His expression was carefully light, but his heart was in his throat as he reentered the bedroom. Taking a rag, he did the one thing he remembered overhearing his mother say had gotten her through her labors. He tied it on the post near Cara's head and knotted the free end into a fat knot. This he handed to her and directed her to grasp it when the pains came.

The next hours crept by as though dragging heavy irons. Noah was forced to stand by, feeling utterly helpless, as his best friend's wife struggled to bring forth new life. She tried to be brave. She tried to quiet her groans, but the pain was stronger than her will, and by the end she was screeching and yelling at him as if he were the vilest creature on earth. Noah was glad Will wasn't there to hear the new endearments his sweet wife, now turned she-devil, was ascribing to him.

He was starting to worry that the boy he'd sent in search of a doctor hadn't understood his instructions. Someone should have come to help them by now. The room was hot and stuffy and the afternoon sun was fading to a hazy twilight. Just as he was about to go back outside to elicit more help, Cara, during a brief lull in the pains, said groggily, "I hope the boy finds Doc Sanders, Noah. The other doctor, Clem Barker, probably left for the Klondike. And if not, I don't know that I would want him anyway." She started to sniff. "He doesn't wash his hands often enough to suit me, and . . . and he's creepy." As another pain came on, she started to cry in earnest, "Noah, I've changed my mind. I can't do this. I don't want to have this baby. Stop the pain. You have to stop the pain."

He'd never seen her look so sure of anything.

Noah looked frantically around in desperation. There was only two ways he knew of to lessen pain, knock her out with a left hook to the chin, or give her some whiskey. The first was unthinkable, though he didn't think she'd object at this point, and the second, well, he would just pray the liquor wouldn't harm the baby. She had to have something.

He went downstairs, straight to the bottle Will kept in the cupboard, and poured a stout glassful. He stared at the bottle for a moment, wondering if it was the right thing to do, then shrugged. If nothing else, it would ease her suffering and let her relax some. He needed her to stay awake, though—he couldn't possibly do this alone.

It took several gulps of the fiery liquid before Cara seemed to relax a little. Noah's tense muscles eased somewhat in relief too. It was such a long struggle, this bringing forth new life. He hadn't realized the full strain of labor until now. It was a wonder women lived through it time and again.

Then, as the sun was setting beyond the edge of the horizon in a brilliant array of pinks and purples, a sudden change came over Cara. With renewed energy, she began to pull her chest toward her knees and push. Noah positioned himself between her legs with a sheet covering most of her and waited. Her whole body heaved with the pressure of pushing the head out. After three hard pushes he saw a dark head of hair, another push and out slid, straight into his big hands, a tiny baby girl.

Noah gasped, wonder and surprise filling him. She was so small . . . so perfect . . . a tiny breathing human. It was like nothing he had ever imagined experiencing. As he watched, the baby screwed up her face and let out a tiny cry.

He just stood there, afraid to move. Red and slightly wrinkled with lots of dark hair like her father, she moved in his hands, turning her head toward him. He was spellbound, so caught up in the moment that he didn't remember Cara's presence until she said in a tired but happy voice, "Let me see my baby."

Noah quickly cut and tied the cord. He cleaned the baby with hands that felt too large and clumsy and wrapped her in a soft blanket. He would never forget the look on Cara's face as he placed the baby in the crook of Cara's arm.

Noah was momentarily nonplused when he saw Cara lifting off the blanket. Then he realized he'd forgotten to tell her the sex. "A girl, Cara. You did real good."

Cara smiled at him with tears in her eyes and said, "She's so beautiful, isn't she Noah?" At his nod, she said, "Thank you. I don't think I could have done it without you."

Embarrassed, Noah turned away to clean up. He laid a fresh bowl of warm water and a cloth on the table for Cara to use and a fresh nightgown. "I'll just go downstairs for a bit. You call when you want me to put the baby in her cradle, OK?"

Cara nodded. "Thank you."

Noah, arms laden with dirty linen and other supplies, was walking down the stairs when he heard what was left of the door scrape open and excited voices filter up the stairs. He quickly lowered the bundle and met the stare of a plump, chattering woman. Will and Jacko were right behind her. "Good heavens, are we too late?" the woman asked.

Noah smiled and looked at Will. "Why don't you congratulate me, Will, I just delivered my first baby." He'd never seen Will's face so white. He didn't even comment on the busted door.

"Is Cara OK? Is the baby OK? What happened?" He was halfway up the stairs when he turned back around to stare at Noah incredulously. "*You* delivered the baby?"

"Everyone's fine. Go and see for yourself," Noah said with a laugh.

The matronly woman took the dirty clothes and said, "I'm Mrs. Woolsey. I run a bakery two streets down. When that boy couldn't find a doctor, he came to me. I'm sorry I didn't get here in time, Mr. Wesley, but it looks like you did just fine."

"We did our best. I'm sure Cara will appreciate your help though. She's worn out. Thank you for coming." He said it with such relief that the older woman laughed. She patted him on the shoulder and said, "You look worn out yourself, young man. Go have yourself a rest, and I'll take over from here."

Noah turned toward Jacko as soon as the woman went up the stairs.

Jacko shook his head. "Sorry, but we haven't found Elizabeth."

"Where have you two been?"

"I showed up at the post just as Will was leaving to search for her, so I went with him. He thought she would go to Sitka, to catch the next steamer out of Alaska, but we must have been wrong. The next ship isn't scheduled to leave for two more days, and we checked all the passengers to make sure she wasn't using a different name. We scoured that town, Noah. She wasn't there."

"You went to Sitka? I could have told you she wouldn't be there. If she's gone anywhere, it's to the gold fields in Dawson City. Why didn't you come for me?" Noah was pacing up and down the length of the post in agitation.

"I would have gone for you next," Will said as he walked down the stairs with the baby in his arms. "At the time, I thought if I could catch her before she got aboard a steamer to Seattle, it would save us a lot of time and effort." He looked down tenderly at the baby in his arms and wiggled the finger his daughter was clutching. "As it turns out, it doesn't matter. If she has gone to the Klondike, as you say, I would have wasted as much time coming after you as I did going to Sitka. Besides," he said, smiling warmly at his friend, "I think you make a better midwife than I do. Cara said you probably saved her life, or at least her sanity. Noah, I . . ." He paused a moment, his eyes sheening over, making both Noah and Jacko gape at him. "I can't thank you enough."

Noah ran a hand through his hair and mumbled. "I didn't do much. Cara did all the work. I'm just relieved they're both OK. I feel terrible that you had to leave Cara here alone."

Will stopped at the bottom of the stairs and asked in his usual direct manner, "What are you going to do, Noah?"

"I have to go after her. I have to find out what she is running from."

Will walked gingerly to the rocker, sat, and smiled down at the baby. Looking back up at Noah, he asked, "Are you sure she would go to the Klondike?"

"I'm sure. Cara mentioned that a man from the Hawk Eye Saloon came to the post saying Elizabeth had been there asking for Charlie McKay. He and a steamer full of men left for the Klondike the next day. Combine that with the fact that she gets gold fever as bad as anyone I've ever seen, and I'm sure. The question is, why so suddenly? I really thought I had her convinced to prospect my land with me."

"I don't know why, but I know it has something to do with that fella she talked to the day before she left. Cara tried to pry it out of her, but Elizabeth wouldn't say a word." Will frowned and looked Noah in the eye. "Whatever it is, it's bound to be ugly. Are you sure you don't want to just wash your hands of the whole affair?"

Noah shook his head. "I can't." He sighed and looked into the fire. "Sometimes I wish I could, but I won't give up on her. This man, what did he look like?"

Will shrugged, "I suppose some would think him handsome. He was well-dressed and clean-shaven, with black hair and fair skin . . ." He frowned. "Now that I think of it, he looked a little like Elizabeth. I wouldn't guess it by the way he was staring at her, but it's possible he's a relative."

"How was he looking at her?" Noah asked sharply.

"Like he'd like to have her for dinner . . . hungry."

Noah turned away in disgust and anger. "If we know where she went, then there's a good chance he does too. I have to get to her before he does."

Will nodded. "If that's the case, you'd better start packing. She has a two-day lead on you as it is. The next steamer doesn't leave for a week. Are you going to wait for it, or should we hire someone to take you up to Skagway?"

Jacko cut in. "I'd go with you, buddy, but I'm due back in Seattle this week. I could postpone it . . ."

"That's OK, Jacko." Noah knew Jacko and Will would support any decision he made, but it was good to hear them voice it. "I think I can manage alone, but if you know where I can borrow a good canoe . . ."

Jacko laughed and Will replied, "Don't be stubborn Noah, you'd lose precious time and energy canoeing to Skagway. I'll find you a little steamboat. I have enough folks around here who owe me, and you're not unheard of in these parts. It shouldn't be too hard to scrounge up a boat."

Noah nodded. "OK, I'll take the boat."

He walked over to Will and held out his hands for the baby. Balancing her carefully, he cradled her in his arms, staring at the tiny, unspoiled potential of a new human, thinking how lucky she was to have a wonderful mother and a daddy who was already blindsided with love for her. What kind of woman would Elizabeth be if she'd had all that? He didn't know and, really, didn't care, because he simply loved her and he thought that she had begun to love him too. It would take more than a man from her past to stop him from finding her and winning her and bringing her home.

April 27, 1890
Dear Mrs. Rhodes,

Your lack of presence here leaves me with little choice but to keep researching on my own. Thus far, I have not been able to obtain the name of the adoptive family. I received the letter you sent regarding the reward. It is quite generous. While this approach may work, I wonder if you couldn't make the trip?

I remain your devoted servant.

Sincerely yours,
Jeremiah Hoglesby
Private Detective for Hire

Thirteen

The chilly breeze that blew off the ice-laden water of the Gastineau Channel stung her cheeks as Elizabeth leaned against the railing of the river steamer *The Stars and Stripes*. Dark forests passed by, stark against the white backdrop of the mountains. Everything was so startlingly contrasted here, the colors of the land and the water vivid and opposing, as if they were competing to see which one could outshine the other.

Turning from the natural resplendence, Elizabeth's eyes swept over the passengers on deck. She saw two of her party, the twins, playing a game of poker around an overturned wooden crate. She had hoped the pair wouldn't get themselves into trouble but was convinced they wouldn't smell danger if it sat down in front of them, which looked to be the case now. Her gaze shifted to the dark-haired man sitting between them. He had the slow, lazy smile of a professional gambler, complete with thin mustache and cigar clamped between his teeth. With a sigh, she turned from the brilliant view of the ice-strewn water and strolled over to the boys.

Tilting her head to one side, she fluttered her lashes and drawled in her best southern imitation, "Now boys, I just know one of you promised to escort me around the deck. Why, I feel just perfectly silly standing here all by myself." She let her gaze slide to the man in black and saw him staring thoughtfully at her. He winked. Turning her attention quickly back to the twins, she said, "Come on, fess up, which one of you promised? Ya'll know I can't tell you apart."

She waited patiently, eyebrows raised, hands on her hips, tapping one foot, while they looked stupidly at each other. When Josh started sputtering, she held up a hand and puckered her mouth. "Now I know you're real involved in this here card game, but boys," she leaned down and whispered, "I'm getting stares, if you know what I mean. Standing around all alone and all." She almost grinned at their sudden scramble to rise. "Since you can't decide which one, why don't you both join me?" They looked uncertainly at the other players. Elizabeth turned back to the gambler and dimpled. "I'm sure you'll spare these gentlemen from the game? I am in such dire need of their assistance."

He placed his fingers on the brim of his black hat and drawled mockingly, "Of course, ma'am, I'm sure I'll sleep better tonight knowing you are in such . . . capable hands."

"Thank you, sir," she replied tartly. Like most gamblers, he was too sharp for his own good. He may have seen through her ploy, but more importantly, the twins hadn't. Men didn't like to be rescued by a woman. They would be appalled if they knew she had likely just kept them from losing all their supply money. She'd seen more than her share of eager, green miners lose everything before they ever saw the gold fields, and these boys were like ripe berries to a marauding bear. She'd have to keep her eye on them. Aside from their puzzling over her sudden accent, they were thrilled to be in demand. Being the only woman within miles did have a few advantages. Grasping each by an arm, she strolled them a safe distance away to the railing.

As the three stood on the deck, Elizabeth watched the twins as they were courted into awe by the scenery. Nearly everyone aboard was out enjoying the view. The air was misty and she could hear the groaning of the ice. Occasionally in the distance an oversized hunk would break away from a glacier and slide into the water, causing a monumental splash and cascade of snow. It looked too beautiful to be dangerous, but Elizabeth knew better and shivered, remembering her own near-death at the hands of the elements.

As the mist cleared and they moved away from the trees, all on deck collectively inhaled as a mighty glacier rose into the pale blue sky. She had never seen anything like it. It was fantastic . . . and blindingly white. The glare hurt her eyes. She lifted her hand in reflex, as did many of the others, but to no avail. Relief could only be gained by turning away, and yet she couldn't bear to miss it.

Charlie joined them at the rail just as Ben, one of the twins, was excitedly pointing out a herd of Dall sheep on a slope in the distance. Seconds later, another crowd on the other side of the boat proclaimed their awe as a humpback whale rose twisting from the water. The splash and spray that followed was all Elizabeth could see.

"Pretty easy trip so far, eh boys?" Charlie eyed Elizabeth shrewdly for a moment and touched the brim of his tan slouch hat. "Ma'am."

"Hello, Charlie. I'd have to agree everything has been comfortable up to now." She looked pointedly at the twins' backs and mumbled, "Perhaps a little too comfortable."

Charlie nodded in understanding and turned to the twins. "You boys keep a sharp eye out for those gamblers. They'll take your savings before you can say Jack Frost."

Josh wrinkled his nose. "Ah, come on, Charlie, we wouldn't let a fool thing like that happen."

Charlie winked at Elizabeth, and she sensed the first sprouting of respect from him. She breathed an inward sigh of relief. She needed him on her side.

"You be careful, all the same. And don't underestimate these professional fellows. They know how to work the best of us," he said.

Changing the subject, she asked, "Charlie, you said we should get to Dyea today." She looked at the low midafternoon sun. "Do you think we'll make it before dark?"

"Yes, I do, Miss Smith. And if you'll look up ahead you'll see why." Charlie pointed. "We just passed through the Lynn Canal, and Skagway is just up on the right. If you look close, you can make out that dark spot there on the bank. That's Skagway."

Ben piped up. "Why did you say we weren't going to stop at Skagway? We're going on to Dyea, right?"

Josh elbowed Ben in the side. "Because of Soapy Smith, isn't that right, Charlie?"

Charlie laughed and exchanged glances with Elizabeth. "Soapy isn't anyone to tangle with, but that isn't why we're not going to Skagway. There are two trails to choose from to get to Lake Bennet and the Yukon River. Each trail has a different mountain pass. This time of year, with spring just getting into full swing, the White Pass is a treacherous beast. And that's the path from Skagway. It turns into a swamp and a giant mud hole. Packhorses can't get through. Dogs can't get through." He shook his head and spit a line of chew over the side of the boat. "It's the best trail in the winter, without the steep incline that the route we're taking has, but it's the devil in the spring. No boys, better prepare yourselves for Dyea, then Sheep Camp and the Chilkoot Pass."

Elizabeth had already heard the details of both routes from all the men going through the post, but the twins were as excited and curious as children.

"How soon till we get to Dyea, then?" Ben wanted to know.

"And tell us about Soapy Smith," Josh added with bright eyes.

Charlie slapped his leg with his hat, letting it dangle in one hand while he scratched his graying brown hair with the other. Squinting at the sun, the deep creases showing around his eyes on his tanned face, he replaced the hat and began. "Dyea is only three miles around the bend from Skagway—it shouldn't take over an hour." He grew suddenly serious. "As for Soapy Smith, he pretty near owns Skagway." He looked sternly at the twins. "He would have a couple of *cheechakos* like you boys in his clutches within minutes." They started to protest, but Charlie went on. "They coax men fresh from the steamers to an out-fitting office, and by the time you leave 'outfitted' you haven't a cent left to your name. He even owns the docks. If you happen to cross his dock it'll cost you fifty cents, and if you rest your bags on one of his boards, it'll cost you a dollar for 'storage.'

That's what they call it. And that's just the beginning. He owns the bank, the newspaper, and any law trying to go on in that town. We'd do better to steer clear of Skagway."

Elizabeth grinned at the twins, who were looking at Charlie like he had just saved their lives. Elizabeth joined their appreciation. "It's a good thing we have you with us, Charlie. I know I'm grateful." She meant it. A knowledgeable guide could save their lives and could mean the difference between the easy and the hard way in many difficulties.

Charlie turned a little red, gazing off into the distance.

Turning, Elizabeth saw the other two members of their group standing behind them. They looked odd standing together—the tall preacher, William Cleary, with his light-brown hair, beard, and mustache all neat and trim; and the hard, tanned half-breed, Skookum Billy, with his long, black hair and scowling features. She had tried to avoid Skookum and, so far, he had only watched her, but she knew if she was going to have any real trouble from this group, it would come from him.

THE BOOMTOWN DYEA didn't yet have a pier, so most of the passengers paid for their provisions to be paddled over on a small boat. Some of them, though, jumped into the freezing water, whooping and hollering their way to the shore. Elizabeth paid for herself a ride. It would take hours for the fools to dry out, and she had no intention of freezing all night in wet skirts. What she wouldn't give for a pair of pants!

Charlie gathered their group together on the bank with their belongings piled around them like the beginnings of

buildings. "Everyone has a tent, right?" He was looking at Elizabeth. He looked relieved when she nodded. "Good. There's a spot up on the hillside where we can set up camp. We'll need to set watches. While our supplies are probably safe from the other miners, they aren't from the animals. There are six of us, that's two-hour shifts each." Again he looked at Elizabeth doubtfully. "Can you shoot a gun, if need be?"

Again she nodded.

"Well, that's everything then. We'll set up camp and eat some supper. I don't know about you boys, but I sure am hungry." He looked at Elizabeth again and grinned. He didn't ask if she could cook.

After setting up her own small tent of white canvas and lining it with a fur and blankets, Elizabeth looked morosely at the cooking utensils scattered across the slope around the fire. They had each set out a ration for themselves and left it for her to cook. She tapped her foot against the ground as she saw the different varieties of fare each man had set out. The twins, thankfully, had jerked beef—that she wouldn't have to touch, so she knew at least they wouldn't go hungry. They had also set out two raw potatoes, some carefully measured flour in a hide bag, and sourdough starter dough in a little clay pot. What was she supposed to do with that?

Charlie had set out beans and flour, and William Cleary had some kind of smoked meat. She smelled it, wrinkling her nose. Some kind of salt-pork. Mr. Lynn—she still couldn't think of him by the first name of Skookum—had two whole fish (from the looks of them, freshly caught, though she couldn't imagine when) and some dried corn. Well, that would challenge anyone's teeth.

Sighing, she turned to look for water and something to carry it in. If Noah had taught her anything about cooking, it was that everything seemed to require water. If she had to fetch it herself she would never be done with this task. Where had all the men gone off to? Searching the camp, she felt her anger rise when she saw Charlie and William Cleary sitting propped up against trees, their hats down over their faces, snoring. The twins weren't around, probably down in Dyea getting the latest news. Skookum was busy smearing some sort of grease from a small pot on his arms and face. She could smell it from where she stood. Clearing her throat loudly in the direction of the snoring men, she said, "Excuse me, but I could use a little help getting the water? Hello?" When they kept right on snoring, Elizabeth marched over and tapped them on their hats. Charlie continued sleeping, but William woke up. "I'm sorry, Miss Smith. You need water? I'll see what I can do."

As he left, Elizabeth went back over to the fire and stared at the food. She idly hoped it would jump up and cook itself and then laughed at herself for thinking such a thing. Charlie had placed an iron spit with a large black kettle hanging from it over the fire. William brought her the water. She poured some in the kettle and added the beans and the corn. They would just have to share. The potatoes she shoved under the nearest glowing log and then she looked dubiously at the meat. Walking around, she found a stick with a good point on it. Turning her head and batting her eyes quickly, she stabbed the fish with the stick until they were impaled on the end. How did women do this every day? The one job Margaret insisted on doing herself had been the cooking. She wouldn't let Elizabeth near the food stores, hoarding the supplies like a tight-fisted miser.

The smoked pork was already cooked, but she supposed she should do something with it, since Mr. Cleary had given it to her. Shrugging, she tore the bark from the other end of the stick and stabbed the pork on that end. Then she balanced the stick across the pot. Finally, with everything cooking she turned to the flour. She added water until it was sticky and then added some sugar from her small stash. Anything with sugar in it would have to be good, she reasoned. After all the "cooking" Elizabeth no longer had an appetite.

The men started prowling around like hungry bears half an hour later.

Skookum was the first one to comment. "You have ruined my food. You cook them unclean. I will eat yours."

He looked at her so accusingly, Elizabeth wanted to cry, but she dared not. Instead she got mad. "Well, you should have cleaned them before you gave them to me. I don't take the guts out of fish. And since I didn't fix anything for myself, I guess you'll go hungry."

"Other women do this. Why do you not do this?"

His face was so stern she was almost afraid to answer. "It's . . . it's disgusting. Besides, you still have the corn. It's in the pot with Charlie's beans. I only had the one pot so you'll both have to share."

Charlie looked like he might choke but said nothing. Elizabeth tried to retrieve the potatoes from the fire, but she couldn't find them at first. Finally, she spied two round black things and rolled them out with a stick. She looked apologetically at the twins. "Just scrape off the black," she said irritably when they stared at her wide-eyed. They chewed on their jerky instead and remained silent.

The preacher pried his pork off the spit, burned on the side closest to the fire, and looked hopefully into the skillet tilting precariously on a log. Elizabeth looked at the bread in the skillet and sighed with relief. At least one thing had turned out. Using her skirt, she gripped the handle of the skillet and pulled it off the fire. The large white pancake was lightly brown on either side and looked wonderful. It even smelled good. Taking her pocketknife out of her pocket, the one she had stolen from Noah, she attempted to cut it like a pie. She grimaced. It was a little harder than it looked. With determination she tried again until there were four big pieces broken off. Stony faced, she passed out the bread and watched while Charlie, the twins, and William Cleary tried to chew.

It was too much. With tears rising to her eyes, she fled down the hill and into the edge of Dyea. The last thing she heard was Charlie saying, "Well, boys, can any of you cook?"

February 2, 1891
Dear Mrs. Rhodes,

I have placed advertisements in newspapers across the larger cities of the east and midwest. The letters I have received in response have been colorful to say the least. Twenty thousand dollars is bound to bring a varied response, but I am sad to report that no one knows the last name Greyson. It is possible that the orphanages renamed Elizabeth, which has led me to consider some of the letters of inquiry and investigate their claims. Upon arriving at one town

*I discovered five Elizabeths, three in the same family as
with each of my rejections, they brought out another. I regret
that, thus far, I have only discovered charlatans. As I mentioned previously, this tactic may work, but we, dear lady,
shall have to wade through fields of chaff before finding our
sought-after kernel of wheat.*

*My own stepson, Clyde, has decided he must learn to
drive the automobile, a contraption that his employer, the
town banker, recently acquired. Please pray my limbs remain
intact as he hasn't mastered the sense of staying on his side of
the street.*

I remain your devoted servant.

Sincerely yours,
Jeremiah Hoglesby
Private Detective for Hire

Fourteen

Ross Brandon glared out the window of the bakery. She'd tricked him. He should have known she wouldn't show up. After a few carefully posed questions, he learned she had disappeared two nights ago. His head pounded. Rage flowed through his body in a pulsing throb that he felt in his temple. It took every ounce of restraint he had not to smash the shop's only window with his elegantly gloved hand. He wanted to put those black gloves against the creamy skin of her throat and squeeze. He calmed himself by imagining it. Composing his features, Ross turned and asked the stout woman behind the counter, "Madam, you said she worked at the trading post? Was she very close to the owners?"

The woman's round face lit up. "Oh, yes. She was like a daughter to them." She frowned distractedly. "Or maybe a younger sister. Will and Cara are young folks themselves." She cocked her head. "Though Will may be in his late thirties by now. But in any case, they were very close."

"You have no idea why she might have left?" He paused and added silkily, "Or where she might have gone?"

The woman just shook her head. "I'm sorry, young man. I don't have any idea . . . Wait a minute . . ." She gazed at the far wall for a moment. "She did have another close friend, Noah Wesley. He's the fellow that brought her here. Lives out of town, on the mountain. One of the first here, I believe." She smiled. "I thought there might be a romance going on between them, but I don't know now. It seems not."

Ross clenched his hands into fists and tried to conceal his impatience. "Would she have gone to this Wesley's place? Do you know where it is?"

She pursed her lips and shook her head until her brown curls bounced. "I don't know exactly where his place is, but Will Collins would know. You go on over to the post, dear, they can answer all your questions over there."

"Thank you, I will." Ross turned to go. He would find Elizabeth Greyson and when he did she would pay dearly for this deception. No one had ever stood in the way of what he wanted, and a little slip of a woman, no matter how delectable, wasn't going to be the first. He would have his revenge and it would be sweet enough to make up for this trip into frozen hell. The knowledge he had of her real mother, Jane Greyson, searching for her long lost daughter sent thrills of excitement through him. Right before he watched the light of life die in her eyes, she would know who she really was, her real name, and how she'd never live to see the loving arms of her true family.

IT WAS GOOD to finally be underway. After questioning the bartender at the saloon where Elizabeth was last seen, Noah was sure she had been aboard *The Stars and Stripes* and was now in Skagway or Dyea. How she'd convinced old Charlie McKay to take her with him, he would like to know, but at least she wasn't alone. He knew of Charlie's reputation and thought he would do well to watch over her.

Noah's gaze passed over the new sawmills along the banks as they steamed by and casually remarked to the boat's owner, Mr. Kawatuk, with a nod toward the bank, "That would be a good business to be in right now."

The Indian grinned, showing big teeth, and nodded at his boat. "This is pretty good business now, too."

Noah agreed. If he could get a message back to Will, he just might build a sawmill himself, closer to the diggings. He would rather make his money with a mill or some such enterprise. Panning seemed a hard, monotonous way to earn a dollar. He knew fortune hunters stood a better chance of making money from supplying the gold towns with goods and services than actually mining for gold. But speculating had its risks. He would have to check out the area when he got there. Gold rushes had short lives and those who got there first usually won the prize.

"We stop at Skagway first?" Mr. Kawatuk asked, interrupting Noah's reverie.

"Yes, but we may have to go on to Dyea. I'll scout around the town and then come back to let you know. You wait for me, OK?"

"Sure, I'll wait."

The man had been pleasant and quiet during the trip, and Noah was glad. He was in no mood for idle conversation.

As Skagway came into view, Mr. Kawatuk steered the craft as close as he could to the shore. A small canoe paddled out and a boatman asked if they would like to pay for passage over to the docks. Noah accepted and the boatman settled in to wait.

The pier was quiet today, with only a few people milling around, but Noah could hear the commotion coming from the town. His boots rang out on the wooden planks of the dock.

A citified looking fellow walked up to him and said, "Mister, you just crossed a toll dock. That'll be fifty cents."

Noah looked at the man as if he'd lost his mind. "A toll dock? You must be kidding me."

"Nope. Soapy Smith, maybe you've heard of him, he owns this dock. He built it himself and expects people to pay for the use of it."

"I've heard of him. You tell Mr. Smith that if he wants his fifty cents, he can come looking for me. Docks are public property in my book."

The man's face turned red but he didn't say anything, just watched with sullen eyes as Noah walked away from him.

The town was nestled in a forested valley, with bluish-purple mountains shooting up above the tree line, the snow-filled crevices tracing white lines on the face of the rock. Things were turning muddy at ground level though. The streets were filled with a mixture of snow and ice and mud, forming ruts so deep a cart could hardly navigate the length of it. Noah watched in amazement as a team of four horses slid and skidded their way down the crowded thoroughfare.

He stopped and took his hat off, running his fingers through his hair, and studying the town, he sighed. He hardly knew where to begin the search, but one of the best places to hear gossip was in a saloon, and there must be over thirty saloons just along the main road. Noah lost count.

Replacing his hat, Noah started for the nearest saloon. Loud music and an awful smell hit him in the face as he walked in. Noah had a fleeting desire to cover his nose with his shirt as the combined odors of unwashed men and filthy back alleys greeted him. Instead, he stepped up to the long mahogany counter. The place was well outfitted, with a huge mirror behind the bar. Tall cabinets with fancy beveled glass doors held rows of amber and dark-colored liquor. The stool he sat on was upholstered and there was even an iron footrest that ran the length of the bar. The bartender walked up looking pristine in his black suit coat, white shirt, and black string tie.

"What'll you be having, sir?" he asked politely.

Noah said, "I'm looking for someone who came over on *The Stars and the Stripes* about three days ago. A woman. You know of anyone aboard that ship?"

The man shook his head sternly. "I don't ask, and they don't tell me. I just serve drinks."

Noah could tell this man wasn't going to help even if he could and wondered if this was one of Soapy Smith's establishments. Outsiders weren't allowed to ask questions in that organization.

After four more saloons had given him a similar response, Noah was beginning to feel genuine despair. He decided to take a different tack and question the patrons of the saloons instead of the employees. At the fifth saloon, he finally found a man who had been aboard the steamer and was well enough into his bottle to talk.

"Sure, I remember the lady. She was a pretty thing. I heard she was joined up with a party of Charlie McKay's, but I just remember seeing her with this set of twins. You don't see twins much, so they sorta stood out."

"Did they get off here or go on to Dyea?"

The man's glazed eyes dazed off into the distance as if concentrating on the question. "Not sure, mister. But I didn't see them get off here, and I haven't seen them since. I'd guess they went on ahead." He looked around the room and then whispered, "You haven't got a dollar you could spare, for the exchange of my information, so I could get some supper, would you?"

Noah dug in his pocket and handed the man a couple of bills. "Don't spend it all on liquor," he advised. "Thanks for the answers."

The man smiled wide at him. "Thank *you*, mister. Oh, I almost forgot. Somebody else was here yesterday asking about the same woman. Black hair, mustache. He seemed in a big hurry to find her, just like you."

A day ahead of him. Noah nearly ran to the waiting boat. *Dear God, let her still be in Dyea and let me find her first.*

It was almost dark when they arrived in Dyea. The sun was out longer now that it was spring, but it was still a long way from the twenty hours of daylight that graced their summer days. Noah didn't waste any time sightseeing in the stump-filled flatland of Dyea. The town had the same temporary, thrown-up-in-a-day kind of feeling that Skagway had, only it was a bit smaller. And like Skagway, it was full of men. Noah scouted around and finally found someone willing, for a price, to talk about Elizabeth and then take him to the place where she had camped. One thing was becoming very clear: it was relatively easy to track a pretty woman on a trail full of men. She didn't go unnoticed. The only problem was, if it was this easy for Noah to track her, it would be this easy for the man she appeared to be running from.

After searching the slope, Noah was satisfied she'd gone on with her group toward Dyea Canyon, then onto Sheep Camp. He went back to the little steamer for his provisions and then made a hasty camp on the outskirts of the town. Had she slept in this spot only nights ago? Was she really on this trail, about to tackle the Chilkoot Pass? She was headstrong and stubborn enough to try it, but he worried that she lacked the stamina. It would be hard on her. He would sleep a few hours and then follow. He hoped to catch up within two days if he pushed hard. Alone, he thought he could manage it.

June 1, 1893
Dear Mrs. Rhodes,

I regret that I have no further leads on your daughter. The letters of inquiry have dwindled to a trickle. I have expanded the reward notices to all the orphanages and schools in several surrounding states, concentrating on the East Coast. I would greatly appreciate any further direction. Your lack of response since the instructions as to the reward has me faintly worried that you've given up hope, dear ma'am, though your payments are prompt and appreciated. Please advise as to any further action.

I remain your devoted servant.

Sincerely yours,
Jeremiah Hoglesby
Private Detective for Hire

Fifteen

The first few miles of the trail from Dyea had been on a wagon road through the forest and deceptively easy. The six in the party were each loaded down with supplies, as were the three packhorses—one led by Charlie, one with a twin, and the third led by Skookum. Elizabeth was packing equal shares as the men. Her lower back ached and her legs trembled with fatigue, but she was determined they wouldn't know it.

By midmorning they reached the Dyea Canyon. It was about two miles long and only wide enough to travel single file, hugging the cliff wall. Some places were almost completely blocked by trees, outcrops of roots, and boulders, which they scrambled and slipped their way through until the two miles seemed like an eternity. Sticks and brambles grabbed at Elizabeth's skirts until they were torn and ragged. Her old half-boots felt as thin as paper; she was sure they would fall to pieces around her stockinged feet at any moment. It was long past noon before they made it to the other side.

After the canyon, they plodded through a narrow trail, two steep mountains on either side. Elizabeth could look up and see a small patch of blue sky between the peaks. She took a deep breath of the clean, cool air, thinking that Alaska was a land full of hidden treasure, continually awing her with its rugged beauty. It sure did challenge her strength though. She hadn't stretched the limits of her body this hard since the blizzard. Alaska was like a living, breathing force that was out to see what kind of mettle a person was made of. Elizabeth was determined to beat it or, more wisely, somehow make peace with it.

Finally, Charlie called a halt and Elizabeth sank thankfully down to the ground, throwing off the bedroll. Closing her eyes for a moment, she let her body go lax.

"Better hurry and eat, Elizabeth," Josh said anxiously. "Charlie says we aren't stopping long. He wants to get to Sheep Camp before nightfall."

Elizabeth roused herself into a sitting position. "I will. Thank you, Josh."

Josh hunkered down next to her. "Ben and I could take some of your load for you, Elizabeth. Pardon me for saying it, but you're too small to be packing all that. Charlie must be a fool if he thinks you can pack as much as the rest of us."

Elizabeth smiled tiredly at Josh. "Charlie didn't insist I pack all of this. I did." After the cooking disaster Elizabeth was determined to prove her worth.

"Come on, Elizabeth," Josh insisted, "Ben and I can easily lighten your load. No one else needs to know."

Elizabeth saw the understanding in his eyes and sighed. It was hard to admit defeat, but she needed to be smart, not stubborn. "Thank you, Josh. I hope to be able to repay your kindness."

Josh cocked his head to the side and grinned. "You already did on the steamer on the way over here. Ben may not know what you did, but I figured it out. We probably wouldn't even be here now if it wasn't for you."

The praise helped assuage her pride. Elizabeth handed him a piece of jerky and said with a half-grin, "I didn't cook it, I promise."

While they ate in companionable silence, another group of travelers came into the little clearing. "Look," Josh said pointing, "there's another woman in that group."

Elizabeth smiled wryly and rolled her eyes. "You'd think we were an exotic animal the way you men go on when you see one of us." She stood and dusted off her dull gray skirt as best she could. It didn't take this new woman long to approach her. She was tall and sturdy-looking, but pretty with chestnut-brown hair and wide green eyes.

"Hello." She held out her hand briskly. "I'm Mary-Margaret Sinclair. You must be Elizabeth Smith."

Elizabeth's eyes widened. "Yes, I am. How did you know that?"

Mary-Margaret shrugged. "There aren't that many of us, women that is, so it isn't too hard to hear about the others." She frowned. "As a matter of fact, I heard there was a man looking for you. He was in Dyea asking questions."

Elizabeth's heart skipped a beat. "Really? What did he look like?" She tried to remain calm under the woman's scrutiny, but Mary-Margaret was one of those commonsense types and hard to fool.

Her sharp eyes narrowed. "I don't know. I didn't see him. My new husband"—she pointed at a good-looking, dark-haired man with a long, droopy mustache—"Pierre told me about it. I'll ask him if you like." Her mouth turned down and she murmured, "He's certainly more of a gossip than I ever thought I'd see in a man."

Elizabeth didn't know quite what to say to that, so she shrugged and smiled, feigning nonchalance. "Oh, no, don't ask him. It's probably no one I know."

Mary-Margaret put her hands on her hips and stared pointedly at her. "If you need some help, you let me know. We women have to stick together out here." She eyed Elizabeth up and down. "You're awfully small. What are your plans, anyway?"

Elizabeth bristled. She was getting pretty tired of everyone commenting on her size. Brown eyes flashing, she responded, "I was raised on the gold fields and know what I'm doing. I'm going to get a claim and pan like the rest of you."

Mary-Margaret cocked her head to one side and grinned. "Just as long as you're determined."

Elizabeth decided she might like her after all. Charlie whistled and she saw that her partners were gathering to leave. Turning to Mary-Margaret, she said, "I've got to go. It was good to meet you. I'll probably see you in Sheep Camp." Turning, she slung her considerably lighter load unto her back and brought up the rear of their group.

The load on her back might have been lighter, but the load on her mind had grown much heavier. She hadn't let herself think or worry about Ross following her. She'd reasoned that if he had been watching her, he would have been on the steamer with her. She had carefully checked every face and knew he wasn't. He was on her trail, though, just a day or two behind. It wouldn't take him long to catch up, and then what? Her steps faltered just thinking about what he might do to her.

She couldn't let her mind run on like this or she'd never make it. She needed a plan.

Sheep Camp was a tent camp. White tents dotted the landscape like the patches of melting snow. It was tucked into a valley about a half mile wide with the Chilkoot Mountains looming in the background. The main street had the usual saloons, hotels, laundry services, and restaurants. The town had the same excited energy that Dyea had, but Elizabeth had lost her eagerness.

She had the night watch between two and four. It really wasn't necessary, but Charlie had insisted they keep up the habit. Elizabeth thought he was trying to keep the twins sober and out of the saloons. One was always assigned the ten-to-midnight shift and the other the midnight-to-two. They'd complained, but Charlie had given them a load of rubbish about how they were such good shots and it was the most dangerous time of night. Elizabeth knew that her shift was the most dangerous, with all the men staggering back to their tents in all displays of temper. She had borrowed a pair of pants and an old slouch hat to stuff her hair into, making her appear from a distance to be a man, or at least an older boy. William Cleary had turned out to be the hardest to convince of the need for her to wear pants. But Charlie and even Skookum had agreed that it was far wiser.

But would it be enough to fool Ross? If he could locate Charlie's party among the thousands of would-be prospectors, he might easily see through her disguise. She didn't have a ready solution except to keep moving as fast as she could. Tomorrow they would leave for the pass. Charlie had said it was a thousand-foot incline that shot straight into the sky. It was close, within four miles of Sheep Camp, so they could be there in an hour or two. Now that she knew just how determined Ross was, she had to admit that eventually he would find her. She couldn't keep running forever. Her only hope was that inspiration would come, that she would know somehow what to say and what to do when that moment came.

In the meantime, she needed to get her hands on a good claim and some real gold. She imagined the shiny rocks in her hands. She'd heard men were finding up to four hundred dollars worth of gold in one pan. And it was all placer mining—panning—which she knew, which she could do alone. No one had yet found any hard-rock veins and so the big companies hadn't come thus far. She thought they might, eventually, but for now the creek beds were oozing with the kind of gold that could be picked up off the ground, and she was going to be one of the lucky ones. If she could just get her hands on a fortune's worth of gold, even a small fortune, everything would turn out all right. She knew it would.

NOAH WAS TIRED. He'd been in every saloon in Sheep Camp and hadn't found a trace of Elizabeth. Everyone was tight-mouthed as clams. He didn't know why or even how, but he suspected they were protecting her. While it irritated him that they wouldn't trust him, he was also glad. If they weren't telling him anything, then they weren't telling Ross anything either. Ross Brandon—thanks to a fellow in Dyea, he finally had a name to go with the picture in his mind.

Noah looked around him and couldn't believe where he was. He'd never had the slightest desire to make this awful trek to the gold fields, and now just look at him. He was one of hundreds in a snake-like line that was climbing, heavily loaded with provisions, to the top of the Chilkoot Pass. It was a steep mountain, and if you wanted something at the top, you had to haul it there on your own back. Horses, mules, and dog-sleds couldn't make it, especially in the slippery snow-and-mud mixture of spring thaw.

During the winter, some enterprising fellows had carved out a line of almost vertical steps in the hard-crusted snow, but now the bottom was a mess. Most had to carry a stick or pole to help maintain their footing and balance. Further up, where the air was colder and the ground still frozen, the makeshift stairs were in better shape. Midway, the men were jumping on the frozen stairs for the remainder of the trip to the top. A person was lucky to make three or four trips a day up and back, carrying sixty pounds of provisions, caching them at the top and then sliding back down for another trip. Noah had to hand it to Elizabeth—if she made it over this pass, she could do just about anything. It was his first trip up and his legs were burning, his lungs working hard. He didn't envy the packers, men who made pennies a pound doing this job for others. Noah thought they earned every cent of it.

When he finally made it to the top, he looked over the edge at the descent and groaned. It was steep and he wasn't fond of heights. Grooves in the snow, tunnels almost, existed for the men to slide back down to the bottom. He turned from the sight and watched the others at the top while he caught his breath. They were busy caching their supplies in piles that they marked with sticks or stones or whatever else they could find. Noah had heard that anyone caught stealing from another's cache was as good as dead. The miners held their own court, when needed, and stealing was the same as murder in these conditions.

One young man planted his pile close to Noah's feet and smiled lopsidedly at him. "Only thirty-four more trips to make. It's a heck of a view though, isn't it?"

Noah looked into the man's sparkling eyes and nodded, breathing deeply of the cool air. "This land will take a hold of you and never let go, if you're not careful."

The young man grinned back and nodded. "I'm already under her spell. Maybe I'll stick around after the gold rush."

Noah took off his pack and started stashing his goods near the young fellow's. "How do you suppose you'll like the ride down from here?"

The man squinted into the sun and pointed. "I've been down a few times already. It's a rough ride near the bottom, though, with the mix of snow and mud."

Noah grinned at the men sliding down the slope by way of the tunnels. One fellow slid down three-quarters of the mountain and then ran into a bare patch and came to a sudden stop. He was launched up and over the path, landing in a mess of slush. Noah watched with relief while the man got up, dusted himself off, and scurried out of the way of another coming down.

The young man laughed with him and said, "Did you hear about the avalanche that happened here last month?"

Noah shook his head. "What happened?"

"Some say thirty feet of snow came crashing down the Chilkoot. Killed over seventy men." He paused and shook his head. "Buried alive."

Noah slapped his thigh with his hat, shaking his head, and placed the hat back on his head. "It's a hard trail. I don't imagine most folks knew what they were getting into when they left the States to come up here."

"But you don't feel that way, do you?" he asked. "You lived here awhile?"

Noah smiled. He liked this young man. Holding out his hand he said, "Name's Noah Wesley. I'm from Juneau. Lived in Alaska eleven years." His eyes scanned the land, the view from atop a mountain pass—like the rest of Alaska—imposing. "I'll tell you what I think of Alaska. It's neither heaven nor hell, but it'll make a man of you. It will test you and try you and tell you what you're made of," he shrugged. "And then when you think it has taken all you have, it will give you something back that more than makes up for it." He clapped the youth on the shoulder. "Stick around, you'll see what I mean."

The young man nodded, drinking in every word Noah said. "I will, Mr. Wesley. I will. The name's Jack. Jack London. I plan to write about this place . . . and these people."

Noah nodded. "It's a worthy subject. People will remember this event for a hundred years or more."

"I plan to see they do," Jack said determinedly. He nodded once more to Noah and joined the line of men sliding down to the bottom.

Turning back to his supplies, Noah lifted his hat and ran his fingers through his hair, sighing. He had really hoped he would find Elizabeth by now and wouldn't have to go into Canada. At the Canadian boarder sat the scales of the North West Mounted Police. No one would get into Canada without a year's supply of provisions and equipment totaling about two thousand pounds. He had started out with less than half of what he needed and had reluctantly bought the other half in Sheep Camp. He'd hoped he wouldn't have to use it, but now he knew he would. If he could only borrow some of the gold fever surrounding him. To him the next thirty or so trips up this mountain were a precious waste of time and effort. He didn't want to pan for gold in Dawson. He just wanted to find Elizabeth.

ELIZABETH'S LEGS WERE trembling to the point that she thought she would have to get out of line and rest. She'd done that once before, and it had taken her an hour to get back in. No one, not even a woman, got any breaks on the Chilkoot Pass. It was just too hard to make it yourself. There was nothing left inside a person to help another. So instead she lectured herself. It's only a little further. Don't look. Never look at how far it is to the top. She'd learned that lesson the first two times up. If she just kept her eyes on the man directly in front of her and mindlessly put one foot in front of the other, she could make it. She was only carrying forty pounds, as opposed to the men's sixty, but still, it grew heavy and became increasingly hard to climb the icy steps. Her lungs felt ready to burst from the exertion.

Their group had made a total of seventeen trips up the pass, cached their goods in designated piles, prayed it was too late in the spring for a sudden snowfall to cover their supplies, and slid back down to do it all over again. After this, the backbreaking work of panning would seem like child's play. Charlie was helping her with her gear since he was staying on at Sheep Camp and hiring out as a packer. She had a new appreciation for the endurance an occupation such as his required and privately thought Charlie was crazy.

❄ ❄ ❄

AFTER TWELVE DAYS and no sign of Elizabeth, Noah and his gear had reached the other side of the pass and had entered Canada. Here, the North West Mounted Police could be seen all along the road, ready to help the flood of gold-seekers to reach the creek beds around Dawson City. Noah was glad for their presence.

Next up was nine miles of sloping land to Lake Lindeman, then a treeless, windy valley. It was quiet here. All that could be heard was the sound of heavily loaded sled runners skidding over the snow. A hush had descended on the group of men Noah was traveling with. He felt his sixth sense, the one refined from years of living in the wilderness, rise up and demand notice. His eyes scanned the area, but nothing . . . then in the distance he spied the prints of a bear. The beast was just out of hibernation and looking for food, no doubt. Noah wished him well. He had met up with a bear once and would never forget the fear and awe. He'd had his gun at the ready, but man and bear had only stared at each other, both surprised, both interested. Then the bear had sniffed the air and turned, wandering away, his backside swaying back and forth as if to say, "I'm not sure what you are, but you don't smell good enough to eat." Noah had chuckled silently.

As they cleared the valley and the bear, his traveling companions became increasingly loud and excited. They had a destination and couldn't wait to get there. Noah seemed to be the only man in these parts not suffering from gold fever. What he had was just as bad, though. In one sense, he was glad to witness and be part of such a grand event, history in the making.

While he enjoyed the hiking and camping and living off this great land, he knew he was different from the others. He didn't share their passion for gold. They were single-minded in their avarice, but that didn't dim his respect for them. They had a code that they lived by and a flame of hope—a dream that, after meeting Elizabeth, he was beginning to understand.

Upon reaching Lake Lindeman, Noah copied his fellow hikers and rigged up a sail on his sled. The waters of the lake were still frozen solid, enabling the heavy-laden sleds to glide across the hard surface. Ice boats, they called them. Rigging up a sail of sorts with a movable boom, one could steer and speed along with the aid of the strong winds whipping over the lake. After a short portage the prospectors would reach Lake Bennett and wait for it to thaw, if it hadn't already. Lake Bennett fed into the mighty Yukon River, its very name meaning "great river." There they would begin the 550-mile journey on the Yukon to Dawson City and the gold.

It took five trips to haul his provisions to Lake Bennett, but Noah thought they were the easiest of the entire trip. Finally, three weeks from the time he had left Juneau, he was ready to make camp on the shores of Lake Bennett in what the miners called the boat-building camps.

Everywhere, men were chopping down trees, whipsawing the wood with a long, large-toothed saw. Some had moved on to the next stage. Noah watched two men argue about the best way to nail the lumber together to form a boat. Noah casually scanned the crowd as he was accustomed to doing. Among the thousands of men in this place, a woman should be relatively easy to spot, he thought, so why was he having such trouble? Then, from the corner of his eye, he saw the swish of a skirt.

Nodding to one of the men he had been walking with, he said, "I'm going check out the lumber over there." The man nodded back, and Noah made his way to where he thought he'd seen the woman. His heart sped up as he rounded a semicircular camp and came upon a woman stirring something in a pot. She turned toward him and Noah's face fell. It wasn't Elizabeth.

"Well, it's nice to meet you, too," she said to him tartly. Tilting her head, she smiled at him and said, "You were hoping for someone else?"

Noah slipped his hat off. "Yes, ma'am."

He fumbled for the words to explain his mission. The woman just kept staring at him in that odd, direct way, until he flushed.

She held out a hand and said briskly, "The name's Mary-Margaret Sinclair."

He cleared his throat. "Noah Wesley."

"Are you a miner?"

"No, I mean, sort of. Heading to Dawson City like everyone else."

She looked around and smiled. "If you're looking for lumber to build a raft, good luck. I think these boys have chopped down just about every tree for ten miles." She pointed to a hodgepodge pile of wood that resembled firewood and said with disdain, "That's all my husband has been able to round up. After supper, I'm planning to go and saw my own wood. We would sink within a mile on those sticks."

Noah nodded, agreeing with her, looking around the clearing. He'd never seen so many different types of homemade boats in all his life. Some looked like big wooden boxes; others were supposed to resemble canoes; most were just pine logs roped together to form rickety rafts. If folks made it through the rapids on those things, it would be a miracle. He remembered someone calling them "floating coffins."

"I'd be glad to help you. I haven't joined up with a group yet, but I'm something of a carpenter, and I know how to build a good, tight craft. Would your husband be interested in the help?"

She lowered her voice and planted her hands on ample hips. "My husband's a handsome devil but drunk most of the time. I doubt he'd even notice you."

Noah nodded and felt bad for her. She was a handsome woman who obviously deserved better than she'd gotten. "It's settled then. I'll go get my gear."

A week later the three of them boarded one of the finest-looking crafts in the camp. Mary-Margaret had helped him whipsaw the lumber but had not been able to help him much with finding Elizabeth, except to say that she'd met her once and that Elizabeth had appeared to be just fine at the time. So with little choice and like the hundreds of others, Noah had dug a hole in the ground and set up scaffolding. After constructing the craft, they waterproofed it with tar. Within a week, they had a good, watertight raft, wide and flat with plenty of room to lash down their supplies and a shade screen, like a small lean-to, providing shelter from the elements. From now until Dawson City, the journey would be by water.

They left the dark-blue waters of Lake Bennett and headed out on the Yukon River, which wound 2,300 miles from British Columbia to the Bering Sea and the north Pacific Ocean, with numerous lakes, streams, and tributaries branching from it. The journey would take more than a month, requiring them to traverse several rapids to reach Dawson. Noah took in the sight of the hundreds of boats and smiled, his emotions rising with hope. It was like being part of an expedition, a fleet even. So many men, so much excitement, you could feel it in the air. A small, bowl-like boat passed them and three men from inside waved. Noah grinned. They looked like the butcher, the baker, and the candlestick maker from his mother's nursery rhymes. The air was crisp, but the sun was shining and the sky was blue. It felt good to be alive today.

"Look up ahead!" Mary-Margaret shouted some time later with glee in her eyes and a big grin on her face.

Noah followed her pointed finger and his eyes widened. Not a half mile away was Miles Canyon. Canyon walls shot straight up in the air, blocking out the light. A rush of white, foamy water squeezed through the narrow opening.

"Hold on!" Noah warned as he shook Pierre awake.

Mary-Margaret yelled in excitement as the boat sped into the dark canyon amidst the frothing water. They were swept along like dead leaves over roots and outcroppings and hidden clusters of rocks of all sizes waiting to topple them. Suddenly, they broke out of the canyon into the bright daylight and the rocky Squaw Rapids.

Noah had heard of the rapids they would traverse on this trail, but for some reason he hadn't visualized just what they were. The reality was a jolt. Pierre was clinging fearfully to the side of the boat, staring in stultified shock as the world whirled by them. Mary-Margaret, on the other hand, was worrying Noah more by her excitement. At a sudden dip, they were all drenched with frigid water. He heard a crash to the right and looked just in time to see the three men in the bowl wreck into a jagged wall. The craft split like a melon and the last thing he saw before they were swept on was the man he'd called the baker, clutching a piece of driftwood. Everywhere were pieces of wood and disintegrating bundles of supplies whirling in the water around them.

Just when they thought they were safe and nearing the end, they were shot forward into the Whitehorse Rapids. Pierre was crouched low in the bottom of the boat, his dark hair drenched, darker eyes terror-filled, but Mary-Margaret was glowing. Noah didn't know if he admired her or thought her crazy. He was in the back, operating the rudder and trying to navigate the craft with what little control he could muster. He would not fully breathe until this rushing ride was over. He was jolted out of his thoughts by a sudden swing to the right. They collided with another raft, which promptly tore off two of their logs. Noah looked toward Mary-Margaret to find her . . . gone! Searching the water, he saw her bobbing like a cork in the foaming mass. Diving for the rope, he fashioned a quick lasso and threw it at the next rocky outcropping they passed.

"Pierre, for God's sake, get up! Your wife was thrown over," he yelled at the cowering man. "Hold the rope! Try to keep us steady until I can reach her."

Pierre finally snapped into action. His pale face strained with the effort to hold the raft against the current, curled mustache wet and drooping, while Noah threw another rope to Mary-Margaret. He soon realized she wasn't going to be able to grasp hold. She was doing all she could just to keep her head above water. As she came closer, Noah dove into the water. Fighting the current with his powerful arms and legs, he fought his way to the woman. She was sinking, her body limp and languid by the time he reached her. Grasping her around the waist, he searched for their boat. It had disappeared among the swirling mass of the wreckage around him.

An unfamiliar voice called out to him. Someone in another raft had thrown out a rope. Noah struggled toward it, reached it, and hung on for dear life. They were dragged along behind the raft for several minutes while their rescuers struggled to reel them in. Finally, just when Noah thought he had swallowed too much water to go on, someone lifted Mary-Margaret from his arms. He was heaved on board where he lay on his side, choking up water for several minutes while someone beat him on the back. He sat up to find Mary-Margaret's body stretched out beside him, eyes staring blankly into the sky. Her face was pale with a water-logged look to it. "Sorry, fella, but she didn't make it." The voice sounded a million miles away, and Noah had to shake his head to see if his ears were clogged.

Scooting up to her, he laid his head on her chest. There was nothing, no heartbeat, no breath. He put his hands together and pressed on her chest. Water spilled from her mouth. Her lungs were full. He pushed again and again, until there was no longer any water coming out. Leaning down, he said, "Come on, Mary-Margaret, breathe, breathe." He tried again and again until finally someone reached for his arm and pulled him back.

"You did all you could," someone said.

Noah turned away, feeling sick. "Close her eyes," he said harshly. He rubbed his hands over his face. Anger overtook him. Women didn't belong in a place like this. Nobody did. What were they all doing out here risking their fool necks for the promise of a little gold? It was crazy . . . deadly. If a woman with strength and endurance like Mary-Margaret could be taken down so suddenly, so swiftly, how was his little Elizabeth going to make it? For the first time, he let himself think it. *She might already be dead.* He should have found her by now, should have caught up to her. The thought of her buried in some shallow, unmarked grave took hold of his mind until he thought it true. His shoulders started shaking with pent-up sobs.

Someone patted him on the shoulder. "I'm real sorry, fella. Was she your wife?"

Noah gazed up at the man with bleary eyes. "No, but she could have been. She could have been."

* * *

January 1, 1894
Dear Mrs. Rhodes,

Your continued payment for my services is the only indication that you are receiving my letters. I fear you have despaired of finding your daughter and have continued on with your life. It is difficult, I know, to hope unceasing without any real evidence that we will ever find her, but I must encourage you not to give up.

My son Clyde has developed an attachment for a local girl, a good and sweet girl I'm sure . . . but he is so young. Tillie, my daughter, calls her favorite doll Elizabeth. She is a topic often on our minds and hearts.

I remain your devoted servant.

Sincerely yours,
Jeremiah Hoglesby
Private Detective for Hire

Sixteen

Elizabeth crawled up the banks of Lake Laberge, the borrowed wet pants clinging to her legs. Her body ached with cold and sore muscles. She was chilled to the bone, soaking wet and hungry. The slicker Charlie had given her before they left had helped a little on top, but the pants were cold against her calves. They'd been on the water for two days and a night without stopping. She had never been on such a ride in all her life. They'd taken shifts sleeping, but Elizabeth didn't know why it mattered. The river took them where it would and there was little they could do about it until they reached the calm, glassy blue waters of Lake Laberge.

It was the first camp they'd made since the boat-building camp, and it felt good to be on land again. Hundreds of men were camped around them along the bank, busy with repairs. They were the same men she'd been traveling with since Dyea, but now their faces were sobered and exhausted. The hardness of the trail was sinking through their veneer of excitement. Still, they had hundreds of miles to go and they all were feeling a keen desire for better, watertight boats. Elizabeth stood and stretched her aching muscles, reaching to the sky.

"Hey, Elizabeth, how are you holding up?" Josh asked with his boyish grin.

Elizabeth turned and grimaced. "I've been better." She smiled. "A fire and some hot food would do me more good than anything."

"Yeah, me too. Ben and I will get the fire going if you can unpack. Maybe we'll get lucky and talk Skookum into cooking for us."

Elizabeth frowned. "I'm not asking him." After losing Charlie at the Chilkoot pass, he wanting to stay and earn money by packing other people's goods up and down, the group had undergone a power struggle. "Let's wait and see what he does."

The twins agreed and wandered off to look for wood. Elizabeth looked around the camp for Skookum. She saw William Cleary heading in the direction of the camp's hospital. He always tried to be where his services might be welcomed and needed. She didn't think he was really here for the gold; he didn't even own a pan, his pack loaded with food, medicine, and books, a small Bible always handy in one of his deep overcoat pockets. Her gaze skimmed the shoreline. There, off in the distance, stood Skookum talking with someone . . . He moved slightly to one side and Elizabeth inhaled sharply.

It was Ross.

Ross was here and Skookum was talking to him. She glanced around the clearing frantically. In a panic, she turned and walked fast and hard toward the hospital tent.

It was dim in the tent. There were several rows of cots, mostly full. She found William Cleary and picked her way over to him. He had his eyes closed and was mumbling. Elizabeth looked down at the person he was praying for. The sheet was drawn up over the face.

Elizabeth asked, "Who was he? Did you know him?"

William slowly pulled the sheet down to reveal Mary-Margaret's face.

Elizabeth gasped. "Oh, no . . . what happened?"

The preacher just shook his head. "A man brought her in. He said he tried to save her but she drowned in the rapids, fell overboard."

"How terrible! Did you speak to her husband? A dark Frenchman?"

William shook his head. "A big fellow brought her in. He was looking for the husband. Did you know her?"

She stared down at the white face, her stomach rolling. She shook her head. "I met her . . . once. She was kind to me." Looking up into the preacher's face Elizabeth said in a helpless and small voice, "She seemed so strong."

Mr. Cleary put an arm around her shoulder as they stood staring at the dead woman's face. She started to reach out to touch her and then pulled her hand back. Mary-Margaret had been so full of life, so determined. It was hard to believe anything like this had happened to her. The reality of their circumstances was sobering.

William squeezed Elizabeth's arm reassuringly. "Come, there is nothing more we can do here."

Elizabeth studied William Cleary out of the corner of her eyes as they walked. Her gut told her that here was a man who could be trusted, and she'd seen nothing to cause her to think otherwise since meeting him. She would have to risk it.

The twins would just make a mess of it. She lowered her voice. "I need to talk to you. It's important."

His focus shifted to her face and sharpened. "All right," he said softly, "let's take a walk."

Elizabeth steered them away from the shore where she had seen Ross. Talking over the din of hammering and sawing, she explained. "I saw Skookum just a few minutes ago and he was talking to someone . . . someone I know." She looked at the ground. "This man . . . I have reason to believe he isn't here for the gold. He's come for me." She looked pleadingly into Mr. Cleary's eyes, hoping a man of God didn't have some special sense to know she was telling only part of the truth. "I can't stay here." She rushed on in anxious agitation. "I have to go on to Dawson alone. But I need your help."

"Elizabeth, have you done something that you need to ask forgiveness for?"

Her shoulders slumped. She needed some practical help, not a sermon. "Many things, I'm afraid. And I will, when this is all over." She gave him a sad smile. "I'm afraid it's too early to ask for forgiveness."

"It's never too early, Elizabeth. On your best day, that most perfect day when you think you've done everything right, it will be no better to Him than this day."

Some part of her heard him, latched onto the hope he held out to her that God would love her no matter what she did, but another part was scrambling to save herself, making her grind her teeth. "First I must leave this place. Will you help me?"

He laid a hand on her shoulder, looking at her with assurance. "What can I do?"

"As soon as you can, gather my supplies together and take them to . . . behind the hospital tent. Stash them under a blanket there, and as soon as it's dusk, I'll retrieve them."

William Cleary was frowning. "I can do that, but Elizabeth, you shouldn't go alone." He was silent for a moment. "That fellow, the one who brought in Mary-Margaret, he said he would be leaving after he found his supplies and purchased a boat. He seemed in a hurry too. I think he would take you along if you take our raft. He was a good man. I'd trust him with you." He looked at Elizabeth sternly. "Don't try to pass yourself off as a boy, though. It wouldn't take him long to figure it out, and he strikes me as the type who values honesty."

Elizabeth shrugged. "All right, but what about you and the others? Skookum will be furious if you give me the raft. How will you go on without it?"

"Don't concern yourself with us. We'll find our way. I have extra funds, and many are turning back at every camp. There are always boats to be bought." He gazed around. "Anyway, I feel needed in this place." He shrugged. "It's a mystery how God's work unfolds for each of us, Elizabeth."

A FEW HOURS later, Elizabeth met William Cleary behind the hospital tent. He handed her a handkerchief full of warm flapjacks. "I have the raft packed with your supplies. I haven't had any trouble thus far. The twins are somewhere playing a game of cards, and I haven't seen Skookum all afternoon. He may be fishing."

"What about the man you told me about? Has he agreed to take me?"

William nodded, pointing toward the lake. "He is waiting with the raft beyond that stand of trees. I will take you to him."

The raft was nestled among tall grasses, shielded from obvious view. She really didn't want to get on another boat. Just one night's sleep on solid ground would have been nice, but she had no choice. A dark shadow was hunting her, and she didn't know if its name was Ross or fear, but she would stay ahead of it for as long as she was able. Elizabeth strained her neck toward the water, across the grasses. A man was leaning down, roping something . . . his movements sure, causing a flicker of recognition in her. He stood and turned just as she reached the edge of the bank.

Noah . . . he had come for her.

Tears instantly sprang up in her eyes. Emotions rose so high that she felt she might choke on them. The world started to tilt, making her dizzy, then blackness began on the edges of her vision until it completely closed in. She forgot to put her head down between her knees in her shock. She forgot everything except that he'd come and what that must mean. She sank to the ground in a crumpled heap.

NOAH HAD HEARD a startled sound and witnessed the collapse. He scrambled up the shore. "What happened to him?"

William Cleary grimaced, looking up at Noah from his crouched position next to Elizabeth. "I didn't want to have to be the one to tell you this, Mr. Wesley, but he is a she. And I believe she's fainted."

Noah crouched down and looked into the woman's face. His hand reached out involuntarily as his heart started its heavy drumming. He wiped the smudged dirt from her face and whispered, emotion clogging his throat, "Elizabeth. No wonder I couldn't find you."

"You know her?" William asked, alarmed.

Noah hung his head for a moment and then looked up at the preacher. "Yes, I know her. I've come for her. She's going to be my wife."

"Your wife? Do you know about the trouble she's in?"

Noah's eyes narrowed. "I know a man named Ross is looking for her. I don't know why, but I aim to find out. What do you know about it?"

William Cleary stood, patted Noah on the shoulder. "Only that she needs someone like you. She'll come to soon enough, and if she is fighting you, it might be providential that she's fainted. Let's get her to the raft, quickly."

Noah picked up Elizabeth and carried her to the raft, laying her on a blanket under the raft's shaded side. Turning, he said, "This is a good raft. It's yours, isn't it?"

"It was hers as well. She was a valuable member of our group." He smiled. "She's the one that insisted we build the lean-to on the raft for cover. It was one of many things she brought to us."

"Let me pay you for it." Noah reached into a pouch under his coat.

William Cleary shook his head. "I have money if we should need to buy a boat. I think I'll have the twins build another one and use the time to stall this Ross fellow. I believe God wants us to be here for a few days."

Noah didn't question his words; he only nodded and shook hands with the man, feeling like he'd found a friend who understood. Taking a wood pole in his hand, he pushed off the bank while the preacher shoved. The raft floated out onto the glossy lake. Noah busied himself getting them quickly downstream. He couldn't seem to look at her again. It did something to him that he couldn't quite identify, so he concentrated on the raft and poling down the river into the long stretch called Thirty-Mile.

A bald eagle screeched from its perch atop a tree and spread its wings, one second cleaving and the next soaring, leaving in its wake a swaying branch and falling leaves from the force of its impetus. Noah watched the great bird until it was just a black spot in the sky as it gained the height of mountaintops. Here was magnificence, he thought, breathing in the awe of the grace, the majesty. "How great you are," he whispered to the Creator.

Even though it was evening, the pale sunlight hung on. It was the time of year for light, the time for staying up and soaking the sun's rays deep into the skin, into one's bones in preparation for the inevitable long winter to come. In Alaska this was a magical time, when the sun rose and stayed just above the horizon, making an arc around them in the sky. It was a time for renewal, and they all—plants and animals and man— lingered with the light, not wanting to waste it on sleep, not able to completely forget the cold darkness to come. Noah would hunt and walk his property well past midnight this time of year when the land would see only a couple of hours of darkness in the wee hours of the night. But not this year; this year he had another mission. He glanced back at her still asleep and wondered if he should wake her. But something told him not to, he needed to wait. And wait some more.

With a gentle, warming breeze and the soft current all around them, it was a leisurely ride. The only hindrance was the occasional boulder in the water or mound of earth to navigate around. Noah gazed at a part of the landscape he had never seen before, the beauty and immensity never ceasing to astound him. The calm water was soothing to his turbulent emotions.

He'd found her! A part of him rejoiced, and yet another part made him ask what had possessed him to chase a wisp of a woman into this land. He knew the answer, but he didn't know if it was the right one. All he knew was that when he quieted himself, all he could hear was the rejoicing of his heart. *I found her . . . found her . . . found her.*

"Noah, is it really you?"

The question was as soft as a whisper, but it hit him in the stomach like a swift kick. He turned from his vigil and stared at her. She was sitting half-up, rubbing her eyes with a small, pale hand. Her hat had fallen off to reveal her thick mass of wavy hair—the same hair that when she wore it down and loose made his stomach do a slow turn. Rising, she stood and moved toward him. She looked good—so good and sweet. It was all he could do not to reach for her.

"Where's your coat?" he asked.

Elizabeth looked around her. "I'm not cold," she answered softly. "Noah, I can't believe it's you. Why are you here?"

She didn't sound particularly glad to see him. Maybe she had been glad to be rid of him. "Seems I just keep turning up when you need me most." It came out sarcastically and when she smiled at the truth of it, he growled inwardly.

"That's true. No one has ever saved me like you have."

Her eyes were all softness, and he felt a tightening in his chest.

"I can't believe you came all this way. Did Cara put you up to it? How is she?"

She moved alongside him and grasped his upper arm, smiling happily into his eyes. He felt a heady rush of excitement.

"No, I came on my own, but she was worried about you. She and Will both. She had her baby the day after you left. A girl."

Elizabeth beamed. "Oh, Will must be so proud. Is Cara well? Did she have any trouble?" She shook her head, still clinging to his arm in a way that made him want to wrap himself around her. "Oh, you probably wouldn't know all those details."

"As a matter of fact," he said, gritting, "I delivered the baby."

Her eyes grew round. "What?"

Noah shrugged. "Will was gone, looking for you. We couldn't find a doctor in time. I'd just arrived to . . . see you and found the post locked up. After breaking down the door, I found Cara trying to deliver the little package all on her own. There wasn't time to do anything but help."

Her shoulders slumped as she looked into the water. "It's my fault. Will would have been there if I hadn't left."

Noah laughed. "It was a good thing Will wasn't there. If I remember right, he wasn't her favorite person at the time." When Elizabeth looked confused, he changed the subject. "Elizabeth, why did you leave so suddenly?"

She turned her head away. "I . . . I had a chance to join

Charlie McKay's party and I took it. You know all I ever really wanted was to come here . . . to be a part of this."

"Yes, but I thought we had an agreement. I thought you were going to prospect my land with me." He thought of Mary-Margaret and said his next thoughts out loud. "This isn't any place for a woman."

She turned on him. He should have expected it by now, but it came like a surprise attack. "I've just as much right to be here as anyone. I deserve a chance." Then she spoke fiercer, to match the fire in her eyes, "I deserve a chance." She looked down, shaking, then back up at him. "Why don't you just admit it—*you* don't want to be here. I didn't ask you to come for me, Noah."

Her gaze locked onto his. What he read in her eyes he could no longer endure. All the pent-up fears and frustrations of the past month exploded inside him. Reaching out, he pulled her to him and lowered his head. With an urgency born of desperation to reach her, to show her, he kissed her like he'd dreamed of kissing her for so long. Noah forgot the river, the raft, the night sun twinkling at them, the mountains, the land . . . his land even . . . he forgot everything except the woman in his arms. He drowned himself in the taste and feel and touch of her. It was like coming home—to an explosion.

When he finally lifted his head and looked into her eyes, she flushed and sighed softly, "Oh."

Noah's voice was firm. "I'll take you to Dawson City. But after you've had your fill of this blasted gold mining notion, I'm taking you home—as my wife."

She looked blankly at him for a moment, myriad emotions playing over her features. Finally, her face grew hard. "No," she said simply.

Noah was stunned. "No? Just . . . no?"

"I can't marry you, Noah."

He took hold of her shoulders, gripping them firmly so that she had to look up at him. "Why? Tell me why not." Softer, pleading, he demanded, "Tell me you don't love me." His throat tightened as he watched her struggle with the question.

She looked away. "I'm . . . Noah, I'm already married." She looked back into his eyes, her face hardened now. "That man, Ross Brandon, the one looking for me. He's my husband. I . . . I lied about my name being Smith. It's been many things, but never Smith."

The air whooshed out of him as though he'd been punched. His stomach rolled, the crumbling of his heart overshadowing it all. Noah wished he *had* been punched. God help him, he was in love with a married woman.

❋ ❋ ❋

ELIZABETH FELT SICK. She watched his face turn ashen before he dropped his hold on her and turned away. Turning away herself, she fought back tears. It was better this way. He had a right to someone better. She wouldn't let him be destroyed.

"Why?" he croaked out. "Why didn't you tell me? And why aren't you with him?"

Her emotions switched off and the lies came easy. "I've been running away from him. He beat me . . . and more. I didn't think he would follow me here," her voice dropped, "but he has."

Noah turned around. "Elizabeth, why didn't you tell me all this?"

"Why? What can you do? You can't save me this time, Noah Wesley. If he comes for me—and he will, I know that now—there's nothing you can do about it." She turned her back on him, burning her safety net and knowing it, but there was no other way. It was the only decent thing she had ever done in her life. She would save Noah from herself if it killed her. And it very well might.

The silence was stifling on the little raft as the night hastened on. Elizabeth didn't know if she could endure it any longer. She shivered and hugged herself and adjusted her sitting position. It was a tranquil stretch of the journey. Silt from the Teslin River slipped into the water, giving it a low, hissing sound that droned in the background. They sat in stillness, bathed in the long twilight, filled and straining with longing toward one another. It lent an eerie feel to the journey, as though the torturous silence would go on forever and the combined aching of their hearts would never stop.

"It's getting cool. Why don't you put on your coat?"

His voice was so deep, struck such a chord within her, that she closed her eyes and inhaled, soaking it in. Finally, she managed, "It's not among my things. I must have left it behind."

She heard him stir and then felt a blanket being wrapped around her shoulders. She turned her head slowly to look at him and felt such sadness, saw only sadness in his eyes. On a breath she said. "If you would get angry and shout at me, it would make this easier."

"I *am* angry. You should have told me, then maybe I wouldn't have . . ."

"Wouldn't have what?"

He shook his head. "It doesn't matter. It probably wouldn't have made any difference." He motioned toward the lean-to. "Why don't you get some sleep. We're on calm water now, but there are bound to be more rapids. I'll wake you then."

Elizabeth shook her head and looked into his tired eyes, seeing his wretchedness. "I couldn't sleep. Why don't you rest, and I'll keep watch."

Noah ran a hand through his hair. "You sure?"

She nodded.

After he lay down she said softly, "Noah?"

"Yeah?"

"I guess you'll head back home at the first camp we get to?"

He lifted his head and rested it against his palm. After a moment's hesitation, he said, "I'll see you to Dawson City first. I don't want you going alone."

She tried to express her gratefulness. She tried to make herself turn around and tell him the truth—all of it. Instead, she just stared out at the dark water and forced the tears to remain behind the knot in her throat.

July 20, 1895
Dear Mrs. Rhodes,

I regret that I have little news on our search. Nothing has opened in the case to lead me to believe that Elizabeth is in New York, Illinois, or the vicinity. I have had many cases over the years and all have been resolved but this one.

Sometimes I, too, despair over it, but something about your description of her in that first letter, when she was such a young child and still with you, it haunts me. I cannot give up.

This morning, in a moment of prayer, I felt the urging to expand my search. Upon finishing this letter, I will broaden the investigation, placing ads in various newspapers across the country, expanding toward the south and further west. I will also continue to try to uncover the name of the adoptive parents. Elizabeth must be approaching eighteen now and has perhaps left her home and journeyed out on her own. Regardless, in this last great effort to serve you, I pledge to leave no stone left unturned.

I remain your devoted servant.

Sincerely yours,
Jeremiah Hoglesby
Private Detective for Hire

Seventeen

Dawson City. Nestled in forested hills, it was the noisiest, muddiest, most crowded place Noah had ever seen. The waterfront was packed with every kind of floatable craft imaginable, most for sale, having reached their destination. The beaches were covered with hundreds of tents, flags of the unlucky, unable to get their hands on a claim.

He was dumbfounded, shaking his head in wonder at the extremes. Beggars rubbed shoulders with the newly rich and their fancy clothes and weighted pockets. A man in a pristine suit and bowler hat walked among the crowd, hawking The Palace Grand, boasting it was so large it could sleep 2,200 people, its accommodations so lavish you would forget your wretched journey, its pillows so soft you were guaranteed only dreams of gold. Signs lined the sides of buildings, depicting a variety of amusements to waylay the loneliness, giving prospectors reason to spend their gold as fast as they could pan it from the icy streambeds. There were gambling halls and dance halls, such as the Monte Carlo where men could buy a dance for a dollar. On the racier side was an area called Paradise Alley that housed prostitutes in what was called the "Dawson

194

cribs." Noah would have to be sure to steer Elizabeth away from there before her natural curiosity demanded she take a look.

Nicknamed "Paris of the North," Dawson was no ordinary tent town.

Noah knew lonely men were easily drawn to the base entertainments. Those prone to gamble could wager on dog-fights, a badger fight, or prize fighting. The resistant could join a social club or pay dearly for a play or local musical evening sponsored by one of the hotels. Dawson could boast a certain amount of culture, and yet it all had *bite* to it. Dawson City was a gutsy town, made up of the kind of men and woman who dared a man-eating trail to get to it.

"Have you ever seen anything like it?" Elizabeth turned toward him, her eyes dancing with excitement. They were standing in a long line at the Canadian Registry Office to register her a claim. Noah felt the familiar pain in his chest when she smiled at him like that. They'd called a forced truce for the rest of the river journey and hadn't mentioned her circumstances again, but Noah thought of little else. He hoped it would get easier to breathe once he was away from her and back home. And he could have left her by now, should have, but he just couldn't leave her to that man. He had to be there when Ross came for her—even though he was afraid of what he might do to him when they came face to face.

After a lengthy wait, they drew up to the window of a tall, thin, balding man with round spectacles who directed his questions to Noah.

"Name?"

"Elizabeth Smith," she answered.

"And your husband's name?" the man asked pointedly.

"He isn't my husband, and I'd like to file a claim in my name, if you please. It's Elizabeth Smith."

"Very well. I'll tell you what I've told the last fifty people. There are no claims left to be had, miss."

Noah watched her face fall.

"Nothing? Nothing at all?"

The man looked genuinely sorry for her as he shook his head, his white bushy eyebrows raised almost to his hairline.

She looked down at her hands for a long moment and then back up at the man. Tears glistened in her eyes as she gazed up at him and said in a choked voice, "But I've come so far . . . I can't just give up. Please, do you know of anything?"

The man was obviously distressed and some sixth sense told Noah to keep quiet. He watched Elizabeth blink hard as a single tear raced down her cheek. The man pulled his pristine white collar away from his throat. Elizabeth just stood there, rooted to the ground gazing at him. Finally, he cleared his throat and fumbled in his pocket for a handkerchief. Handing it to her, he leaned down and whispered, "There is a claim that was just vacated. I bought it myself and was planning to sell it to a friend of mine. It's on Bonanza Creek but . . . I will let you have it for seventy-five dollars."

Elizabeth gasped. "Bonanza Creek? Isn't that where they first struck it rich?"

"Yes ma'am. One of the first places. Like I said, I was saving it for a friend of mine, and he'll likely have my neck if he learns I've sold it, but . . . if you have the cash, you can own it."

Elizabeth gave the man such a blindingly joyous smile through her tears that he flushed. She quickly pulled out the bills and counted them into the man's palm. There were fifty-four dollars and some change in all. Noah wordlessly added the rest. Elizabeth handed over the money, saying, "Thank you, sir. Thank you."

Noah could only shake his head at her, convinced the man would have done just about anything for a pretty woman in tears. Turning her, he led her away with his hand in the small of her back. Once outside, he turned her around and looked into her sparkling eyes. "Happy?" he asked.

She smiled up at him with elation in her eyes. "I have a claim! Can you believe it? I'm so happy I could do a jig right here in the street." Grasping hold of his upper arm she squeezed it and demanded, "Let's go see it."

"It may not be much," he warned.

"It will be perfect," she returned solidly.

Nothing, not even sound reasoning could daunt her enthusiasm. She was convinced she would strike it rich. He sighed. "All right, let's go have a look."

Number 17 on Bonanza Creek was the standard size of 500 yards and positioned parallel to the stream. It looked as if it had already been dug up, several times in fact, and had the beginnings of a shaft showing in several different places. There were mounds of black earth waiting to be washed and a broken-down lean-to at the top of a rise. Noah thought he could make it into a small one-room cabin if he could find the lumber. People were breaking up their boats for lumber, but Noah didn't want to do that. What he wouldn't give to own a lumber mill in this town.

Elizabeth was busy unpacking. "I know, I know, it doesn't look like much," she said over her shoulder, "but we're really lucky." She pointed toward the muddy water. "See that sandbar?"

Noah walked over to the edge of the grassy bank and looked at the stream of water before him—it looked the same as a thousand others he'd seen before, but he didn't say so. "Yes, I see it."

She grinned good-naturedly at his lack of enthusiasm. "Gold collects in spots like that. A bend in the stream, low gravel banks. It's a good sign, very promising."

Noah couldn't resist asking, "If it's such a good claim, why isn't someone already mining it?"

She shrugged, undaunted. "Who knows? It appears that whoever had this claim before didn't know what they were doing. They couldn't decide where to sink the shaft and, in my opinion, should have been concentrating on the streambed."

"Maybe they did that first and, finding nothing, decided to try farther up the bank." He took a heavily packed bedroll out of her hands while he talked and carried it to where he thought he would build their camp. He was still unpacking when, moments later, he heard her squeal.

Running down to the raft, he stopped short in amazement. She had the back hem of her skirt pulled up between her legs and tucked into the front of her waistband, revealing white calves. Her little black boots were completely submerged. Noah made a mental note to buy her some good mukluks— knee-high, sealskin, waterproof boots—next time he went to Dawson. She was swirling a gold-pan. Looking up, a thick wave of black hair hanging in her face, she shouted, "Come see! I've found a nugget."

Noah shook his head and smiled as he sloshed into the river. Standing next to her, he looked into her open palm. There, lying in the middle, was a small, yellowish rock. He raised his eyes to her excited face. "This is it, isn't it?" he asked softly.

"This is what you really want." For the first time, it truly sunk in just how much this meant to her.

Her hand closed tightly over the nugget. "Yes," she said fiercely, "this is what I want."

As he stared at her radiant face, he felt the last grains of hope slip away. What was he doing here? Was he going to build her a cabin? He was just making excuses to stay indefinitely. Abruptly, he turned away and walked up the slope to start supper. He had to leave soon. Ross Brandon was her husband, and there wasn't a thing he could do about that.

ELIZABETH WATCHED HIM go, confused. He had been so nice. After that first awful day and night, he had acted like a friend, and she needed a friend. Why did he have to blame her for wanting gold? She was far from the only one. Sighing, she carefully wrapped the nugget in her handkerchief and stuffed it into a pocket in her dress. Bending down, she scooped up some of the sandbar into her pan and started swirling it around and around, just barely submerged in the water, until all the sand and light rock had washed away leaving the heavier rock at the bottom. She poked around at the rocks and debris in the bottom of the pan, searching for golden flakes or, better, nuggets. It was an art, panning, and it had come right back to her. The cold water swished over her reddening hands. The flat, shallow pan, as wide as her hips, grew heavy. She could feel the familiar ache in her back, arms, and neck and knew her whole body would be tired and sore tonight. At least she still had a partner who could cook her a decent supper. She really did need to learn to cook.

By the end of the afternoon, she was weary and feeling a little defeated. It would take her a year to sift through all that sand and dirt alone with a pan. She needed a sluice or at least a rocker to speed up the process. The only problem was, she couldn't operate one alone. Maybe she could persuade Noah to stay until the twins arrived. They didn't know the first thing about mining and would probably be glad to share her claim since she'd likely gotten the only one around. She grimaced inwardly, thinking that then she would have to make them partners, as she couldn't afford to pay them the average dollar-a-day wage for hired help. Hopefully, there would be more than enough wealth to go around.

It was dusk when she finally dragged herself to the camp Noah had set up. The lean-to was repaired and all of her supplies organized underneath it, with her bedroll laid out and ready for sleep. His bedroll lay to the other side, a respectable distance away. Both bedrolls had a pile of gauzy mosquito netting next to them and two tall, whittled sticks—one at the head and one at the foot—to form the bones of a tent. A brisk fire blazed, and the smell of dinner made her stomach remind her just how hungry hard work made her. Noah ignored her after he handed her a plate of what miners called the three B's: beans, bacon, and bread. But she was too tired to try and sweet-talk him out of his mood. As soon as she finished eating, Elizabeth fell into her bedroll and drifted into a dreamless sleep.

SHE WOKE TO the first threads of daylight and the sounds of Noah packing. Panic assailed her. "Where . . . where are you going?"

He shrugged, not meeting her eyes. "The lean-to is fixed up. You will have to get someone to build a cabin if you plan to stay here all winter, but the lean-to will get you through the summer."

She stepped closer to him, tentatively touching him on the shoulder. When he turned and looked into her eyes, she saw a momentary flash of pain. Then his eyes shuttered and he stated briskly, "I need to get home."

Her arm dropped to her side. What could she say to convince him to stay? In his eyes she was a married woman. She reminded herself why it had to be that way, why she couldn't let him see her true feelings. "Noah, I . . ." She faltered, not wanting to beg him. "I know you have little interest in gold mining, but couldn't you stay until the twins arrive? I plan to offer them a partnership; but until they get here, I could really use the help."

Noah shook his head. "I can't."

Elizabeth could sense how badly he wanted to say yes. Pressing, she found herself pleading. "It would only be for a few days. I'm sure they are close behind us. And, Noah, you said you wanted to learn how to pan. I could teach you. Then, when you get home, you could prospect your land." She held her breath, waiting.

He looked torn, in anguish. "Elizabeth, you don't know what you're asking. It's killing me . . . being with you like this."

Raw pain shone from his eyes, making Elizabeth's heart ache. She could not make herself drag him into the mistakes she'd made. Resolved, she took both his hands into hers and pressed her fingers into his palms; even now, torn with so many emotions, the feel of his strong hands making her breathe differently, she willed him to hear her sincerity. "You must go, of course. It was wrong of me to keep you here so long. I'll be fine."

He looked so undecided, so ravaged.

She looked into those clear blue eyes, not as steady or peaceful as when she'd first met him, knowing she was the cause of that. "I'm sorry, Noah. For everything." She had never meant anything more, but the words seemed too little. How did one tell a man he had opened her eyes to a new world? That he had made her see mankind in a new light. That now she had hope for the side of good. A tear rose, unbidden, and she fought it. Now was not the time to soften; she must be firm and resolved for them both.

His jaw flexed and anger blazed from those brilliant blue eyes. "What will you do . . . when he comes? What will *he* do, Elizabeth? Will he take you against your will? Will he drag you back to wherever he's from and force a life upon you that steals your soul? Tell me, Elizabeth . . . what will you do if I leave?"

"I have a gun." The words popped out softly and she hadn't even realized her plan until she said them.

"You'd kill him, then?"

"If I have to. I won't go back with him."

"No. I won't allow you to become a murderess. You couldn't live with it—not with everything else you're carrying."

She wasn't sure what he meant, but she was sure he believed it. "I can live with it. It would be self-defense and justified."

"Do you think killing a man is that easy? Don't be a fool. He'd likely kill you . . . or worse." He turned from her and stared at the flowing water of the stream, its peaceful trickling belying the scene it witnessed.

He wrestled with the silence and then, looking up to the sky, he growled out, "You would see me drawn and quartered, then? Stretched out on this rack indefinitely?" He laughed harshly then turned to Elizabeth. "So be it. I'll stay." He swung away from her and stalked out of the camp.

Elizabeth watched him go, feeling wretched. But she couldn't speak; she was too relieved.

After three days of mostly silence from Noah, Elizabeth decided she had to do something to goad him into talking again. She had shown him some basic mining techniques, but he was more interested in working on the lean-to, which was beginning to take the shape of a cabin. She would pan all day, with little results, and he would hunt and build and cook.

After dinner one night, she stood and stretched. "I think I'll take a bath."

Noah scowled. "No, you won't."

Elizabeth ignored him and moved to the lean-to, gathering clean clothes and soap.

He growled at her. "You can't take a bath in that muddy creek with all of these men around. It's crazy. And the water is too cold."

Elizabeth slanted him a coy look. "Call me crazy then. I haven't had a real bath in weeks, and I'm taking one."

She thought if he glared at her any harder his eyes might just pop out.

"Fine. But don't yell for me if you need help. I warned you."

"I wouldn't dream of it," she replied tartly.

Dipping her toes into the water, she called herself a thousand kinds of stubborn fools. With a sun that now never slept, just faded for a few hours, there was entirely too much daylight to guarantee any modesty. And the water *was* freezing. But she was determined. Stripping down to her drawers, she waded quickly to her waist, teeth chattering, and began soaping herself. She grimaced as she felt the bottom of the creek bed oozing mud and rocks between her toes. Swallowing hard, she tried not to think about what might be in the water, swimming around her bare legs. It was amazing the comfort and sense of security one's boots provided. Redoubling her speed, she bent at the waist and wet her hair, lathering it quickly with soap. Something brushed against her calf, making her shiver. She was just about to scramble out when she heard it: the laugh that haunted her nightmares and sent tingles of alarm along the bony column of her back.

"You didn't really think I would just give up, did you?"

She sank down into the water, covering herself with crossed arms. Teeth chattering, she demanded in a low voice, "Get off my claim, Ross."

He laughed again, low and menacing. "The claim bought with my money? You are sadly mistaken if you think I will leave until I get what I want, my dear."

The cold water numbed all but her fear and anger. She knew anger to be her ally here and latched onto it. "You got what you wanted. What do you think I have left?"

"I want what is rightfully mine, Elizabeth. You cheated me and you will pay for that."

"I'll pay you back the money I took as soon as the claim pays. I don't have anything else to give you." She backed up until the stream reached her neck.

"I think you do. And this time, when I'm finished with you there won't be anything left for that big fellow you are currently with." He eyed her body through the water. "You have been playing the whore, haven't you, Elizabeth? I'll have to find some special way of compensating myself for such used goods." His face hardened with a look that made her stomach twist. He picked up her blouse from the ground and held it in the air. "Get out."

She shook her head in terror. She would freeze to death first, and from the lack of feeling in her legs, she very likely would. "I'll make a deal with you," she blurted out in desperation. "If you will leave me alone, I'll give you half of any gold I find."

His laugh was a wolf's snarl. His eyes, black and deadly, glittered in the pale light. "You don't really think I came all this way for the money, do you? You are more of a fool than I thought, Elizabeth. We have more to settle than that, you and I. Your hasty departure ruined all of my carefully laid plans. You will pay for that, don't ever doubt it. Now, get out."

Marshalling her anger, her hate, she spat, "You will never touch me again. Now, get off my claim." What she wouldn't give for her pistol right now.

"Such bravado from a lone, naked woman. You are not thinking your friend will save you, are you?"

She heard the click of a gun and saw a shiny glint in the pale light as he waved it in the air. "By all means, please, call your precious Noah Wesley. He will come charging to your rescue and right into my hands." He shrugged. "If he persists in hanging around, I'll have to get him out of the way at some point, anyway. Why not now?" The smile was back. He was so confident, so evil, she felt her strength drain away.

He leveled the gun on her. "Get out. We can't have you freezing to death and ruining all my fun, now can we?"

With her chest pounding with fear, she took a step forward.

"Stop!"

Elizabeth felt a rush of relief as she recognized Noah's voice. He had a long rifle pointing mere inches from Ross's back. "Drop it, Ross."

Elizabeth watched as Ross's face changed from leering expectancy to composed rage. Slowly, he lowered the gun to his side.

"Lay it on the ground." Noah's voice was as calm and steady as the gently lapping water. When the gun was on the ground, he said, "Turn around and face me."

Ross turned.

"Now, Elizabeth, get out and get dressed. Go straight to the fire and stay there. I aim to settle this once and for all."

Elizabeth didn't like the sound of that, but she was happy to obey. What would he do? Moving as fast as her frozen limbs could carry her, she reached the bank and her clothes. Quickly, she wrapped the towel around her and scurried through the grass. Back at the fire, she threw on her clothes then ran to her bedroll, searching wildly beneath it. She firmly grasped the pistol and hurried back to the bank. The tall weeds shielded her from view as she crouched down and strained to hear.

". . . I'm telling you now, if you hurt her, I'll see to it that you're behind bars. You don't have any right to treat her that way, even if you are her husband."

Ross laughed low and fearless. "Her husband, eh? Is that what she told you? The little fraud. What is she taking you for? Quite a ride from the looks of things. I never knew what to believe with her either, but her husband? That is a good one." He laughed again. "Don't look so glum, fella. You must have been a prime target for her, living alone in the frozen wilderness like you do. Me? I should have known better. She and I are cut from the same cloth, you know. Did she tell you about us? Probably not everything, and you do want to know, don't you? Let me tell you what she did to me."

Elizabeth's heart hammered harder, shame filling her, as he ruthlessly continued. "She made a bargain with me back in Seattle. Nothing hidden, a straightforward business deal. In return for the favor of her," he stretched out his arms at the great expanse, "Alaskan holiday, she would, shall we say, share my bed until I tired of her. Then she decided to cheat me. She stole all of my money and ran off without even a good-bye. Imagine my heartbreak. I figure she owes me. As for being her husband . . . ha! What kind of fool would marry a lying, conniving little thief like Elizabeth Dunning?"

Elizabeth's heart wrenched in the long silence that followed.

"I don't believe you," Noah answered back, but he didn't sound certain.

"Don't you?" came the smooth reply. "Think about it. Doesn't it make some of the pieces to the puzzle fit?"

Elizabeth clenched her teeth, waiting for Noah's response. She jerked as she heard the gun go off.

"Get out of here and don't ever let me see you again. I'll kill you if you come near her."

She heard movement and then Ross's laugh farther off. "Sorry, she will never want you. I have what she wants and she will come to me for it." A short pause and another laugh, farther off, then . . . "I know her real name."

Elizabeth sat there in the tall weeds for a long time, waiting . . . feeling numb.

"Is it true?"

His voice was closer. She couldn't answer, couldn't even move.

Suddenly, he was grasping her by the shoulders, kneeling beside her. "Is it true? Did you lie about him being your husband? Did you agree to such a bargain with him and steal yourself a ticket to Alaska? Elizabeth, tell me."

She looked up into his eyes, tormented eyes, and saw the depths of the pain she had brought into his life. A sob broke from her throat. "Yes, yes, it's true. It's true and more."

He pulled her close, forcing her to hold his gaze. "Why?"

When she didn't answer, couldn't answer, just stared at him, he let go of her and backed away as if he'd touched something unclean. His last words slipped out in a whisper, fell to the ground with a dark thud and rolled through all her protective walls to pierce her heart.

"And to think I almost married you."

Scorching pain made her fall back. "And now you know why I wouldn't let you," she whispered.

NOAH RUSHED BACK to their camp, his breathing heavy and sick. What had he done? Chased a stranger halfway across a continent? Yes, a stranger—that's what she was. He could hardly contain his feelings. Looking up into the night sky he railed, "Why? What was all this for?" The stars twinkled back at him, so sure and bright in their creation.

Forgiveness is not for the good.

He hadn't heard the voice in a long time and didn't really want to hear it now. "Forgiveness? For what? Being someone she's not? For making me believe she was someone she's not?" He felt like shaking his fist but set his hands on his hips instead—daring God to answer.

Seeing only what you wanted to see, perhaps?

Noah felt the words hit to his core. Was it he that needed her forgiveness? Yes, she had lied to him—broken his heart even—but hadn't he stubbornly clung to what he thought Elizabeth should be instead of seeing her as she really was— a survivor of terrible circumstances. A woman with strengths that he had only seen as hardness, something to change and fix. It was just those circumstances that had made her who she was . . . and he loved who she was. Her fierceness . . . her vulnerability . . . her laughter and her face with laughter on it. Her determination to be strong . . . her elation when she was . . . her tears when she was weak and the willingness to let him see her weakness . . . her very self. Elizabeth. Then he realized . . . he loved her just as she was.

Before he had time to change his mind or even reason it through, he rushed back to the tall grass where he had left her.

She sat in the twilight, her knees up and her head down on them, her arms curled protectively around her legs. She looked so fragile, her slender shoulders weighted with burdens she should not be carrying, a burden he had added to. Something inside him broke, like a dam, and he felt a rush of compassion for her. Kneeling next to her he touched her gently on the shoulder, tears of his own making cold, wet tracks of sorrow and repentance on his cheeks.

She jerked up and away from him. "Go away . . . go back to Juneau where you belong." Her words were strong and he marveled at her strength—hard won and tempered like steel to a deadly sharpness. He smiled a slow, sad, happy smile, realizing that in knowing its source it could not pierce him. He remembered suddenly what she had last said to him, why she had lied about being married. "And now you know why I wouldn't let you," she had said. If she loved him at all, he suddenly understood what that lie must have cost her.

"Elizabeth . . . I'm sorry. I didn't mean it. It was the shock, and my own weakness. I haven't wanted to see the truth anymore than you've wanted to say it."

She stared up at him, confusion evident in the endless pools of her deep brown eyes.

"Listen to me," he said, "it doesn't matter. Not Ross or your past or anything else you could tell me. Elizabeth . . . I love you."

Suddenly Elizabeth was a she-cat, clawing and kicking at him. "Stop it! Don't say something you will regret."

He let her thrash for a moment and then quieted her in his strong embrace. "I won't regret it."

She stilled and then lashed out with a better weapon. "You don't know the half of it. What if I told you I've learned the backside of honesty like you know your land. Loving grandparents are for fairy tales, and profitable farms in Illinois are pipe dreams. Black, dark voids live in me where silent orphanages and parent slave owners dwell. I've stolen more than food or money or anything I could put my hands to. I've stolen courage and honest work from the backs of others. I've stolen truth from situations that weren't working to my advantage. I'm a past master at knowing how to work people—get what I want from them. It's as natural as my breath, and I did it to you and Will and Cara and every living soul who has ever touched me. Ross said we were cut from the same cloth and he's right. Living with me would mean sucking the life out of you until you had nothing left to give." Her voice lowered to a mere harsh whisper. "I would use you . . . not love you."

He felt it again, that searing pain that connected him with her emotions. It was overwhelming, overpowering. With fresh tears in his eyes he whispered back, "Take it. Take my love . . . even unto my death. I'll give it all for you."

She let out a sob that turned into a wail. "I would destroy you," she choked out.

Taking her face between his hands he looked deeply into her eyes, willing her to believe him. "No . . . no you wouldn't. My love is strong enough for both of us. Let me love you . . . Elizabeth . . . the woman you are right here, right now. If I could take away the pain of your suffering I would, but I can't. All I can do is suffer it with you, help you carry it. Elizabeth, let me love you."

She gazed at him, unbelief in her eyes, for a long moment that seemed an eternity. A cool breeze blew in, drying their tears, bringing with it an unearthly calm. She breathed heavy and long breaths. "All right, Noah . . . but never say I didn't warn you."

He laughed long and loud, with a kind of relief that sent his heart soaring—a victor's laugh. Stroking the top of her silky head, he pulled her into his arms. "It's going to be OK." He kissed the top of her head and squeezed her tight. "I promise."

❄ ❄ ❄

January 16, 1896
Dear Mrs. Rhodes,

I have received several responses from the many new advertisements regarding the reward, but nothing of substance. In reviewing my accounts, I am sad to report that I don't feel I am earning your generous payments. Would you like me to continue, dear ma'am? I could place advertisements in the newspapers of the far west. It is the only area of the country yet unturned.

My son Clyde marries this year. It is an event in the life of a child that I wouldn't want you to miss. Let us not give up hope.

I remain your devoted servant.

Sincerely yours,
Jeremiah Hoglesby
Private Detective for Hire

Eighteen

he room was poorly lit and thick with the smells of tobacco, sweat, and whiskey. Noah stalked over to the bar of The Grand Dame Saloon, a man on a mission. Ross's parting taunt of some hidden knowledge of Elizabeth's real name still rang in his ears—he had to find out what Ross had alluded to. He was just about to question the bartender when he heard that unmistakable laugh. Turning, he saw Ross dressed in a black suit, white shirt, and thinly knotted black tie at a table in the back. He was facing away from the door and hadn't seen Noah come in. In spite of the fact that Noah had been looking for him most of the day, he was surprised to actually find him. Noah wasted no time striding over to the table.

Ross looked up as Noah's booted steps stopped across the table from his chair. Ross had a thin cigar clenched between his teeth, his manner conveying his usual impeccable appearance. His face darkened when he saw Noah, but he remained seated.

Noah looked around at the other occupants at the table. "Excuse me, fellas, but I need to borrow one of your players for a moment." He looked at Ross. "I need to speak to you, Ross. Let's step outside."

Ross smiled. "What kind of fool do you take me for, Wesley? I don't think so."

Noah wasn't in the mood for this. Meaningfully patting the pistol dangling from his side, he ground out, "We have unsettled business to finish. Let's go."

The other men at the table were held frozen, eyes wide and wondering. Ross just smirked at Noah. "If you shoot me, you will never get the answers to your questions." Slowly, he rose to face Noah. "Tell you what, buddy. Elizabeth is a pretty piece of skirt, but she's not worth this much of my time. I'm sick of this town and sick of seeing you, so tell me what you want to know."

"Not here. Let's take it outside."

One of the other players started to guffaw, but when Noah turned his steely gaze on him, he stopped abruptly.

Ross shrugged as if he didn't care and rose. Noah turned toward the door. It shouldn't have come as a surprise when he felt the knifepoint in his back and heard Ross say breathlessly, "I'd rather not kill you in front of all these people, so I've decided I *will* go outside with you. Now walk."

Noah took one step as if in acceptance and then, leaning forward away from the knifepoint, he kicked back, hitting Ross in the knee and causing him to fall back. He turned swiftly, as Ross recovered and came at him with the knife. The man might be smaller than Noah, but he was quick and wiry, and Noah had to keep his eyes on the blade darting close to his face.

A crowd spread out around them, jeering and cheering, picking sides and laying bets. A side argument broke out between two other men and soon they were brawling in another corner of the room. Noah had just reached for his gun, thinking to shoot in the air, when a big man bumped him and sent the gun flying across the room. Great, now he would have to disarm Ross. Noah hated knives. Concentrating on the shiny metal, he lashed out and landed a hard blow to Ross's shoulder, knocking the knife from Ross's hand. Just when it looked like he had gained the upper hand, two other men jumped into the fight. Noah pushed one of them back onto a table, crashing it to pieces, while the other man was hurled into a cheap mirror on the wall, sending a shower of glass to the floor.

The crash was like a signal, and the fight became a free-for-all. Every man in the place dove into the fray, sending bottles and furniture and glass flying around the room. In the midst of it all, Noah lost sight of Ross. He pushed and punched and shoved his way around the room, trying to find him, but Ross had disappeared. Finally, Noah was able to force his way to the door and out into the bright sunlight. He shook his head to clear the fuzziness, wondering if his face was cut up bad; he could feel blood running down from a busted eyebrow. His right eye was swelling fast and his bottom lip was cut, but aside from that, he seemed to be in one piece. Lumbering down the sidewalk, he scanned the street for Ross. As he passed an alley, he glanced down it, turned to walk away, then felt a muzzle of cold steel in his back.

"This time, we'll finish this," a voice hissed.

The gun, his gun he suspected, was shoved into his back, and, for a moment, Noah thought this was it.

"Turn around, slowly, and start walking toward that grove of trees outside of town. No tricks this time, Wesley. If I see one suspicious move, I'll blow you away in front of the whole town. Now walk."

Noah walked. As Ross pushed them deeper into the brush and farther from Dawson City, Noah tried to come up with a plan. This man, with his smooth exterior and handsome face, had the core of a serpent. Noah was not looking forward to what was coming. He had seen Ross's kind before, the type that enjoyed watching living beings suffer, whether animal or human, friend or foe. He knew Ross derived some kind of sick excitement from seeing fear and pain in others. With this in mind, he buried his apprehensions and took on the careless demeanor of his good friend Jacko. Jacko was a different kind of devil. The kind that had no sense at all, as far as Noah was concerned. He laughed in the face of danger and scoffed at mortality. He wouldn't have even recognized Ross's sinister soul and would, in turn, be outrageously cock-sure.

Noah smiled to himself as he trudged through the increasingly thick brush and thought to borrow a little of his friend's bravado. "Since you're going to put a bullet through me, Ross, you may as well tell me what you know about Elizabeth."

Ross jabbed the gun in his back. "Keep moving. And don't worry about your precious Elizabeth. She'll be in good hands."

Noah swallowed. "What are you going to do with her?"

Ross laughed. "I thought I already made that clear." He paused. "But, if you want details to take to your grave, I'll be happy to oblige." He laughed again and Noah felt the hairs on the back of his neck rise up.

Shrugging, Noah said, "Sure, if you want, but that wasn't what I was referring to. I know you're smart, Ross, and smart men don't track a woman thousands of miles just for sex. You're holding out on me. What else do you want with Elizabeth?"

Ross chuckled and pushed Noah toward a fallen tree, motioning for him to sit down. While holding the gun steady on Noah, Ross pulled a cigar out of his pocket and lit it. Puffing several times to get it going, he contemplated the big man. "You poor sod. She's had you in knots since you first laid eyes on her, hasn't she?" He didn't wait for an answer. "I remember the first time I saw her. She was coming out of a little dress shop, looking very prim and proper. I remember being surprised she was such a pretty little thing." He smirked. "If you could have seen those awful people who raised her, you would know why." Sniffing, he took another puff on his cigar, his elegant fingers extended. "They were horrid, backward people. Anyway, I put on my best charming manner and set out to win her. I hadn't planned on seducing her when I first took the investigation, but after seeing her," he raised his brows twice at Noah, "well I'm sure you, of all people, can see why I decided to change my plans. She *is* so delectable." He paced a little, the gun growing slack in his hand as he warmed to the subject. "The really funny thing is that she made it so easy. Under that prim dress lay the reckless heart of a dreamer. She wanted to go to Alaska and," he lifted his arms wide for a moment, "participate in the great gold rush going on here. She was barely scratching out a living, near starvation she was so thin. You should have seen how she dreamed of gold, how she positively glowed when she talked about it. She was feverish with it. So, the seduction took a business turn. She wasn't interested in flattery and fine manners like most girls. Not coy or shy either. She needed fare to Alaska and I offered it. Not for free, of course, but then I told you how she was to pay me."

Noah ignored his feelings and said with deadly calm, "You were never going to give her the money though, were you? No matter how many times she . . ."

Ross bared his white even teeth, perfect like the rest of his appearance. "Eventually. I was hired by Margaret and

Henry Dunning, her parents. I would have wired them the moment I tired of her and collected my money, which I must say is amazingly substantial considering the looks of them."

Noah scowled at him. "Elizabeth's parents are dead."

Ross cocked his head and smirked at him. "Are they? Have you believed everything she has told you? You poor, besotted fool." He flicked an ash and continued with relish. "Elizabeth was raised an orphan until the aforementioned Dunnings adopted her." He showed his teeth again. "She was better off in the orphanage than with them, I assure you."

Noah tried to keep his boiling emotions at a simmer. He took a breath and then asked evenly, "What do her parents want with her now?"

Ross smiled and walked closer. "That's the best joke of all. Elizabeth is terrified of them, probably that claim-jumping business, but that's not the reason the Dunnings are looking for her. If Elizabeth only knew, she would have never come to this God-forsaken country."

Ross leaned down, his elbows braced on his thighs, the gun dangling unheeded from the tips of his fingers between his knees. As much as Noah wanted to ask, as badly as he needed to know what the Dunnings wanted with his future wife, he knew that the time would never be better. Ross could move away at any moment, destroying this opportunity. With lightning quickness, he kicked the gun out of Ross's hands and rolled toward it. They both scrambled for the gun in the tangled weeds. Ross reached it first and, cocking it, turned it toward Noah who was right on top of him. They rolled, struggling for control of the gun. Noah was larger by far, but Ross possessed an evil strength. With a jerk, Ross wrenched the gun away, slithered from under Noah, and stood. He quickly aimed at Noah, breathing hard, his face a mask of rage.

Noah was rising and jerked as the gun went off. He mentally searched for pain and found none. Ross was pointing the gun at him again.

"You missed," Noah said simply as he dove for the arm holding the gun, wrestling Ross back to the ground. It went off again and then skidded away into the grass. Noah put his hands around Ross's neck, demanding, "Tell me. Tell me everything."

Ross stared back at him with blank eyes. Noah watched in stunned stillness as the thin man stopped breathing. He scrambled off Ross, seeing for the first time a large red stain spreading across the white shirt. Somehow . . . someway . . . Ross had been shot. Noah had not pulled the trigger.

Now he might never know why her adoptive parents were looking for her. Now he would have to find *them*.

❄ ❄ ❄

"NOAH WESLEY?" A voice called out.

He had just left the Canadian Police Headquarters, having given full details of the accident to a grim-faced Mountie. He turned and shielded his eyes against the sun to see William Cleary and the twins walking up the main street.

"That is you, isn't it?"

Noah stopped and waited until they reached him. Nodding, he held out his hand and said, "Pastor Cleary, it's good to see you." Turning to the twins, he regarded them. "This must be Ben and Josh. Elizabeth has told me about you. She'll be glad to see you."

"Did she get a claim?" Ben asked excitedly.

"Has she struck gold?" Josh chimed in.

Noah couldn't resist a grin. They had gold fever as bad as Elizabeth. "Yes, she managed to get hold of a claim. If you boys want to come back with me, you can see her and take a look at it. As for the gold, she's no doubt panning right now, so who knows what we'll find when we get there."

The twins enthusiastically agreed and went to find the Recorder's Office to check on any new openings. After they left, William Cleary fell in step beside Noah as they walked toward Noah's raft.

"We haven't seen a sign of that Ross fella since you two left us. Have you seen him?"

Noah nodded solemnly. "Yes, I've seen him."

William looked grave. "If your face is any indication of the encounter, I'd guess it didn't go very well. Do you know what he wants with Elizabeth?

Noah shrugged and turned away from the man's direct gaze. "He came to our camp last night and nearly took Elizabeth at gunpoint. I . . . I just had a fight with him." Noah looked into the preacher's eyes and sighed heavily. "He was going to kill me, and while I was trying to wrestle the gun away from him, he was shot. Ross is dead."

The preacher inhaled sharply and looked up toward heaven. "Does Elizabeth know yet?"

"Not yet. I'll tell her when we get back to camp. Could you come too? I think she would like to see you."

"Of course. The twins and I have been very concerned for her. It's terrible, but at least now she no longer has that threat hanging over her." He sighed, looking at Noah. "There are others, though, aren't there?"

Noah only nodded and guided the preacher over to the raft.

It was a good thing demon fighting was fast becoming his specialty.

❅ ❅ ❅

April 22, 1898
Dear Mrs. Rhodes,

It is my great joy to send you the enclosed letter from Margaret and Henry Dunning. The advertisements have gleaned many letters over the years, but I feel this is the one we have been waiting for. I believe, dear ma'am, that we have found your daughter in the far west. I will await your further instructions. Please write or telegraph soon.

I remain your devoted servant.

Sincerely yours,
Jeremiah Hoglesby
Private Detective for Hire

Nineteen

New York City

 isting, cold rain pattered against the black umbrellas surrounding the gravesite. Jane Rhodes clenched hers with a thin-boned hand as she watched them lower her father into the earth. She didn't listen to the intonations of the priest, that one-tone monologue that had kept her father dozing off every Sunday. Instead, she felt driven to really consider Howard Greyson for the first time in years.

She'd never forgiven him for making her give up Elizabeth. There was still a pain in her heart when she thought of her baby girl, though not so sharp now; it didn't steal her breath away like it used to. Now it was just a dull ache that never seemed to go away completely. But as she looked upon the ornate rosewood coffin, with its shiny brass trimmings, that he had picked out for himself years ago, she was faintly surprised to feel a fluttering of sadness that he was gone. It was as if a little piece of her had been cut away, and she wondered that it should be so.

Howard Greyson had been a hard man, a determined man. She couldn't remember a time when he had ever been afraid or unsure of himself. He was a man of action, and she supposed that was one of the characteristics she had inherited from him. She had been a whirl of action after Elizabeth was taken.

What he had done to her was wrong. If her mother had been alive, and oh, how many times Jane had wished it so, things would have been so different. But Jane knew that her father had truly wanted what he thought best for her, not what made her happy. Happiness to him was success, both financial and social. His image was everything to him, and she had nearly destroyed all that by showing up pregnant and unwed. He had done what had to be done, in his eyes, to rectify the matter. Giving away her baby and marrying her off to a respectable, up-and-coming lawyer was the only solution, no matter that it had broken her in the process.

She felt the umbrella being taken from her hand and looked up at her husband, Benjamin Rhodes. Jane smiled tenderly at him and once again marveled at the irony. A less ambitious man would be hard to find. He was quite the opposite from everything she'd known—open and generous, keenly intelligent but humble and with modest aspirations. But mostly he'd been patient, waiting for her to notice him, waiting for love. Her father had gauged Benjamin by his prestigious family and had not clearly seen the man himself. For that, Jane was intensely thankful.

Her thoughts shifted to the man she would have chosen for herself—Elizabeth's father. When she thought of him, through the hazy glasses of time, she remembered a devilishly handsome young man from the less desirable side of town, but with a blazing desire to change all that. She marveled now how very like her father he was. He had craved power and wealth and acceptance. She saw now that she would have been miserable with him, but the cost of gaining Ben was still sharp. It had been so horrible in the beginning.

She squeezed Ben's hand. It fit outside her own so well as to seem molded for that express purpose. He'd been a stranger when they had married, and she, like a wounded animal, so hurt and frightened and furiously, stubbornly determined not to ever love another living soul again, had viewed him as another enemy. She hadn't let him touch her for the first year. Then, seeing him give up, eat his quiet dinners alone, and pour himself into his work, she'd begun to feel wretched in her neglect, sorry for their stilted conversations, the way he couldn't meet her eyes. Finally, her heart was able to agree with the logic that he wasn't the cause, that he was suffering because of her, that he'd married a shadow-woman, and it wasn't fair at all.

She had tried then. Turned her body, if not her soul, toward him. And for a long time that had been enough. He loved her. From the first moment he saw her in that mocking-white wedding gown that she'd hated, he'd seen only beauty and had fallen in stomach-wrenching love. He'd made her laugh—and sometimes even forget—binding him to her and bringing her a few stolen moments of happiness. It was an ebb and flow that still ruled them, though softened with time. Now he was her best friend and only comfort in her life. Besides Elizabeth, they were childless.

She had begun looking for Elizabeth immediately, selling her jewelry and then her mother's heirlooms to hire a private investigator. After her marriage, Ben had helped and that was the one area where she'd let him. She'd been obsessed, almost destroying her health to find her lost daughter. She'd spent every dime Ben made, and he had given it to her with an open hand. On what would have been Elizabeth's tenth birthday, she pulled out every scrap of paper she had been able to gather over the years and then collapsed across her dining room table, a living corpse on unburned ashes. They were living like paupers, they had next to no friends, and her father had thought she'd lost her mind. He wouldn't even see her, not that she cared at the time.

In the years of searching they'd had only one real lead— the name of the orphanage in New York where Elizabeth had first been sent. Jane had been frustrated with her private investigator's inability to find Elizabeth there. Then he'd written that Elizabeth had simply disappeared and while he would continue to look, it appeared there was no trace of her to be found. It was her last letter from him, and so many years ago.

But that day, on Elizabeth's tenth birthday, among the blank walls of her stark dining room, she'd decided that she couldn't go on like she was anymore. It was time to rejoin the living. She didn't give up hope—never that. She didn't stop looking at every dark-haired young girl she crossed paths with in the hope of seeing her face, but she did let go of the heavy burden. She'd gone shopping, took an interest in her clothes and furnishings. She'd made friends, stiff and uncomfortable at first, but with growing success. And most of all, she found herself again. She liked Jane, and Jane was glad to finally be alive once more.

Now, as she watched the cause of all her suffering being buried beneath the wet earth, she was faintly surprised to feel something akin to forgiveness welling up inside her. She didn't understand her father, but she couldn't hate him anymore, and she thought perhaps he had loved her, in his way. The crowd around her started moving away, causing her to realize that the ceremony was over. Looking up into the hazel-green eyes of her husband, she said, "Just a moment alone with him, please."

He kissed the top of her forehead, his hand a comfort on the back of her head as he handed her the umbrella. She watched his straight back, the rain dripping from the brim of his hat as he strode to the carriage. Turning, she walked to the mound of fresh earth, squatted down as close as she could get to his last resting place, her gloved hand brushing lightly across the loose earth, the air smelling of wet dirt and the flowers that surrounded the site. She had brought only a small bouquet of forget-me-nots, nothing compared to the showy blooms from all his rich friends, but they had just seemed right.

Laying them on the brown earth, she murmured, "I'm sorry it was so hard for both of us," the first tears since his death springing to her eyes, her voice tight and tear-clogged. "I'm sorry I wasn't perfect and you weren't perfect . . . and we messed it up so terribly." She swallowed hard. "I wish . . . I wish we could have talked before, but," she smiled through her tears, "we're both so stubborn and prideful. It wouldn't have gone well." She laughed a shaky, crying laugh. "So if you can hear me . . . I'm sorry. And . . . I forgive you." She sniffed and then stood, brushing off her skirts, trying not to let the held-in sob overtake her. Taking a shaky breath, feeling the control borne by many hardships sustain her, she cocked her head to one side and, with a half-smile, finished. "I'll do my best to spend my inheritance on something lavish. Just for you."

Turning, she held her skirts up with her free hand and followed after Ben. He was waiting in the carriage for her with open arms, a tender smile, and a broad chest to lean against.

*** ** **

WHEN THEY RETURNED home from the dinner held in her father's honor, Jane found a box of her father's legal papers on the table in the foyer. She opened it casually and glanced through the documents while at the same time taking off one of her gloves with her teeth. A copy of her father's will, which they'd already seen, some deeds and records of his accounts, and then, at the bottom, letters, a stack of string-tied letters addressed to her. She froze, a white glove fluttering to the floor as she saw the return address. It was from the private investigator she'd hired years ago to find information about Elizabeth—Jeremiah Hoglesby. She hadn't heard from him in years. She opened the top one with shaking hands, scanning the clean handwriting, seeing the name Dunning. Margaret and Henry Dunning. Another, smaller folded paper was inside. She looked up at Ben who had just walked in, her face suddenly drained of all color, her mouth pressed into a thin line.

Ben laid his hat on the table and asked urgently, "What is it, Jane? You look as though you've seen a ghost."

She held out the letters with a trembling hand. "You read them. I can't. I don't . . . how could he have these?"

Ben glanced at the return address. "Are these from the private investigator you hired?"

Jane nodded, looking up at Ben. "He must have kept them from me. What does this mean?"

Ben searched the box for other letters, finding another stack, crisp and neatly refolded in their opened envelopes. He looked through them, reading the addresses. "This doesn't make sense. There are reports sent every year . . . to you . . . so many of them. Have you had any reports from him in that time?"

"A few, in the beginning. I—I don't understand. They all said the same thing: 'Nothing yet. I'll keep trying.' I stopped paying him years ago." She looked up at Ben. "What has my father done?"

Ben gathered the letters in one hand, put the other on the small of Jane's back and led her into the parlor. "Get me the letters you received."

Jane nodded, numb, but with a hole opening inside, a vast hole that could suck her into it and leave a shell of a woman, a babbling fool, the woman she'd been on the brink of becoming before escaping her father's house. She forced her legs to walk to the elegant desk, dug in the top drawer for the slim key she knew so well, as imprinted on her fingertips as her fingerprints, so often had she reached for it. Then she found the strongbox in another, deeper side drawer. Unlocking it, she clasped the few letters, her treasures, so well read they were spiderweb fine, her hands looking white, blue-veined, and thin as she grasped them. She walked over and held them out to Ben, knowing every line by heart.

Ben opened the first letter, the oldest one. He picked up and opened one of Jane's letters, held the two papers side by side, comparing the handwriting. The writing from the letter in Howard's box was small and neat, the kind from an analytical mind. The one from Jane's desk looked vastly different, flowing, long lines, like a woman's. He scanned them both. Jane's letter was terse, stoic, and for the first time, as Ben read it aloud, they both caught the underlying meanness, the slight turn of phrase that said the writer was glad he had no good news. A sentence of hopeful nonsense and then a line that snatched away any hope, an ending with the promise to keep trying. The letters from the real detective were detailed accounts of where he'd gone, everything he'd found, little clues here and there, with a tone of sure knowledge that eventually, with enough time and persistence, Jeremiah Hoglesby would find her.

"God help me, I can't breathe." Jane sank onto the pink-and-white-striped divan, her hand clutching her chest.

Ben's face was a mask of stark anger.

"How could I have been so stupid? I should have known he would do something like this," Jane gasped.

"No." Ben rose, bringing Jane a glass of water, the false letter crumpling into a ball of rage in his fist. "*I* should have known. I didn't watch him closely enough." He looked at his wife. "Jane, I knew what he was capable of. I've seen him in the courtroom. He was the most dreaded judge in the city, showing no mercy." He looked at the floor, the creases in his forehead pronounced, then grieved aloud, "I didn't want to see it."

Jane shook her head. "Read the others. Read them all."

Ben let the crumpled paper fall to the floor. "I don't know if I can right now. If he weren't dead . . . I think I would kill him."

Jane walked over and took the stack of letters. She pulled the next one from the envelope, reading it aloud, her hand shaking so that she could hardly see the words. It was the same tone. He sounded excited, having found the orphanage in New York where Elizabeth had been taken. "I received a similar letter. Remember? I wrote to this orphanage but didn't receive an answer." She laid it on the sofa and unfolded the next one. Jeremiah had spoken to a woman from the orphanage. Yes, Elizabeth was there, had been there for two years; she was four now. He planned to travel there. He was sure he would find her now. Jane's letter around that time said that no one at the orphanage knew of an Elizabeth Greyson, that it was a dead end. It was the last letter she ever received from her investigator.

The next one from Jeremiah read with disappointment. He had arrived, only to find the woman he'd corresponded with gone, the other employees claiming they'd never heard of her. Elizabeth, too, was nonexistent—any sign or record of her had disappeared. Two more letters and then another lead. The woman had contacted him again, overheard where Elizabeth had been taken. It was an orphanage in Illinois. He should have her soon. Jane broke at that, crying, holding out the stack for Ben to take over.

Ben was shaking too, more angry than Jane had ever seen him. "Read them," she cried out. "Read the rest."

Ben unfolded the next letter. There had been an accident. Jeremiah had been hit by a wagon on the streets of an Illinois town on his way to the school. His legs were broken and then, in another letter, he said he'd contracted food poisoning, which was forcing him to move to a small town nearby. Jane looked at Ben with horror in her eyes. "Do you think my father tried to kill him?"

Ben shook his head, opening the next one. "Nothing is beyond him now. Your father must have been paying him, somehow intercepting our letters and his, and then giving you these fake letters. He was leading us all along, controlling our every move."

"But why?"

Ben looked helplessly at her, his eyes slashes of pain. "I don't know . . . to keep you apart. He's been controlling our whole lives, Jane."

Jane hung her head, her arms protectively crossed over her stomach in her lap.

Ben slowly unfolded the next letter. Jeremiah apologized profusely, not blaming anyone for the accident, like some guardian angel whose wings were clipped, who was being guided and duped by evil, blissfully ignorant but completely undeterred. It seemed while recuperating he'd met a woman, a widow with four children, and had married. He was living in Illinois now, had enclosed his new address, which Jane had never known about, and was ready to take back up the challenge of finding Elizabeth, even going to the extreme of posing as a custodian to glean inside information. Jane could only shake her head, lips compressed in shock.

The next letter said that Elizabeth had been at the school and she'd recently been adopted. Could Jane come to the school and demand the name of the adoptive parents?

Jane's eyes filled with tears. "I could have gone. She must have been twelve or thirteen then, and I could have gotten her back."

Ben just stared at her, sharing this shock. He looked through the remaining letters. Unable to endure any more, he picked up the last one . . . the one Jane had already opened but not read. He read it silently, knowing he had to shield her from further betrayal. A deep quiver moved over his body as he read it. He looked up into her shattered eyes, his head tilted to one side, a sheen of tears in his own. "Jane, he says they've found her. He says the letter inside explains everything."

Jane took a quivering breath. "When? Is it too late?"

Ben shook his head. "It's dated only a month ago. From the state of Washington." He opened the small, grubby letter that had been tucked inside the neatly folded one. Ben cleared his throat as he read.

> *Dear Mr. Hoglesby,*
>
> *We read in a paper here that you are offering a reward of twenty thousand dollars to anyone who can help you find a girl named Elizabeth. My husband Henry and me adopted a girl from the Illinois State Orphanage in spring of 1889. She went by the name of Elizabeth. We were not told her last name, but one time I saw a paper saying the name Elizabeth Greyson.*

Ben's voice faltered, but he quickly read on.

> *If you think this might be the girl you are looking for, telegraph us at the Sweet's Hotel in Seattle, Washington.*

He looked up at Jane. "It's signed Margaret Dunning."

Jane clutched the edge of the sofa with one hand and held the other against her mouth. "Could it really be? After all this time?"

"I don't know." He studied the letter then looked up at her. "After everything he's done, I fear this is another trick. What if this," he motioned to the letters with his arms, "what if it's all a grand plan to destroy you? What if he's destroyed Elizabeth already?"

Jane stared open-eyed at him. "Oh, my." She inhaled. "What if he's killed her, leading us on this chase to nothing but a grave?"

Jane sank down from the divan onto the highly polished floor. She stared through blurry eyes at the wood grain, seeing in its patterns an evil face, feeling the malevolence rush over her, as if her father were still alive and here, breathing, watching, in this house with them.

"And I'd just forgiven him," she whispered into the room.

Twenty

"We have to reply immediately to the Dunnings' letter. A telegram. And Jeremiah Hoglesby, we must write and tell him everything." Ben stood, fury and deep resolve in his steps as he helped his wife from the floor. *He* would not forgive Howard Greyson for this abomination. Not ever.

"If she's alive, we'll find her," Jane said. "We will find her, won't we, Ben." It wasn't a question.

Ben looked hard into his wife's eyes, the wife he'd almost given up hope of ever having whole. And now, years later, as they'd found their quiet way together, he saw it all crumple into the fine sand it really was. They would never have anything as long as this evil ruled over them. It had to be stopped; it had to be resolved. It was *his* battle now, now more than ever before, and he would see Howard Greyson's sneering eyes fade from their lives and lie with his body, dead to them. He would end it one way or the other, but they would not live another day waiting. His patience was at its end.

"We will find her."

He walked over to the desk, his wife's elegant desk that ill-fitted him but that he had loved because it was one of the first things she had chosen in her determination to pick up the pieces of herself and her life. He sat in the spindly chair, loving the elegant curve of the wood on the back, remembering her excitement when she'd brought it home, his breath catching anew as he remembered the shadows leave her eyes in that moment. His throat clogged as he poised the pen, then he swallowed it and narrowed his eyes, every muscle tense for battle. "To the Dunnings, we'll say . . . *Interested. Stop. Will be on next train to Seattle. Stop* . . ."

Jane stopped him. "We're going ourselves? Together?"

Ben nodded once. "Yes. And if we have to spend every dime your father left you to find her, we will. We won't stop until you see her face."

Jane wept. "God help us," she wailed toward him, toward heaven.

"Yes. God help us."

"HAVE YOU EVER seen anything like it?" Jane breathed as they pulled into the Seattle train station. She had been saying that exact phrase over and over as they crossed the country. The trains going west were bulging with men, and it seemed they were all affected with the same sickness—gold fever.

"I suppose the closest thing I've seen to this is when Gloria Parkins let us pay her a penny to see her drawers," Ben drawled and then gasped as Jane's sharp little elbow poked him in the ribs.

"I'm sure that didn't hold a candle to the gleam in these fellows' eyes, my dear. I've never seen anything like it. Do you think any of them will really strike it rich?"

Ben shrugged and stood up as the train came to a stop. "The odds are slim. Only a handful really strike it rich during these rushes, but each man here thinks he'll be among that handful, so who knows?" As he eyed his wife he added, "I see that gleam in your eyes, Jane. Don't go getting any ideas. We're getting too old to scale frozen mountains."

Jane moved ahead of him, following a young man dressed in miner's garb, carrying a heavily loaded canvas pack, and clanking his way down the narrow isle, and whispered, "Speak for yourself, Ben Rhodes."

Ben laughed, thinking she was right. She probably could scale a mountain if her daughter was on the other side of it. She was looking younger every day, vitality of purpose filling her face and her body with energy. They should have done this years ago.

As they came to the door, they paused and looked out at the city. Each town they had stopped at had its own distinctive feel, a personality it seemed. Seattle looked intriguing, sophisticated. Not like the last few dusty western towns they had stopped at, most of them looking as if they were thrown up in a day and made from tumbleweed. This town had a look of permanence about it.

"Just smell the air, Ben. It's so clean. Doesn't it smell of pine and the sea?" She took a deep breath, moving down the steps of the train onto the wide platform where they collected their luggage. "I suppose we should find a hotel and get something to eat," she said wistfully.

Ben smiled, reading her well, as he always did. "Yes, we should. We'll look up the Dunnings first thing in the morning. I, for one, would like a bath. I feel as if I haven't had one in days."

Jane smiled. "That's because you haven't." Shaking her head she said, "I'm just so anxious. I won't ever be able to sleep tonight."

With his arm around her lower back, Ben led her to the waiting hackney and whispered in her ear, "I'll do my best to keep you occupied in your sleeplessness."

❄ ❄ ❄

THE NEXT MORNING brought with it rain and gusty winds. Dressed in long, black coats with their black umbrella raised above their heads, Ben and Jane followed the directions the hotel clerk had given them and picked their way through the side streets to the Sweet's Hotel. Finding the street name they turned, walked up the windswept, narrow lane toward the foretold blue sign.

"Ben, are you positive of our directions? This place looks so . . ."

"Seedy? Yes, it does. But, it seems we found it, so the directions must be right." Turning, they walked up the wooden-plank steps and through the door. The entry looked to be a parlor room done garishly in red—a faded and stained red carpet, red draperies, and dark paneling making up the backdrop. The furniture was of red-and-gold damask, with dark mahogany frames, the kind in Jane's Great Aunt Eulalie's house, a place she had hated to visit as a child because it smelled of old people and the lemon oil and vinegar that her aunt used to clean everything. This room reeked of tobacco and something else distasteful that Jane couldn't quite put a name to. Taking a firm grip on her elbow, Ben pulled her further into the room and cleared his throat.

A blonde woman appeared. Her girth was squeezed into a tight, pink chiffon evening gown that swayed dangerously from side to side as she approached. "Yes?" she drawled. "Would you like a room?" She was looking at Ben like she would like to have him for dinner.

Jane cleared her throat, gaining her attention, but only for a moment. "We are Mr. and Mrs. Rhodes from New York City, and we have come to see the Dunnings, Margaret and Henry. They telegrammed us that they were staying here. Are they still here?"

The woman eyed her and then Ben again, pouting her lips. "Sure, they're here." She touched her hair and tilted her head. "Are you friends of Henry's?"

She was looking at Ben again. "Not exactly, Mrs. . . . ?"

"Oh, Miss Hart. But you can call me Bess."

Jane resisted the urge to grit her teeth. "Miss Hart, are you employed here?"

Irritated eyes shifted momentarily to hers. She shrugged an exposed, plump shoulder and grudgingly answered, "Why yes, would you like me to tell Henry you're here?"

"Please, and his wife. We would like to see them both," Ben said with authority.

Bess motioned to the chairs. "Just make yourselves comfortable, and I'll see if they're up . . . that is, if they can see you." With an exaggerated sway to her hips, she made her way up the stairs. She would have been disappointed to learn that Ben wasn't appreciating her efforts, as he was busy dusting off one of the chairs.

Jane sat beside him with a *humph* and said, "Tell me this isn't a brothel, Ben."

Ben raised his eyebrows, looking around. "At one time it may have been, judging from the decor. But it's only a seedy hotel now. I never would have brought you had I thought otherwise."

"If the Dunnings were here, I would have come anyway," Jane muttered.

"No doubt."

They stared in tense silence, hearing only the loud ticking of a clock as they waited. After what seemed an eternity, Bess came back down and said, "They're ready. You can follow me."

At Ben's nod they followed her down a narrow hall and into a small room at the back of the building. Jane sighed in relief at the spare furnishings and simple embellishments. She had feared the deeper they ventured in the house, the more brothel-like it would appear. Sinking down into a chair, she summoned a smile. "Miss Hart, might we have some coffee while we wait?"

Bess seemed more amiable after her visit to the Dunnings'. "Of course, ma'am. And some tarts if you like. Freshly baked, apple or blueberry."

Glancing at Ben, Jane shook her head. "No, thank you, Miss Hart. Just the coffee will do."

The door had just closed when it opened again. In walked a tall, reedy man, his face gouged with pockmarks, his hair thin and gray. Standing beside him was a gaunt, hard-looking woman. Her face hung in lines of bitterness. Jane felt her heart lurch. Fighting down feelings of despair, the inability to connect these two with her precious child, she forced a smile and stood with her husband. Ben regained his composure first and in his usual friendly way extended his hand. "You are the Dunnings, I presume?"

Henry shuffled his feet and handled the brim of his hat, nodding, his eyes darting around nervously. Margaret eyed them with a greedy glitter. "Yes, sir, we are. Margaret and Henry Dunning you're talkin' to."

Jane felt as if nothing escaped those beady eyes and shivered. Ben drew her forward, her arm stiff as she reached out to shake their hands. "This is Jane, my wife, and I'm Ben Rhodes. Please, sit down. Coffee should be here any minute."

After they were all settled, Ben began his interrogation. "Your letter indicated that you adopted a girl from the Illinois State Orphanage."

Margaret nodded, quickly agreeing. "That we did, sir. She was nigh on twelve when we got her. Pretty thing, wasn't she, Henry?"

Henry jerked his attention to her and scowled. Speaking for the first time, he said loudly, "We did the best we could by her. Times were tough and we might 'ave worked her a mite hard, but she thrived."

Jane sought and found Ben's hand for strength. Her eyes closed briefly for a moment before she could speak. "You said her name was Elizabeth. Could you describe what she looked like?"

Margaret was quick to answer. "She was the spittin' image of you, ma'am. Only maybe a bit prettier, beggin' your pardon, ma'am." She smiled, revealing black rot on her teeth.

Jane turned her face toward Ben's in a silent plea for help. She hadn't known this would be so difficult.

Ben squeezed her hand. "You say she looks like my wife. Can you be more specific?"

Margaret shrugged. "She had black, wavy hair. Thick and unruly it was. Fine, creamy skin. I never could figure out how it stayed so nice out in the goldfields like we was . . . but she always did insist on a big hat. Wore one o' Henry's most of the time."

"You made a living mining gold?" Ben asked incredulously.

Henry roused himself to answer. "Farming wasn't feeding us anymore. We had to do somethin'."

Jane's eyes sparked as she asked quietly, "If you couldn't feed yourselves, why adopt a child and have another hungry mouth?"

Margaret stepped in. "Now listen, we done all right by the girl. She wasn't mistreated."

Ben squeezed Jane's hand again and took over the questioning. "Your letter also said you saw a paper with the name Elizabeth Greyson. Can you tell us more about that?"

Margaret answered again. "Well, the day we went to pick her up at the orphanage, we were left in the office there for a bit, and layin' on the desk was her papers." She shrugged. "I was curious what they said and so was Henry. Seein' how he can't read, I sneaked a peek. I only made out the name Elizabeth Greyson, then I heard them coming back and sat myself back down. They told us at the orphanage her name was Elizabeth Smith—till we changed it to Dunning, that is. Does the name Greyson mean somethin' to you?"

Margaret looked hopeful and though Jane didn't want to confirm it, she did. "It's my maiden name and the name Elizabeth was given at birth."

The gleam was back in Margaret's eyes. "Well, if you don't mind me sayin' so, I think you've found her."

"We've found her," Jane repeated softly to herself.

Ben leaned forward, intense. "Not quite, Mrs. Dunning. Where *is* Elizabeth?"

Margaret and Henry exchanged glances. "Well, lookee here," Henry interjected, "we heard there was a big reward for that kind of information. We'd like to see some of the cash before we go and tell what we know."

Jane felt Ben's muscles tense for the battle and relaxed inwardly. Her husband was one of the best legal minds in the country. He could handle the Dunnings.

"There is a . . . reward," Ben said smoothly, "but only for the safe return of Elizabeth Greyson." He looked steadily at Henry. "Not for information."

Margaret perked up. "Well, you won't be findin' her without our information. And we ain't sayin' where the chit is until we see that reward money."

Henry looked at her and scowled.

Ben just stared at her. Calmly he laid it out. "We, of course, are interested in finding the young woman you say is Elizabeth Greyson and desire to know her whereabouts. On the other hand, you have no proof of your claims and could be misrepresenting the facts for your own personal gain. This being the likely case, we shall have to be assured that the girl in question is indeed Elizabeth Greyson before you see the reward money. Is that perfectly clear?"

They both nodded as if spellbound. Henry hesitated and then ventured, "But sir, we can't stay on in this hotel without somethin'. We've been living on credit with the hopes of gettin' this money soon. Couldn't you spare a small sum to tide us over?"

Ben contemplated the man. "Three hundred dollars for the whereabouts of this young woman. After that, you will have to wait until her identity has been confirmed."

Margaret drew a wrinkled paper from her pocket and handed it to Ben. "I suppose that'll do for us until you find the chit. Now this here is a telegram we received from that investigator we hired to find Elizabeth."

Ben scanned the message and passed it to Jane. "It's over a month old. Is this all you have?"

Margaret grinned, showing a missing tooth. "That's true, sir. But if I know Elizabeth, I know where she's at. This telegraph from Juneau proves it."

Jane grasped the paper tight in her hands. "Where?"

Margaret cackled with glee. "To the goldfields in the Yukon. That girl gets gold fever worse than any man I ever saw. She always said she'd be rich someday. Well, I figure she's gone to make her fortune."

Jane felt the paper slip through her fingers as she put her hand to her mouth. Ben interceded. "Is this it?" he thundered. "Are we supposed to search the whole Yukon Territory for her?"

Henry roused himself to answer. "She'll be somewhere between Juneau and Dawson City. A woman'll be easy enough to track in the goldfields." Scorn curled his lip. "Even a couple of city folk like you should be able to find her."

Margaret shot him a hard look and interjected, "We'd offer to come with you and help look, but Henry here ain't been feelin' too well lately, have you, Henry?"

Henry looked down at his hands and shook his head.

Ben rose and pulled some bills out of his pocket. Handing them to Margaret, he said, "Stay here if you want the reward. We'll be in touch."

WHEN THE DOOR closed, Margaret waved the bills in glee. "We were real lucky to hear about that reward when we ran from the law in Utah. That little chit runnin' off worked to our good."

When Henry started to reach for the bills, she jerked them back and crowed, "You ruined the chances of our last fortune by turnin' tail and runnin'. I'll not hand over this and let you do it again."

Henry's eyes narrowed at the reminder. "We barely escaped with our lives after I killed that miner. We didn't have no choice, woman."

Margaret sniffed. "You're lucky to still have your neck. It was an idiot thing to do."

Henry moved closer to her to peer into her thin face. "You wouldn't 'ave said that had we got the gold. And anyhow, we can't keep that money. As much as I'd like to, we have to pay Billy the gold we borrowed to hire that investigator and clear this hotel bill."

The two continued to argue as Ben and Jane went out the establishment's front door.

BEN LED JANE back to their hotel, both numb and unable to say a word. She couldn't talk about it—she couldn't think about it—not out here on the street in front of the world. Once in their room, Jane turned and buried her face in Ben's shirt, gasping, "I hope it's her . . . and yet after meeting those horrid people, I hope it isn't."

Ben kissed the top of her dark head. "I know, I know," he agreed grimly. Leaning back, he tilted Jane's face up and wiped her tears away with his thumbs. "Jane, if it is her, you mustn't expect too much. A hard life could have changed her into someone you aren't expecting. Do you know what I mean?"

Jane nodded. "I know. I've tried not to have any expectations, but it's nearly impossible." Turning from him, she walked to the washbasin and took up a cool cloth. Placing it on her eyes, she lay back on the bed and asked, "What do we do next?"

Ben sat down beside her, staring into the darkening room. "We go to Juneau, Alaska. I'll book passage aboard the first steamship I can, though it will probably be difficult with all the miners heading that way. In Juneau we will see what we can find out." He sighed. "Pray we find her there, my dear. From what I hear, the Yukon Trail is not for the faint of heart."

Jane lifted the cloth and stared at him. "If she's not in Juneau, we'll hire a dozen men to find her. I won't lose her again. Not this time."

Twenty-One

$\mathcal{E}$ lizabeth was so tired when their steamer floated into
the Juneau wharf that she could hardly muster a smile
in answer to Noah's obvious excitement. They had been on the
water the entire journey back, in one kind of craft or another,
mostly a crowded steamer. Elizabeth hoped to never see another
boat for as long as she lived. Now, three weeks after she'd agreed
to become Noah's wife, she was back in little Juneau.

So much had happened. Ross was dead. She'd given up her
claim to the twins. She'd given up gold mining in the Yukon all
together. *Ross was dead.* Noah had taken over the plans, convinc-
ing her a wedding in Juneau with Will and Cara present was
better than a mining town filled with strangers. *Ross was dead.*
Everyone would be so happy for them. *Ross was dead.*

It was all so hard to grasp hold of. She was free! And yet
. . . she didn't feel free. She felt a tightness in her chest and panic
in her breath—especially when she thought of the wedding.

They climbed into a small rowboat that was sent out to
the steamer to fetch passengers. Noah's arms bulged as he took
up oars and helped row, strong and steady, looking over at her
now and then, brimming with anticipation. He looped a rope

over one of the posts of the dock and said softly, "We made it. Come, Elizabeth, let me help you out."

His touch was gentle as he lifted her out of the canoe and set her on the dock. She tried to fight off the desperate need to run . . . run as far as freedom could take her. What was wrong with her? Any woman would want Noah. She wanted Noah, wanted him in ways she didn't even understand, and yet she was terrified. Now here they were, about to burst in on Will and Cara, and Elizabeth felt close to tears. She longed to see her old friends, but so much had happened. Would they still accept her? Be angry with her? Her brow creased with worry as they strapped on their packs and walked toward the post.

Her gaze swept over the town as they descended upon it. It seemed much the same and yet quiet, peaceful almost, after the noise and teeming humanity of the boomtowns.

Slowing her steps, she asked hesitantly, "Do you think they will be surprised to see us?"

Noah slanted her a look. "If you mean will they be surprised to see you, I don't think so. They knew what I was going after."

Yes, of course they knew. Noah wasn't one to fail.

The post loomed up ahead of them, just as her future loomed ahead of her. Soft light flooded out of the windows, and Elizabeth momentarily forgot her apprehensions and braced herself for Will and Cara's reaction.

The door swung open at Noah's knock, revealing Will's startled face.

"Noah. And Elizabeth?" He opened the door wide and motioned them in. "You're back." With a big grin he grasped Noah's arm. Turning to Elizabeth, he took both her hands in his and said sincerely, "I'm glad to see you're all right, Elizabeth. You gave us a scare, but you look none the worse for it." Turning his head he yelled, "Cara, come quick! You'll never believe who is here."

It didn't take long for Cara to appear at the top of the stairs. When she saw Elizabeth she squealed like a schoolgirl, rushing down the steps and throwing her arms around her, hugging her tight. "Oh, my sweet girl, I can't believe it's you. Let me look at you." Leaning back, she took Elizabeth's face between her hands and said, "A little thin, but nothing my cooking can't fix." Looking over Elizabeth's head toward Noah, Cara raised her brows in silent question. When he didn't answer, she looked back down at Elizabeth and asked softly, "Did you find what you were looking for, dear?"

Elizabeth looked down and said, faltering, "I, um . . ."

Cara started to ask another question, but Noah cut her off. "I'll be glad to tell the whole story, but first, Cara, I sure could use a drink. Got any coffee?"

Cara smiled. "Of course. Please sit down and I'll put on some water." Linking an arm through Elizabeth's, she said, "You come with me. I'm not letting you out of my sight for a while."

Once in the kitchen, it didn't take Cara long to ask, "Elizabeth, I have to know, are you and Noah . . . ?"

She left it hanging, but Elizabeth knew what she wanted to know. She took a deep breath. "Yes, Cara. I've come back to marry him. We hope to have the ceremony here, as soon as possible."

Cara's face lit up with joy. Then, as she looked into Elizabeth's eyes, her smile faded. "But that's wonderful . . .

what's wrong?" When Elizabeth didn't answer she continued, "I know I shouldn't pry, but Will and I care about the two of you so much. Tell me."

Elizabeth toyed with the spoons in her hands and looked at the counter. "Nothing's wrong. I . . . I just hope he's not making a mistake." The last came out in a rush and Elizabeth wished she could take it back. It sounded so pathetic.

Cara's laugh was a short *ha!* "A mistake in marrying you? He has known what he wanted the moment he laid eyes on you." Squeezing her hand tight she said, "It's obvious he is in love with you. Is it that you're not sure you love him?"

"How could I not love him? But marriage . . . what if I can't?"

Cara smiled a little sadly. "If the alternative is letting him go, could you? Does marriage sound more terrible than a future without him?"

Put like that, Elizabeth shook her head. She couldn't deny that a part of her wanted to run, run to the safe comfort of independence. But another part wanted nothing more than to stay.

Cara laughed, not unkindly. "You look so miserable. What you need, my girl, is some good old Elizabeth determination. It's fear you're fighting here . . . you've fought that before and know how to beat it down, yes?"

Elizabeth could only nod. She didn't deserve such a good friend, but she was glad she had one.

"My sweet girl, you've climbed steeper mountains than this will prove to be. I have perfect confidence that once you get settled with him, in your own home and together, you'll be amazed that you fought this. Marriage is a gift. And with Noah, it will be a treasure."

Elizabeth felt the first beginnings of hope. "Do you really think so?"

Cara clasped her hands together, eyes sparkling. "Yes, and I have just the gift for you. Follow me out with the coffee and then we'll go upstairs to my bedroom on the pretense of seeing Rebecca."

She grasped Cara's arm. "Oh, the baby. I do want to see her. Thank you, Cara. I . . . I wasn't sure you and Will would ever want to see me again after I ran out like I did. And in your time of need, too. I'll never forgive myself for that."

Cara shook her head. "There's nothing to forgive. It was your time of need more that it was mine. We did just fine."

Taking up the tray of cheese, smoked sausage, little green pickles, and crackers, Elizabeth followed Cara with another tray of coffee, cups, and a fresh apple pie. Setting down the trays on the low round table, Cara made their excuses.

The cradle sat beside Will and Cara's bed, small and bright with a pink, ruffled calico blanket. Elizabeth leaned down and smiled at the sweetness. Rebecca was lying on her tummy with her face turned toward them. In the light from the candle that Cara was holding, Elizabeth could see her chubby cheeks pressed together making a rosebud of her mouth. Gently Elizabeth reached out and smoothed the back of her finger over the curve of the baby's cheek and whispered, "She's beautiful."

"Yes, Will and I think so. She's good and sweet, too. You should see Will strut about with her."

Elizabeth smiled up at Cara and then followed her over to the cedar chest on the other side of the room. Opening the lid, they knelt down in front of it. Cara carefully pulled out several items until she came to a small bundle wrapped in tissue paper.

"My mother gave this to me when I married Will. I wore it at our wedding." Handing it to Elizabeth, she smiled.

Elizabeth slowly opened the wrapping and pulled out the most lavish dress she'd ever seen. Gasping, she held it up in the candlelight. Shimmers of light bounced off it, making it seem alive. It was of the palest blue, shot with silver threads—the most beautiful fabric. It had a round neckline edged in a shade of darker blue satin and a high gathered waistline with a wide satin ribbon that tied in the back.

"It's like nothing I've ever seen. I couldn't possibly . . ."

"Yes, you could," Cara insisted. "You'll look like a princess in it." Excited, she continued. "Tomorrow is Saturday. Pastor Sullivan may be available and perhaps we can even have the wedding in the afternoon."

Elizabeth could only nod, letting herself be swept away on a tide with a life of its own.

NOAH STOOD WITH Will at the front of the church in somewhat of a state of shock that their wedding was finally here, now. Once Cara had heard, he had only to sit back and watch her enthusiastic planning in amazement. She had arranged everything from the ceremony, complete with church and flowers, to the dinner party afterward at the post.

Elizabeth had been kept out of sight since bedtime the night before. He had heard much running to and fro and some laughter upstairs, but he hadn't had even a moment to speak to her. He wanted to ask if she was OK, if she was sure, but then again, maybe it was better that he didn't have the opportunity.

If he was this nervous, it was hard telling what Elizabeth was feeling.

An organ began to play and Noah swallowed hard, trying to force down the knot in his throat.

And then he saw her . . . and all emotion was swept away except wonder.

She came in the back door, brilliant in a pale, bluish-silver gown. Her dark hair was elaborately curled and sat in a rich pile on the top of her head. Her face was radiant, creamy skin, eyes bright and sparkling in their darkness. His body responded to her, straining for the moment to touch her. His soul ached, anticipating the moment when his other half would be one with him. His spirit rejoiced, a rising ripple of joy expanding and overcoming him.

When she reached him, her head was down. He watched her lift her eyes slowly to his, uncertainty and something else in them, something he had never seen in them before now. Was it hope? He wanted to reach out and touch her, to ascertain she was real, that he wasn't dreaming, but he couldn't seem to move at all. It was all he could do to breathe.

In a daze, he heard the ceremony begin. Clearly and solemnly the pastor spoke of the vows and the covenant they were about to enter into. Noah tried to concentrate on the words, but all he could do was drown himself in the fullness of her eyes. They had made their covenant weeks before, on the shore of their brokenness. This was just a formality.

"I do."

He heard her say the soft words and cherished them. They had been so hard won. His own "I do" was triumphant, jubilant even. He felt a war had been won and he was now being crowned the victor. And then he was told to kiss her. It wasn't the kiss he wanted to give her, this chaste peck. That kiss would wait a little while longer and would last the rest of their lives.

❄ ❄ ❄

WITH MIXED EXCITEMENT and dread, Elizabeth slipped out of her wedding clothes and gave herself a quick sponge bath from the pitcher of water on the bedside stand. She had just pulled the nightdress over her head and had begun buttoning the row of tiny buttons when there was a faint knock on the door. *Oh, no. Not yet!* Standing frozen, she heard a voice say, "Elizabeth, open up. It's me, Cara."

Relief pooled through her as she rushed to open the door. "What are you doing? He could be here any minute." The wedding party had ended a half hour ago, and Noah was down talking to Will and giving her time to get ready.

Cara sidled through the crack and whispered, "We have a few minutes, and I wanted to help you." She began working the buttons as she talked. "Now hold still."

Elizabeth's stomach was a mass of quivering nerves.

"You're shaking like a leaf. Now relax, it will go better that way."

Elizabeth gave a nervous laugh. "Oh Cara, must I go through with it?"

Cara's mouth formed a rueful line. "You'll wonder why you ever said that in the morning."

Cara's confidence helped boost her spirits. Once the gown was buttoned, they pulled the pins from her hair. Cara quickly took down Elizabeth's hair and brushed it. It was long now and hung in rich, dark waves around her slim shoulders.

Turning Elizabeth to face her, Cara laid the brush on the dressing table and smiled. "Don't look so worried dear. Everything will be fine."

"I hope you're right, Cara. I really do."

"You hope she's right about what?" came a deep voice from the doorway.

Startled, they both froze. Cara regained her composure first and silently walked toward him. Noah and Cara exchanged glances at the door, Cara handing Noah the brush, but Elizabeth couldn't make out his face in the shadows. She stood like a statue and waited.

Noah walked into the room and shut the door behind him without taking his eyes off her. After what seemed like an eternity, he walked over to her until he was very close. She could feel his breath in her hair. "What are you doing, Elizabeth?"

His voice sounded strained. Tilting her head back, she closed her eyes and said in a husky voice, "I'm not doing anything."

The seconds ticked by, seemingly endless, but she wouldn't, couldn't open her eyes.

Finally, she felt his hand cup her cheek and she turned into it. When she heard him expel his breath in a rush, she let her eyelids flutter open. He looked deep into her eyes, saying heatedly, "I want to kiss you."

She felt the battle within her, fear versus love, and knew she had to make a decision. Noah was not Ross. Noah was not any of the others who had hurt her. Noah was her husband, a man who loved her more than she had ever imagined being loved. How could she give him anything less than her whole heart? Elizabeth lifted her hands, placed her flat palms against his chest, felt the steady rhythm of his quickened heartbeat, slid them up to his shoulders, her gaze rising to his neck, feeling the rush of his breath across her face, and then she bravely lifted her gaze to his.

She gasped, tears springing to her eyes. She had expected to see lust, to see what she'd seen a hundred times in men's eyes, was prepared to sacrifice herself to it. But instead, she saw love. Life-giving, heart-restoring love. Heated and real and masculine.

And hers. He was hers.

She felt the knot inside unravel, felt the stiffness in her spine melt, reached up on tiptoes and coiled her arms around his neck. *God help me, I love him.*

DOWNSTAIRS, THE NEXT morning, Will pulled Noah aside and said quietly, "I hadn't the chance to tell you yesterday, but we had an interesting telegram arrive while you two were away."

Noah raised his eyebrows. "What was it about? Who from?"

"It was from a Margaret Dunning. She said she is looking for Elizabeth."

Noah frowned and sat forward in his chair. "That's Elizabeth's adopted mother, the one who hired Ross. What did she want?"

"Noah, she says Elizabeth's real mother is on her way to Juneau. She's looking for Elizabeth."

Noah let out a breath in a rush. "So her mother is alive . . ."

"It would appear so. She might have been told at the orphanage her mother died. It is a common practice."

"Possible," Noah said quietly. He didn't know what to make of it. All he knew was that suddenly he wanted to get Elizabeth home. "Thanks for telling me, Will. Her adoptive parents are not the kind of people to be trusted, from everything I've heard. Don't tell Elizabeth about this. I don't want to upset her."

Will nodded in understanding.

"If Elizabeth's real mother shows herself, which I doubt will happen, we'll tell her then."

Twenty-Two

Jane shielded her eyes on the Juneau dock and gazed at the mountains. "Oh, Ben, it's so beautiful."

"Breathtaking," he agreed, but he wasn't looking at the mountains.

She blushed when she caught his meaning.

"You have to stop that."

"What?"

"Looking at me like you've never seen me before."

He grasped her hand, lifting it to his lips, brushing her knuckles with a whisper of a kiss. "I've never seen you like this."

She looked up into his eyes, really looked into them like married couples forget to do, and smiled. She looked ready to cry, so he laughed, deep and happy, and kissed her square on the mouth in front of strangers, causing her to pull back, laughing and lecturing him instead. "You're making a scene, Ben Rhodes."

It was true. But she was nearing forty, and she had never looked so alive. Or happy. The steamship had been crowded, their private cabin expensive . . . and it had been the honeymoon they'd never had.

Turning back toward the city he watched her breathe in the mountain air and smile, making excuses for the compliments. "Anyone would feel wonderful in this air. Can you believe how clean and fresh everything feels here?"

He grinned as they climbed into the carriage, feeling young again, feeling young and as though this vast Alaskan sky was their new horizon.

"Where to, sir?" the driver interrupted.

"Oh, take us to the best hotel in town."

"Yes, sir. That'd be the Grand Hotel."

With a jolt they were off, Jane peering eagerly out the window, the curve of her neck so appealing, his wife not wanting to miss a single thing. She turned suddenly toward him, eyes alight with excitement as she said, "Look at that log church. Isn't it sweet? And it even has a log bell tower. I feel like we've stepped back into history here."

Gone were the tall buildings of New York City, the crowds and the busyness. They were seeing America now. And Alaska, the last frontier. As they passed the town trading post, Jane pointed out an odd-looking couple coming out the door. The man was big, tall and broad-shouldered, and the woman was quite small in comparison. She had dark hair and big eyes . . . Jane suddenly grasped Ben's arm. "Look, did you see that young woman?"

Ben nodded but the couple had turned the corner and they lost sight of them. Jane gripped his arm harder.

"What? What is it, Jane?"

"Tha—that young woman I just saw coming out the trading post. Ben, it was her, I know it. Turn around! We have to go back." She pulled on his sleeve. "Tell the driver to turn around."

Ben looked at her wild eyes and pleading face. "OK, we'll go back. But Jane, you have to calm down. It may not have been her. You don't know. You couldn't have gotten a very good look at her."

"Ben . . . I can't explain it, but it was her. I've been looking into faces for years, looking for something that I would know. It was her!"

Ben rapped on the window toward the front of the carriage but the man didn't seem to hear. Soon they stopped in front of the Grand Hotel. Jane stumbled out, yelling up at the driver. "We have to go back to that trading post."

Ben grasped her hand to gain her attention. "I'll just check us in and have our bags taken to our room. You wait here and we'll have the driver take us over to the trading post."

Jane nodded. "Hurry! She was leaving. What if she's gone? What if we can't find her?"

Ben gripped her shoulders. "We'll find her. I promise. We won't go home until we do. Now calm down and wait in the carriage, OK?"

She nodded and climbed back inside while Ben hurriedly gave instructions to the driver and the hotel staff. Within ten minutes they were on their way back to the post. Once there, Jane suddenly became hesitant. "What if she isn't there? What if she *is* there? What will I say to her?"

Ben helped her climb down from the carriage. "You will tell her you love her. Everything will be fine. Now, come."

As they walked in, a bell jingled above the door. An older woman came out of the back room and smoothed her skirts. "Can I help you folks with something?" she asked kindly.

Jane smiled and took a deep breath. "How do you do, ma'am? My name is Jane and this is my husband, Ben. We are looking for a young woman by the name of Elizabeth and, well, I thought I might have seen her here just a short time ago. Do you know anyone by that name?"

The woman shook her head. "I'm just minding the store. All the young people went out to see a new horse one of them bought and then out to dinner. But it does seem like I heard one of them being called Elizabeth. Can't be sure, though. My hearing, you know, it's not what it used to be. But you can come back in a few hours. Will and Cara Collins will be here then, and they'll know the answer to your questions."

Jane's body collapsed with a mixture of relief and disappointment. "Yes, well, thank you. We'll come back later."

Ben squeezed her hand encouragingly as they walked back to the carriage. "It's better this way. We won't be so flustered. We'll be better prepared to meet her in the morning."

Jane sighed and leaned against his arm, looking suddenly tired. "Yes, you're right. Let's go."

❄ ❄ ❄

THE NEXT MORNING Ben and Jane breakfasted early in the hotel dining room. Afterward, they wandered into the lobby. At the front desk Ben was told he had received a telegram. Opening it at the desk with Jane standing pensively at his side, he scanned the message. Then scanned it again.

"What is it?" Jane asked.

"It's from my partner, Herbert. Before we left New York, I gave him Henry and Margaret's name and asked him to see what he could find out about them." He took Jane's elbow, led her over to the window, and lowered his voice. "He says that Henry is wanted for the murder of a miner in the state of Utah. The authorities have been looking for the two of them for over three years."

Jane gasped. "What should we do?"

Ben shook his head. "I'll telegraph Herb with the Dunnings' address. I'm sure they will be there since they are waiting for the remainder of the reward from us."

Jane looked at him with concern. "But . . . what if we need them or," then suddenly, "you don't think Elizabeth was mixed up in this do you?"

Ben looked grim. "We won't know the answer to that until we find her."

"Shouldn't we wait to tell someone? We might need the Dunnings to be cooperative and if they find out we reported them . . . they won't tell us anything," Jane insisted.

Ben shook his head, eyebrows down over his green eyes. "Don't worry, Jane. We'll find Elizabeth without any further help from them. We have to report this."

Jane sighed and nodded. "Yes, of course. You are right." She looked up into his eyes. "To think my little girl was adopted by a . . . a murderer . . . I can't bear it."

He grasped the curve of her jaw in one hand, looked steadily into her eyes, willing her strength. "We know she's alive and we'll find her. That's all that matters now."

After he calmed her, they hurried out the hotel door, headed toward the post. Ben looked over at her with a worried frown for what seemed the hundredth time that morning.

"Are you sure you're up to this right now? You look so pale, Jane."

Jane nodded up at him. "I haven't come this far only to turn back. I'm fine."

The walk to the trading post was short and Ben gave her a reassuring nod before as they reached the front door. They stood for a moment, contemplating the door they'd walked through yesterday, both feeling that something monumental was about to happen. Taking a deep breath, Jane took the first step forward.

The bell jingled as Ben opened the door and allowed his wife in. The shop was well lit, neatly organized, and clean. It had a homey air to it that pleased Jane, causing her to take a deep breath and throw back her shoulders. Striding to the long, wooden counter together, they paused and met the smile of a business-looking man in his mid-thirties or so.

"What can I help you folks with today?" he asked in a friendly tone.

Ben started to speak, but Jane raised her gloved hand. "Sir, my name is Jane and this is my husband, Benjamin. We have traveled a great distance in search of someone, a young woman actually." She hesitated, close to tears, then tilted her head and gave him a shaky smile. "I thought . . . that is, would you happen to know an Elizabeth Dunning?"

The reaction of recognition on Will's face was immediate and Jane held her breath waiting for his response. "Well, ma'am, I might know someone by that name, but you'll have to tell me exactly what you want with her before I say anything more."

Jane liked his answer and trusted him immediately. "Well, you see, I'm her mother. And I've been looking for her for a very . . . very long time."

Will looked at Ben and then back to her with a startled expression and then he shook his head. "Ma'am, may I say you look so much like her that I can only believe what you say is true."

Jane took a sudden breath, raised her shaking hand to her mouth and looked at Ben.

Ben squeezed his wife to his side and asked, "Can you tell us where she is?"

Will whistled low. "You just missed her. She's on her way home, left this morning bright and early."

"Home? Where might that be?"

Will motioned them to follow him to a window. "See that mountain range to the east there. She lives about a quarter of the way up the middle one, with her husband, Noah Wesley."

Jane felt another shock rush through her. "Her husband? I . . . I hadn't thought of that." She'd never even considered the possibility that her little girl would be married. Stunned, she realized that she still thought of her as a young girl.

Will chuckled. "Well, now that's a long story, ma'am. But he's a good fellow, rest assured. The finest, actually, and one of my best friends." Gesturing toward the sitting area in front of the fire, Will asked, "Would you like to sit down? I'll get my wife. She will want to meet you. Elizabeth is like a little sister to her." Will steered them toward the warm fire, where they ignored the chairs and the elegant rocker. They were both too nervous to sit.

Soon a pretty blonde woman came in with a baby riding her hip. She walked up to Jane and held out her hand, smiling a sincere smile that reached her eyes. "Jane? I'm Cara Collins, Will's wife." She paused and shook her head. "Will tells me you

. . . are Elizabeth's mother?" Her gaze swept over Jane and then filled with tears, a compressed smile on her lips. "She does look so very much like you."

Jane found she didn't want to let go of this woman's hand, this woman who knew her daughter. Her voice shook as she answered. "I hope to see that for myself very soon. I have been searching for her for such a long time. I can hardly believe I've nearly found her." Little Rebecca let out a squeal of delight, pointing to the fancy feathers on Jane's hat. Eagerly she reached out to grasp one, squirming in Cara's arms and making Jane and Cara laugh.

"The poor darling, she can't reach them," Jane remarked as she took off her hat and plucked a feather from the brim, handing it to the child.

Cara laughingly said, "If you give it to her, she'll only eat it. She chews on everything she can get her hands on."

Jane looked lovingly down at the child, causing Cara to offer, "This is Rebecca. Would you like to hold her while I get us all some tea?"

Jane nodded and was glad to have another outlet for her emotions, if only for a little while. Rebecca babbled and tried to chew off the end of the feather. Jane caught it and used the fluffy end to tickle the child's cheek and nose, making them both laugh out loud. When she looked up at Ben, she caught a pained expression and her heart ached for him. If only they'd been able to have children of their own . . . but now was not the time to think of such things. This was a moment of gladness and nothing would spoil it.

Cara returned and they all sat around the low table by the fire. Cara looked at Ben and asked, "Forgive me, but you're not Elizabeth's father, are you?"

Ben shook his head. "No, we did keep track of him for some time, in case Elizabeth wanted to meet him when we found her, but he died a few years ago in a railroading accident."

Cara frowned. "I'm sorry. Elizabeth told us her parents had died."

Jane looked down into her lap. "She was raised in an orphanage, Mrs. Collins. I don't know what they told her, but it is possible they told her we had passed away."

"And you have searched for her for all of these years," Cara remarked softly. "It is amazing that you found her here, so far away from anywhere."

Jane nodded. "I had given up . . . and then I received a letter from Henry and Margaret Dunning. They claimed to have adopted Elizabeth years ago. Needless to say, we took the first available train to Seattle to meet them. They directed us here—something about a telegram they received from a detective they'd hired to find Elizabeth. Does any of this sound accurate to you?"

Cara and Will exchanged looks. Finally Will nodded. "Yes, there was a man here looking for Elizabeth. He must have been the one. But I have to tell you, she was very afraid of him. And her adoptive parents, too. I don't think she ever wanted to see them again."

"I can understand why after meeting them," Ben said grimly. "They were far worse than we had hoped. We can't tell you how relieved we are to hear that she made it away from those people."

Cara leaned forward earnestly. "Have no fear. Elizabeth is everything you could want in a daughter. She may not have always had an easy time of it. I know she has suffered in ways, but her trials have refined her into a brave and rare young woman, one whose spirit I'm glad to have the privilege to know. It will mean so much to her to know you both."

Jane looked at Ben and smiled. "It looks like we will be climbing some mountains after all."

Ben grinned boyishly back. "I wouldn't miss it for the world, dear wife. Not for the world."

Twenty-Three

*N*oah was in a hurry to get his bride home. They had only stayed long enough to see the post cleaned up from the wedding party and back in running order before loading up his horse and the new horse purchased for Elizabeth before starting the trek back home. He repeatedly told himself that he was doing the right thing. It would only upset Elizabeth if she knew about the telegram.

As they rounded a bend, Noah urged his mount up the last slope of the journey. Looking back at Elizabeth's horse, he checked the baggage. They had loaded down both steeds with supplies and all of Elizabeth's belongings. She was coming home with him to stay. "Almost there," he called back happily.

She nodded her head in response, tapping her horse with her heels to spur her forward and catch up. They passed the waterfalls above the upper end of the basin and came into a breathtaking grassy meadow where wildflowers danced in the breeze, unseen by anyone save God and, now, them. Noah hoped to teach Elizabeth all their names—purple mountain saxifrage, bluebells, yellow buttercups, heather, wild roses, and flowering berry shrubs dotting the land around Noah's cabin—but not yet. That would all come in time. Noah inhaled the sweet fragrances of home and reined in to wait for Elizabeth. She stopped beside him and looked where he was pointing.

"We're here," she said with surprise. "I thought it would take much longer."

"It's a quicker trip in the summer with the horses."

Elizabeth took a deep breath and smiled, happiness in her eyes. "It looks so different now, without all of the snow."

"You asked if we had flowers and I don't think I answered you at the time, but wildflowers grow all over the mountain in the summer. Do you like them?"

Elizabeth gazed out over the expanse. "I like that *we* have flowers," she repeated softly, wonder in her voice, "like a rainbow on the ground." She gazed up at him, something new shining in her eyes, something he hadn't seen there before. "I love that you speak as if we share it now."

Noah reached over and kissed her. "We do. What's mine is yours." He grinned wolfishly and added, "And what's yours is mine."

"But I don't have anything!"

"Oh yes, you do." He could tell when she finally understood from the pink in her cheeks. Laughing, he motioned her to follow him, nudging his horse into a gallop. In fact, he loved everything about her. Noah smiled, thanking God silently for it all, feeling good to be back on his land in the height of its summer glory, with the woman he loved beside him to share it.

NOON THE NEXT day, Noah headed back to the cabin to grab some dinner after a busy afternoon of checking his traps.

He tried to shake off the disquiet that hounded him. Something was not quite right with his wife, with this marriage. Their nights together had been filled with passion, and their days promised to settle into a comfortable routine, but she . . . again, he couldn't say exactly what it was, but something about her, or inside her, was missing. She was holding something back. Sometimes, it felt like she was just going through the motions of trying to please him. Determined to fix things, to help her trust him more, he reached for the doorknob. It was then, while he was turning the knob, that he heard the sound of approaching horses. Turning, he shielded his eyes from the sun and was startled to see Will Collins riding up with two other city-looking folks. They looked to be in a hurry, their horses tired. Noah turned from the door with an odd feeling in his gut as he watched them approach.

Will dismounted first and walked over to Noah, a big smile on his face. He grasped Noah's hand in a firm shake and clapped him on the shoulder. "You'll never guess who I've brought, Noah. Is Elizabeth around?"

Noah felt his chest tighten even more. Something told him that the next few moments would change his life. "She's in the cabin. Who are they, Will?"

The man had helped the lady dismount. Noah watched as they crossed toward him. The man was a tall, stately looking gentleman with dark hair, graying a little at the temples, expensively and impeccably dressed. He extended his hand, which Noah took in a firm grasp, the man's eyes warm and friendly. Will made the introductions.

"Noah, this is Ben Rhodes. He's a lawyer from New York City."

Will moved over to let the woman in. She held out a small hand and smiled at him. "Hello, I'm Jane Rhodes."

Noah felt his heart miss a beat. His breath quickened as he stretched out his big hand toward her, feeling awkward in the presence of her elegance.

He knew who this woman was.

He was just taking her hand when the cabin door opened and out stepped Elizabeth.

"Noah, are you . . . ?"

Her voice trailed off as she saw their visitors.

They turned as one and looked at her. Noah heard a muffled sound from the woman behind him. He looked from his wife to this Jane Rhodes, this stranger and yet, this known woman. Time seemed to slow and they all stood frozen, staring between the two women who were so alike it was startling. He watched as Jane slowly walked toward Elizabeth, her elegant skirt skimming the grass, and stopped in front of her, their skirts just inches away.

The midafternoon sun shone ruthlessly down on them as they looked at each other, illuminating, not even a thread of a shadow dimming the brightness of the scene. It was truth, finally come to light.

Then they heard Jane's voice, choked but soft, as she finally spoke.

"Elizabeth . . . it *is* you." One of her hands reached up to cover her mouth for a moment as she stood, rooted and entranced. Then she reached out, tentatively afraid but sure, to touch Elizabeth's shoulder. "I have seen your face again," she breathed. "I have finally found you."

❄ ❄ ❄

Elizabeth stood in the woman's rapt presence, this woman whose likeness was frightening, and fought the battle of self-possession. Something within her wanted to crumble—cave in to the knowledge that she had a mother, give in to the feelings that pounded against the walls of her heart. But another part of her held to the mortar, knowing that happy endings only occurred in fairy tales. She had never believed in those.

The woman stepped closer, learning her face like God knew Adam's when He molded it from the dust, the fierce love in it refusing to let Elizabeth look away, reject it as something unreal. And as she looked back she realized it was like looking into a mirror of the future. Where her skin was young and plumb, this women's had thinned, her face more chiseled though still lovely. They had the same coloring, the same cheekbones, the same lips, the same eyebrows, and the same eyes. Those deep brown eyes that almost melded with the black pupils. Eyes so dark they were easy to make unreadable, but these eyes were anything but that—these mother eyes were filled with the culmination of a woman who had waited for this moment her whole life. There was no lie Elizabeth could tell herself to explain it. There was only stark truth: love.

Then Elizabeth felt the woman reach up and touch the curve of her cheek, the slant of her brow, her hand hovering, like a blind man's, wanting to explore but hesitant, knowing that another soul shared this moment and that she needed permission. She settled for words. "I have finally found you . . . my Elizabeth."

Her voice broke, causing tears to spring to Elizabeth's eyes. What *had* she found? *What had she found?* her heart wailed.

Elizabeth stared at her, unable to fully believe what she was hearing. And yet, something within her knew. Something recognized this as the woman who had given birth to her and been a mother to her for a short time.

Anger rose strong and unbidden. Why? Why had she been cheated of this woman? Her past, in all its unholy glory, rushed back over her.

"Who are you?" she heard herself whisper in harsh staccato, wishing these onlookers would vanish.

"Elizabeth . . . I'm your mother," this beautiful, stately woman pronounced. "I'm your mother." She was shaking her head, tears rolling down her cheeks.

Suddenly, a memory came back of being rocked and sung to, of the song Noah had sung in his cabin that first day with him. Then she knew for certain. Elizabeth looked to Noah and saw his shocked amazement, her eyes swept to Will, someone who knew the face of honesty, and she saw his approval, and then she glanced at the stranger-man who had come with this woman and saw . . . oh God . . . she saw such hope in his eyes. He loved this woman so much. He wanted so much that she would accept her. She looked back at the dark-eyed woman and felt such a tumult of confusion—a warmth, a melting in her chest, and a deep denial, an anger. Could she prove it? "The song. Do you remember the song you used to sing to me?"

Jane smiled through her tears. "You remember that? Oh, Elizabeth, do you remember me?" She laughed. It didn't sound like the kind of laugh that would come from such a fragile-looking creature; it sounded hard-won and righteous, ringing all the way through heaven, it was so sure and strong.

✳✳✳

SHE BEGAN TO sing it aloud and loud, with everyone looking on, in the gentle summer breeze filled with the scents of Noah's flowers. With Elizabeth's hand clasped in hers, she sang with all her might.

A victory lullaby hymn.

This mother held nothing back, singing while her gaze roved the curves and hollows of Elizabeth's face like sunlight, filled with life and warmth and truth. It reached her, reached deep into her doubtful, fearful heart, that song, that look, until there were tears on both their faces.

When it was finished there was a moment of stunned stillness. It was as if even the birds dared not speak due to the momentous occasion.

Jane broke the silence with a declaration: "I didn't give you away willingly, Elizabeth." She squeezed Elizabeth's hand tightly in her own. "I've been looking for you for your whole life. I've been waiting for this moment my whole life. I wanted you back."

Elizabeth could only shake her head, not understanding.

Jane demanded her eyes, her full attention. Her gaze was unrelentingly fierce. "I love you. I've always loved you. I didn't give you to that orphanage willingly. You are my daughter. *You are mine.*"

Elizabeth could only shake her head, fighting the tears, fighting the caving-in feeling. How could she believe it? She shook her head at this beautiful woman, unable to stop the tears from escaping down her cheeks.

"It's true," Jane asserted. "I know it must be hard for you to believe. Dear God, I can only imagine all you've been through, and I hate it too, but we're here now, Elizabeth." She stopped and breathed deep, a look of full joy on her face. "I've found you."

She squeezed her hand again so hard it hurt, but Elizabeth welcomed the pain, welcomed this feeling of reality intruding on this unreal scene.

"I'll never let you go again. Never."

Again that fierceness, and Elizabeth recognized it. More than the physical resemblance, more than the faint memories, Elizabeth knew that *fierceness*—it was what had kept her alive for the past twenty years. This woman was her mother . . . and she could only love her beyond all reasonable thought.

THE FIRE HAD died down, but everyone was too emotionally drained to get up and replenish it. Elizabeth looked down at her hand for the hundredth time in the last hour to see her mother's there clasping it. Then she looked up to see this woman's face, smiling at her with so much love shining from her eyes, and then she would start crying all over again. It had taken all evening, but she had told them everything. She'd started from as far back as she could remember, in the orphanages, and had told of every memory she could recall. Then she'd told of her adoption and Henry and Margaret. There wasn't any self-pity in her voice, just bare facts. She hadn't left anything out. She told of the murder, her escape, and then her struggle to make a living.

And then she'd told them about Ross. Her mother had squeezed her hand so hard during that time that Elizabeth had had to wince before Jane realized what she was doing. There had been no condemnation from anyone. They said they admired her courage. Ben and Jane had told them everything they had learned about Ross from Margaret and Henry Dunning, and how they had been forced to turn the Dunnings over to the authorities. Ben assured Elizabeth she would have no further trouble from them or the law.

Noah helped fill in the gaps, once she told about booking passage to Alaska. How he'd found her on his doorstep, how he'd kept her alive that night, breathing his life into her. Hearing him tell it had made her want to fall in love with him all over again.

She hadn't told a single lie or embellished a single truth. She had bared her soul to them, and it was good. She felt whole somehow, and clean.

THE NEXT MORNING, Jane and Ben asked if they could stay awhile. Jane clasped Noah's arm after breakfast and said with a twinkle in her deep brown eyes, "I know you two are newly wedded, Noah, but you'll have to bear our company for a little while. I've waited much longer for her than you have."

Noah smiled down at her and thought that Elizabeth would look just this way when she was older. "You're welcome to move in. You've transformed her. She has needed you for a very long time."

Jane laughed. "I doubt you will be saying that after a few weeks, but we'll see. We'll see."

They soon settled into a routine. Ben was interested in learning about everything Noah did and gave him advice on investments and expansion for the future. Jane spent every waking hour with Elizabeth. They talked and laughed and sewed and cooked. Noah was happy to see Jane teach Elizabeth some of the basics of cooking. Sometimes, while they were occupied, Noah would see Jane stop and just stare at Elizabeth's face as if she was memorizing it. He didn't think he could fathom the pain the separation had caused them, but he was glad to be a part of the joy now that they were reunited. The fact hadn't escaped him that it was going to be hard on them both when the Rhodes left, maybe impossible.

One night, three weeks after they had arrived, they were all sitting around the table savoring their after-dinner coffee when Jane threw down her napkin and blurted out, "New York is too far away." She looked at Ben and bit her lip, just the way Elizabeth did when she was trying not to cry.

Ben reached over and squeezed her hand on top of the table. "We'll work something out, Jane. Don't fret about it."

Jane looked at Ben and then at Noah. Noah felt his stomach churn. "Noah, I know this is unfair of me to ask, but I must. If Elizabeth is willing, can I take her back to New York with us? I want to show her where she was born. Where her grandfather lived. I want to take her shopping and buy things for her. I want to introduce her to all my friends. And Jeremiah Hoglesby . . . the private detective I hired to find Elizabeth.

He loves her almost as much as we do. We have to stop in Illinois on the way home and see him. Noah, please, I have so much to make up for. Let me have her for just a little bit longer."

Noah looked at Elizabeth, but she gave him no clue as to her thoughts. She just stared back at him.

"You're welcome to come, too, Noah," Ben said gently, giving his wife a firm look.

"Oh, of course. Forgive me, Noah. You must come," Jane added quickly.

Noah shuffled his feet under the table and stared at Jane. He knew the right thing to do. Some part of him had even been expecting it, but he hadn't known it would be this hard.

With a short nod he answered, "Short of selling the place, I can't leave the land that long. Alaska's my home. I . . . can't leave it. But, of course, Elizabeth should go."

Jane fluttered her hands and smiled excitedly. "Oh, it will be wonderful. Just wonderful!" Jane hesitated, then smiled softly at her husband. "We have one other announcement." She clasped her hands over her stomach. "I do believe I'm expecting—after all these years." She laughed with such shy happiness, it brought joy to all their hearts. Elizabeth went to her and hugged her tight, and Noah shook Ben's hand.

"Middle-aged and starting over," Ben said, his face alight with happiness.

They all laughed and then Noah asked, "When will you leave for New York?"

Jane bit her lip again and looked at Noah. "Oh, I'm asking so much, aren't I? I'll make it up to you. I promise I will."

Ben answered his question. "We were hoping to leave in another couple of days. As soon as Elizabeth can be ready."

They all looked at Elizabeth and she shrugged. "I could be ready tomorrow since I'll be buying new clothes in New York. It will be strange to have so much money that I can buy anything I want."

Noah frowned. "What do you mean?"

Jane grimaced. "I'm sorry, Noah. I should have told the two of you together. I'm giving all of the inheritance my father left me to Elizabeth. It's a sizable fortune."

Noah felt his heart sink lower as he realized what that meant. She really *didn't* need him now. She had all she could ever want in these kind, loving people sitting at his table.

She would never need him again.

Twenty-Four

$\mathcal{N}$oah watched as Elizabeth packed her things. She had been strangely quiet the last two days and he guessed she didn't know what to say to him. He didn't know what to say to her. It hurt just looking at her. He wondered if he would ever see her again after they left. The tiny part of him that said she'd married him for the security he could give her rose up to torture him. She would be caught up in her new life as an heiress and the weeks would turn into months that would turn into years, until he was just a distant, cold Alaskan memory to her. Sometimes lately, she seemed so wrapped up in her new family, it hardly seemed they were really married at all. Maybe it was for the best.

The arrangements were all made. Noah had hired a friend of his, a Tlingit, to guide them back to Juneau. He knew he would have to say good-bye from his own land. He couldn't bear it in Juneau with the others around.

Now it was nearly time and they were loading their saddle-bags onto the horses. Noah handed Elizabeth a pouch filled with food for the trail and her canteen filled with the kind of cool, clear water that graced his land, and, for a moment, their eyes locked but neither said a word. It was just too hard.

Jane and Ben had left them alone in the cabin for obvious reasons and were milling around in the yard, waiting. Finally, Noah could stand it no longer. Taking the bundle from her hands, he laid it on the table and took Elizabeth by the shoulders. With courage from deep within, he kissed her. It was soft and heart-wrenchingly tender. Then he said, "Go. Regain some small part of what you lost. They need you now . . . and you need them."

She looked up at him and asked softly, "But what of you, Noah? What do you need?"

Why was she making this so hard? He wanted to shake her. Didn't she know this was killing him? With a deep breath, he said one last time, "I love you, and I need what is best for you. Now, go!"

She hesitated for a moment and then, with a final, quick kiss on his compressed mouth, she scooped up the pouch and walked to the door. Turning, she looked at him for a long moment, her face an unreadable shadow, his glowing with stark pain in a shaft of late-afternoon sun. Then slowly, softly, she shut the door.

Noah fought the battle of going to the window and won. Instead, he braced both hands far apart on the counter and leaned heavily against them. With his head dropped forward, he cried, "Oh, God!"

He heard the sound of horses' hoofs pounding away from the cabin and his spine stiffened. They were gone. She was gone. He stood there several more moments and then, raking his hand through his hair, he expelled a big breath and took up his ax.

❊❊❊

THE FOREST RANG with his efforts to block the pain, but he couldn't seem to escape it. His old standby wasn't enough this time. Returning to the cabin, he took up his rifle. He walked his land. Gradually, he remembered it, the width and the breadth of the land, the trees and streams and rocks and animals, the little secret places that only he knew about. Places that quite possibly no other human had walked upon on this earth before. Places he loved. He relived why he loved it and how precious it was to him. He couldn't have left it. Living in a place like New York City would have destroyed who he was. He had made the right decision and the pain would lessen with time. With time, he would think back on her and be able to smile and remember how much joy she had brought him. With . . . time . . .

The night was cold. Autumn was making her grand sweep over the land, and riding on its tail would be another Alaskan winter. The kind that brought challenges most men and woman shrank from, but the kind he, and yes, Elizabeth too, thrived on. There would never be another like her . . . not if he lived to be one hundred.

After a cold supper, Noah put on a heavy sweater and went back outside. The night called to him and complemented his mood. He walked around his yard, watching the stars come out. They seemed brilliant tonight in their sharpness and too numerous to count. The air crackled with electricity, as if expecting some great deed by the moon. He walked and walked, sometimes slowly and sometimes with sudden energy, trying to out-walk the ache in his chest.

The eeriness increased, causing the fine hair on the back of his neck to rise. His gaze scanned the land and then the sky. Then, deep in the sky, to the north, a jade green glow began. It rose, as if by deliberate, slow degrees, and wrapped itself around a shot of pink, the hue unknown on the earth.

Noah smiled. The aurora.

Like rivers of molten jade, a neon green surged across the sky, rising and falling . . . swelling and then receding. It seemed a living, breathing force and Noah marveled that it should be so. The lines whipped and moved and coiled around and over each other. They moved with hypnotic grace, a pulse of life, leaning and swaying and teasing one another. Their colors bright and then fading and then bright again.

Suddenly, in a burst of brightness, a silvery maelstrom opened above him. With an almost achingly sweet, slow motion it began to release ring after ring of silvery light, as though a starchild had thrown a rock in its midst. The movement didn't stop, hypnotic in its seeming infinity, it continued, one after another, each brilliant in its silver hue . . . unearthly . . . fantastic. The center pool of light became even more active as time went on. Then the center disc began to fade, the rings slowed, the light faded away, and in its place he could see two long rivers of green stretching from horizon to horizon, very slowly moving back and forth with sensual grace.

He had to tell himself to breathe again, it was so astounding. Never, in all the years he had lived here, had he seen anything so fantastic. It was unmatched imagination, unfathomable creativity.

For you, my son.

Joy leapt within him, comfort engulfed him. In a sudden knowing, he saw himself as he was—a beloved son of the Creator.

And then he saw an image of Elizabeth too. He saw her as she was. He had never been more righteous than her—to the Creator, they were the same.

As his attention returned to the earth, a soft crying sound reached his ears. He jerked his head in the direction of the cry. There, on the edge of the slope, was a figure kneeling on the ground, face uplifted toward the heavens. Noah's breathing increased as he walked, involuntarily, toward the figure.

She turned her wet face toward his and gazed at him. He felt his heart leap. It was as if he could see into her soul. In a whisper that sounded too soft to be human, she said, "How breathtaking is this land. It stirs my blood with feelings I cannot find the words to express."

He couldn't say a word, could only stare at her, unbelieving. He thought her a ghost. She stood, a pale dress blowing around her and seemed to float toward him. When she was very near, she reached out her hand and placed her palm on his heart. With aching softness she murmured, "I've come home, Noah. I couldn't leave you, or this land, even for a little while. I want only to be your wife and to love you . . . always."

She was the ghost that haunted his heart and his dreams. She was the snow angel he'd found on his doorstep that first night. Only she wasn't an angel or a ghost—she was his wife. His. Wife. He reached out and touched her shoulder. She was real. She had come back to him. With eyes closed, he crushed her to him, his hands moving over her back and arms, telling himself over and over that his Elizabeth did exist and she loved him. Looking down at her countenance, tracks of tears gleaming in the moonlight, he cupped her face between his palms. Who but God could have created such as she, and for him, bone of his bone, flesh of his flesh?

Slowly, still within the enchantment of the land, always within the enchantment of her, he leaned down and kissed her like a husband kisses a wife who was lost but now is found, who was dead but now lives, and who would belong with him . . . forever.